PENANCE

STEHANIE J. BARDY

www.darkmythpublications.com

Dark Myth Publications, a division of
The JayZoMon Dark Myth Company, LLC.
145 S Glenoaks Blvd. Unit #3149 Burbank, CA 91502

ISBN: 979-8-9925038-1-4

First Printing March 18, 2025

Dark Myth Publications is a registered trademark of The JayZoMon Dark Myth Company, LLC.

10 9 8 7 6 5 4 3 2 1

Books by Stephanie J. Bardy:

- **Musing From Me** – Dark Myth Publications – 2022
- **The Chosen** – Dark Myth Publications – 2020
- **Eternally Bound** PCE Edition – Dark Myth Publications – 2020
- **Eternally Bound** – Dark Myth Publications – 2018

Other works by Stephanie J. Bardy:
- **Unwelcomed Stories of Hauntings and Possessions** – *The Entity* – Zombie Works Publications – 2022
- **The World of Myth Anthology Volume IV** – *Penance* – Dark Myth Publications – 2021
- **Natural Instincts Tales of Witches and Warlocks** – *Word Witch* – Zombie Works Publications – 2021
- **Full Moon & Howlin: A Werewolf Anthology** – *Pack Business* – Zombie Works Publications – 2020
- **Monsterthology 2** – *Salla* – Zombie Works Publications – 2019
- **The World of Myth Anthology Volume III** – *The Huntress* – Dark Myth Publications – 2018
- **A Pagan Testament** - Brendan Myers

To Dave.
For always believing, always pushing, and always putting
up with my crazy.
In your eyes.

Table of Contents

Introduction...xi

Never tear us apart...01
What Fresh Hell is This?..11
Roanoke..19
Best Kept Secrets...31
Reese..39
Marlon..49
Trouble Shared...59
Love Obsessive...69
Unremembered Memories...79
Fall into Me..89
Desperate Measures...101
Mother of All..111
Death Is Inevitable..121
There is no life...129
The Road to Hell is Always Paved............................143
Gone, but not...153
Just one night...163
All Bets are Off...177
What have you done?..185
There Will Be Blood..197
The Spoils of War...205
Fear and Loathing...217

Table of Contents (Cont'd)

Best laid plans..227

The silly games we play...............................241

Call my bluff..253

All is not well that ends well.......................265

Do not go gentle...277

About the Author...287

Introduction

I have always had a fascination with the supernatural, and if you have read any of my other books, you will have noticed. I have also denied being a horror fan, vehemently denied. Until it was pointed out to me that I am just not the typical slasher kind, this rocked me. Could it be possible? Me? The one who sought out every paranormal, every supernatural, every psychological thriller I could find, actually be a fan of horror?

It was true. I was a fan. This presented me with a challenge. Could I write horror? Could I compete in the supernatural horror world? So, I set out to write a short story based on horror but with enough supernatural elements to make me still feel like I was in my comfort zone. I had never written horror before. I figured I would write this tale about the beginning of supernatural beings, putting my own spin on the creation stories, adding enough blood and violence to qualify as horror and tick it off my to-do list. I posted it in The World of Myth Magazine Issue 96 and won Member of the Month! To say I was surprised would be putting it mildly. Because I couldn't write a short story and leave it at that, I added to it the next month and kept going. I won again in issue 99 and again in 101. I knew I had something special. I started sending the pieces to a friend of mine, who immediately fell in love with them. She said it had a very Anne Rice quality to it. That blew me away. What started as a short story in 2021 has become something so much more. So, I wrote every month. In every new issue, a new installment of the story would appear, and I gained a following for it. Each time I wrote a new piece, I would call Dave and read it to him. I have a knack for leaving a piece on a cliffhanger, and it drove him nuts. He would have to wait until the next month to find out what happened, just like everyone else. Sometimes, including me.

Every character I have written has contained a piece of me somewhere. Not Reese. Not that I can see, anyway. Writing her was like getting to know a new friend. Each chapter revealed more of her personality. We became friends, and as strange as that sounds when she cried, I cried. I felt guilty when I had to put her in a situation that was going to cause her pain, and I reveled in the times when she was all-powerful and vicious. A lot of this story came naturally; it flowed organically. And then, it didn't.

Reese stopped talking to me. Marlon stopped talking to me, and I fell into a depression. My inspiration was gone. I was drowning in stress and could not find any way to face my responsibilities. So, I let them sit. I let everything sit. Thankfully, those around me saw the trouble I was in and pulled me out of it.

When I sat down to write again, it wasn't on this particular book; it was on another one I have in the works. Nothing came for that; that wasn't a struggle. I kept seeing Reese, arms crossed, tapping her foot, waiting. My boyfriend, who has always been a big supporter of my writing, was asking for more. My friend, who had fallen in love with the story, was also asking for more. I also had a deadline looming. I didn't have a plethora of poems I could pull out of thin air and put into a book like I had the year before. I had made a commitment, and I needed to follow through.

I opened the file and read over what I had already written. I actually let the computer read it to me, and I got lost in the story again. Picking up where I left off felt like slipping on a comfortable old sweater. If it felt right, now, I won't lie, some days were harder than others, and I would have to do what I call writing spurts. Pound out a few paragraphs and get up and go do something else. Then come back and etch out a few more. Some days I would whip out five thousand words, and some days, I barely got out five. But I kept at it. I wrote I deleted, I rewrote, and it all came together. Each chapter took me further and further along until I finally realized this was no longer a novel or even a novella. This little short story had grown and transformed into a novel. I added characters, created bonds, and formed a story that had my readers on the edge of their seats, wanting more with each page.

I say this with each book, and I mean it. This is the one I am most proud of but for different reasons than the others. I started in a genre that I had never written before. I created scenes that fit that genre but didn't feel forced or over the top. I created a monster. Then I created more.

I am in love with Reese and Marlon. I hope you will be too. This was a labor of love, a journey in self-discovery, and of reaching the edge of my mental health and coming back.

Welcome to Penance. This is only the beginning.

Your friend,

Stephanie J Bardy
July, 2023
Ontario, Canada

PENANCE

Chapter One

Never Tear Us Apart

THE SMELL OF decay surrounded Reese as she lay as still as she could. He would be back. He always came back. Something slithered nearby and she cringed just a bit. He had never left her like this before. Just lying on the cold stone. It was always in the hole. This time he had just dropped her like a rag doll and left. She could feel the damp beginning to seep into her bones.

"I have to get up." She thought. She almost laughed out loud because that is what she always thought. "I have to get out of here."

She moved her left hand slowly across the floor until it was beside her. The arm was broken at the joint and she knew it was going to hurt like a bitch to put it back. She gritted her teeth as hard as she could and twisted her arm back to its rightful angle. Bones popped and snapped as she did. The sound of flesh tearing almost made her gag but the searing pain that quickly followed it made all her senses shut down. She neither saw nor felt beyond that pain. Then there was a loud pop, and the arm was again as it should be. She took a moment to catch her breath, tears flowing freely from her eyes and getting lost in her hair. She continued to stare up at what she assumed was the ceiling. She never saw the sun, the stars, or the moon, never felt a breeze or heard the sound of the trees, so she assumed she was inside somewhere.

Slowly she moved her legs and repeated the same process she had with her arm. After what seemed like hours, her limbs were back to rights, and she could push herself up to a sitting position. She looked down and realized that her feet were not where they were supposed to be. Sighing sadly, she turned her head back around to face the right direction. Once she was as she had begun, she wiped the tears from her face, and stood. Her legs shook beneath her, but she remained upright. Sheer determination and the will to survive rode her and she lifted one foot and then the other. When she reached the door at the far end of the room, she gave it a hard push.

Nothing.

She pushed again and still nothing. Not even a slight movement.

Sliding down the door she crumbled onto the small step and lay her head on the cold stone. If she had any tears left, she would have shed them.

The smell of dry leaves, wet dirt, and the cold blew

across her face. She raised her eyes slightly and she could see a small line of light under the door. Every time the wind blew, the line got bigger, then smaller as the wind stopped. She watched it closely. It was blowing inwards, not out.

She stood again, a small spark of hope igniting in her chest. If she had a heart, it would have beat faster as she placed her hand on the door handle and pulled inward.

The door stuck for a second then came loose and swung open. Light burst in and engulfed her. She threw her arm up and shielded her eyes and shrank back into the shadows.

"Get it together Reese!" she said out loud. It almost sounded like words. She hadn't used her throat or her voice in over a hundred years. What came out was harsh, dry, and raspy. She crept towards the light again and felt the warmth on her skin. Paper thin and cold she just stood for a moment and drank it in. She could smell freedom. Feel it. She just had to make her feet step beyond the threshold of her prison. One step and she was free. One movement of her foot. She stood, swaying slightly as she fought with herself.

A deep male chuckle echoed from the room behind her.

"It's always the same Reese. I do not hold you here. You do."

Her head fell forward, and her shoulders dropped.

"You built this prison. Each stone, each board, every nail. Created by each sin, by each life you took. Every soul extinguished by you; built the prison you now cannot escape."

Marlon pushed himself off the far wall where he had

3

been leaning, watching Reese go through the same ritual she put herself through every night.

"Do you not think you have suffered enough?" he asked, "Do you not feel that your penance has been paid?"

Reese stepped back into the shadows, pushing the door closed. The room was engulfed in darkness once again.

"No." she said. "It will never be enough."

She walked over to the stone slab in the middle of the room and lay down on it.

"Begin." She said.

Marlon walked over to the door and opened it. Again, the room was flooded with light.

"No." was all he said and then disappeared outside.

Reese lay on the slab staring up at what she now could see was the ceiling of a crypt. Each stone bore a name. A life. Marlon was right.

She sat up and looked around the room. It wasn't an ordinary crypt although it passed as one from the outside. There were no slots for bodies. No human had ever been laid to rest here. Each stone, each board had a name carved into it. Each name, a life she had taken. A soul she had destroyed.

She slid down off the slab and the sun hit her again. The warmth crept into her. She stood for a moment, again soaking it in. It would be so easy to just walk out, breathe in the fresh air instead of the fetid stench of this prison. She had spent a hundred years trying to do penance for the sins she had been accused of. Marlon had been her jailor at the beginning. Her persecutor. Somehow over time, he had become her guardian.

Each night he would pull her, limb after limb, breaking bones, tearing flesh, rendering unbearable pain upon her, then he would place her into the hole. She would wipe her memory, heal, she would try and escape, and she would fail. Just as all those whose names taunted her from every angle, had. She would clear her mind of the memory of what was to come, clear her mind of her duty to pay such a price, and begin the fear, the anguish, again each day. The night was her reprieve. Her moment of peace. That is how she had come to know Marlon as more than just the one tasked with her sentence.

He was once a man. Not an overly good one, but an honest one. Which is why he had been given the job. He would carry out the punishment, without fail, no more, no less. Until she told him to stop. She had not removed his free will, just the ability to leave her permanently. His body would not allow him to venture to far from her side. She knew he would be just beyond the door, sitting sullenly on the stoop.

She walked to the open door. This was new. This defiance.

"Marlon." She said. He grunted from the sunlight.

"You can't ignore me." Reese stepped closer to the threshold.

"No, I can't. You took that away from me. I have to tear you apart every day, watch you scream and writhe in pain, and then talk to you like an old friend every night." He stood angrily.

"I can't do it anymore Reese. Physically I can't stop, but

inside, I am dying."

Reese chuckled a bit. Marlon glared at her. "You know what I mean."

"Marlon, we are immortal. We can't die. Outside or in. You know what I was accused of. You know that I do not remember my time of change. Until I know for sure one way or another, this is how it must be." She turned back towards the shadows.

Marlon stormed after her. "How are we to find out if we never leave this place? If we never seek out those who know the truth?" he waved his arm, "This is not your prison, I see that now, it is your escape. You don't want to know the truth. It is easier to hide here, bear the pain, and play what they painted you to be, than to seek the truth. You are a coward. Nothing more."

Reese's eyes became slits, a fire burning in them. "Tread carefully jailer. You live because I will it. Should that change, your name can be added to the stones that you stand upon."

Marlon huffed angrily and stormed out of the crypt again. She knew he would pout for a while and come back. He always did. After all the years of torture and pain, there were moments, during the night, as she re-knit her bones and mended her torn flesh, that they had become something akin to friends. He had never loved so when she bound him to her, he had nothing to lose but an honorable death. He had hated her for that for a long time, taking his frustration and anger out on her day after day. She had welcomed it. Sinking into the devastation he caused her, to pay for what she had done. She was guilty, no matter what Marlon said. Maybe not of all she was accused of, but she

PENANCE

had taken lives. Many of them. Each a name now in stone.

She stared at the sunlight streaming in the open door. To just step beyond that threshold, to feel the warmth, to relinquish her penance. It was so easy, but one of the hardest things she would ever do. She inched closer to the door and stepped into the sun. The threshold lay before her, small, insignificant, dull. She stood here every evening, during the "great escape." She always turned away. What if she didn't this time? What if she lifted her foot and stepped over that threshold? What would happen.

"Nothing." Said Marlon from the stoop outside. "Nothing would happen. The world would keep turning, the sun would keep shining, and the souls you took would still be gone. You would remain immortal, and I tied to you."

Reese looked down at him. "Since when did you learn to read my thoughts?" she asked.

He snorted in disgust. "I don't have to. I have seen it every evening for a hundred years. You come to the door, you mimic wanting to escape, you ponder the reality of said escape, then you close the door, and lay on the altar and I tear you apart until full dark. It's not hard to know what you are thinking. It is written all over your face. Your eyes take on this faraway look."

Marlon stood and reached up for her hand. "You are eternal, you have made me as such. Why can we not have a life outside of this crypt? You have paid dearly for your crimes, real and otherwise. You are the Mother of All, let us go and look for your children. Those they created from your flesh. You no longer need to be alone."

Reese stared into Marlon's eyes. Those beautifully gold

flecked eyes. She ached to step out into the light with him. To take his hand, let him pull her out. She closed her eyes, took a deep breath, and lifted her foot. Slowly she moved it forward and put it down. She waivered for a moment and Marlon took her hand and gently tugged her the rest of the way.

Warmth surrounded her. The fetid air of the crypt faded back, and the scent of cherry blossoms filled her. The birds, who always sounded hollow and distant, chirped loudly. The breeze teased her hair and tickled her face. She opened her eyes and immediately squinted.

"We may have to find you a bonnet to shield your eyes until you adjust." Said Marlon. He pulled her close to him and turned her to view the forest they were in.

"It's so...so...green!" She exclaimed. Marlon laughed. "Yes, it is, and in the Fall, it is red, and orange and brown."

Distant barking caused Reese to tense. Marlon moved to stand in front of her as a black and brown dog burst out of the brush and skidded to a halt in front of them.

"Biscuit!" a male voice shouted, "Get back here you fool!"

A man, dressed in britches that were missing the bottom half, and a strange kind of shirt with a triangle on it came running after the dog.

He too came to a skidding halt. He looked around and then back at Marlon and Reese.

"Hey, you guys, ok? Did I interrupt some kind of cosplay thing?" he asked grinning slyly at Marlon. "You know this is private property, right?"

Reese sniffed. "Of course, it is. It belongs to the Duke

and Duchess of Highton."

The man laughed. "Not for about a billion years it hasn't. It's a B and B now. My cousin owns it." His eyes narrowed slightly.

"Who did you say you were?"

Marlon again moved to put Reese behind him, not trusting this strange loud man.

"I am Marlon Gibson, and this woman is my prisoner. Who be you?"

The man laughed. "Dude, you can drop the character. No one is around. Name's Chris. Chris Martin. That's my dog Biscuit."

Reese moved around Marlon and walked toward Chris. She could feel the frailty of his spirit. He would be easy prey, and it had been so long. She licked her lips and suddenly she had Chris's full attention.

"Tell me...Chris...is there shelter and nourishment at this B and B place?"

Chris nodded.

"Wonderful." She smiled, giving just a bit more pull, his energy came easily. "Take us there."

Chris smiled and without question, turned and led them out of the forest to a small country home.

Reese looked around panicked. "What has happened?"

Marlon looked down at her and grinned. "It has been a hundred years. Did you think things would not change?"

Reese looked around again and grimaced.

"Not quite for the better I see."

Chris opened the front door and immediately they were bombarded by loud music.

Reese and Marlon both recoiled.

Chris furrowed his brow. "Megadeath not your thing?" he asked.

"Mega...what?" questioned Reese.

"Never mind, you don't look like you listen to much rock."

Reese stepped close to Chris and captured his gaze.

"Let me make this clear. So, there is no misunderstanding. We are not from this time. The last time we saw the light of day, it was 1921. You will be our guide in this new land."

Chris shrugged. "Sure." He turned and sauntered towards the back of the house. "Kitchen is this way."

Marlon looked down at Reese. "I see your powers of persuasion are still intact."

Reese looked up at him puzzled. "I didn't use them."

They both turned and looked down the hallway towards where Chris had disappeared. Strange noises had started to emanate from the kitchen.

"Strange." Said Reese. "Very strange indeed."

Chapter Two

What Fresh Hell is This?

REESE AND MARLON followed the strange man into the house. The structure still looked as it had 100 years ago. The same crown molding, the same curved railing on the grand staircase, but what had been the front parlor was now combined with what used to be the formal dining room. It was big and spacious, and the fireplace was still intact, but the mantle had been replaced with some strange painting full of color and metal hooks that held tiny milk pails with flowers.

"The fireplace is original to the house, but it has been converted to electric and that ugly mantle was ripped off to make way for my cousin's wife's artwork." Chris had reappeared and was munching on something. 'You flip a switch and boom, fake fire!" he walked over to the wall and showed them. Up, you got what simulated flames inside some kind of covering, down, it disappeared. Chris did this a few times, and then walked over to a strange looking spinning plate and the horrendous sound disappeared as well.

"Any time you want to check out my record collection, let me know. I got some great vintage rock in there."

"You have rocks in those flat books?" Reese asked.

Chris looked at her with a weird expression. "Where did you say you were from?"

Reese leaned towards him and whispered softly. "Here. This is, was my home. You are trespassing."

"Oh, hell no it's not, my cousin bought it from the bank years ago. It was a crappy run-down mansion then. He dumped thousands into this shithole. You are the ones trespassing. Don't think for one second that I don't know the law. Now, try again. Where you from?"

Marlon chuckled quietly. "Maybe you should ask her 'when'?"

"What do you mean when?" Chris was getting agitated. "No one is from *when*. That's sci-fi TV stuff. Unless your ghosts. My place in town is haunted as shit. I want friends of mine to investigate it, but they can't find the time."

Reese just looked at him confused. He was not like any man she had ever encountered before. He didn't seem susceptible to her power but didn't seem resistant either. He had long curly hair which he let hang free. His clothes were unusual, some sort of decorated shirt and pants missing the legs. She had seen shirts similar without the pictures, on the men who fought in the war, but not on someone outside of the military. The poor often wore them as well, under their button shirts.

"Are you poor?" she asked circling around him, trying to understand just want he was.

Chris laughed, "Well I sure as hell ain't rich, the government don't give you enough to live on, but I have my ways of making extra money."

Reese squinted her eyes and sniffed the air around him. "Are you simple?"

"I like simple living if that's what you mean." Chris asked, getting a little suspicious.

Reese looked up at Marlon. "Do you think he is a dewdropper?"

Marlon looked down at the man. Chris wasn't a short man, but Marlon was well over 6'5.

"Do you work?" Marlon's voice was still gruff from lack of use. Reese and Marlon usually communicated through thought, so having to actually speak again was still strange.

"You not listening?" grumbled Chris. "I already told you I get a check. I'm on disability. It's barely enough to cover my bills, but I do side jobs under the table for cash. I make do. Why all the questions?"

Reese waved her hand across Chris's face and immediately it went blank. She had had enough of his chatter for the moment.

Reese had known men like him. Before she had locked herself away, she had 'fed' on many of them. Lay-abouts, with no real purpose other than to collect from the

13

government and skip out on fighting for their country claiming some ailment and paying a back-alley doctor for a note to get them out of the conscription. She locked herself away two years after the war ended. The freedom people felt, the recklessness, had been too much for her, and after fighting her nature and losing, she took Marlon and returned to the family land, and shut herself away. Marlon had been with her since she had landed in Roanoke. He had been her jailer when they tried to hang her for witchcraft. The night she finally decided to leave, she had feasted. The wake of bodies behind her as she walked through the town had been tremendous. The screams of the fearful, trying to hide in their home as they watched their neighbors fall, just made her smile. She spared no one. Not even the children. Those were especially tasty. So fresh, so unmarked by the ugliness of man. Like a savory candy with a sweet gooey center. As she had stood at the gate, one man stood alone in the middle of it all. The only one to have shown her even a small amount of kindness. Marlon surveyed her destruction. A bland look on his face. The shock of it had robbed him of any emotion and he was just numb. Watching over the women that the town deemed evil had taken its toll. Many were kind, innocent women, just trying to survive. He had looked at Reese, standing at the gate, hair blowing in a wind only she could feel, skin glowing a soft pale white.

"You missed a dog I think." He said.

She had laughed. For the first time in many, many, years, she had laughed. That night she bound him to her. They spent many decades after that, crisscrossing the country, venturing to other lands, but always returning to the place that Reese had called home. Marlon had always been her

PENANCE

voice of reason. Her caution. He counseled her on the victims she took. Children were taken off the menu. Much to her chagrin. Over the years, they had gathered information to her existence. For as long as Reese could remember, she had just existed. There was no childhood to remember no parents, no family. Just her. She had always been this age, always looked the same. In the early 1900's they had found a secret society that kept records of a being from long ago. 'She' possessed qualities that you find in the creatures you find now. Vampire, Werewolf, Jinn, Shapeshifter, Witch, Phoenix, she had them all. The records said that a ritual had been performed and pieces of her flesh were taken and ingested by members of the ritual. Each one transformed into a different creature. The subject, as she was called, had then escaped, never to be found again.

Reese had no memory of this, but her body bore oddly shaped scars. In the exact number of the 6 creatures that these records spoke of. They had called her Mother of All. Reese had searched the world looking for others and had come close at times, but they always seemed to stay just out of reach. Hidden from the public and only noticed when an unusual death was reported in the papers.

She paced the floor in front of the fireplace.

"He could be of use to us. We need a guide in this new time. It is strange with things that I don't understand. Things have changed dramatically from the 1920's." she said.

Marlon nodded. "Yes, and he seems to have a fondness for you, whether that is just your natural power, or not, it can be used. You seem to enjoy the attention."

Reese glared at him. "Jealousy doesn't suit you, Marlon.

15

He doesn't seem very bright, which will play to our advantage. This isn't his residence, as he has stated, so I must put a barrier of ill around the perimeter to keep others away. We will learn all we can about this new world and then...dispose of him."

Marlon sighed heavily. "He is an innocent. We've talked about this."

Reese pouted. "But it's been so long."

Suddenly there was a bang that sounded like a gunshot coming from the back of the house. Reese and Marlon both went to investigate leaving Chris standing staring blankly.

They stood at the kitchen window and watched as a young girl ran past. Her face was dirty and streaked with tears. Not far behind was a much older man with a shotgun. He stopped and took aim. The ground exploded by her moving feet.

"Get back here you dumb bitch!" he screamed.

She froze as the dirt rained down around her. The man reached her and slapped her so hard across the face that she dropped like her body had no bones.

Marlon was out the door before Reese could stop him. As the man took aim at the girl, he didn't seen this huge man barreling down on him. Marlon hit him full speed and the two rolled across the lawn. Reese reached them just as Marlon was about to strike the man in the face again.

"Stop." Was all she said.

He stopped and rose up off the man.

"What the hell?" the man said through broken teeth and blood. "You need to collar your damn dog lady."

Penance

Reese smiled at him. She could smell the evil on him, like a foul stench with a bitter undertone. Her eyes began to glow and her skin shimmer in the late afternoon light. The man's outrage quickly turned to fear.

"What are you...?" he breathed.

She smiled down at him as the delectable flavor of fear overpowered the bitterness of evil and she drank it in.

"I am your worst nightmare and the last thing you will ever touch." She straddled the fat man, her knee's several inches from the ground, placed her small hands on his chest and took a deep breath.

His eyes bulged and he began to scream. She took another deep breath, and his skin began to wither and wrinkle. With each breath her knees got closer and closer to the ground until she was flat from knee to foot, in the grass. The man was less than he was when she started. His screams had stopped, and he lay now staring at the sky. No life shimmered in those eyes. She leaned down and licked his cheek then looked up at Marlon.

"May I?" she asked sweetly.

Marlon grimaced. "Do you not smell him? Really Reese? It hasn't been that long."

A scream brought them both back to the current situation. The girl they were saving.

"Besides, I'm sure that girl has seen enough. Even you can't erase everything."

Reese stood and walked to the girl. She whispered in her ear and the girls face took on one of pleasure and she turned and walked back the way she came.

17

"Let's go deal with this 'Chris'." She said.

The two walked into the house together, but Reese had a little more bounce in her step than she had before.

Chapter Three

Roanoke

CHRIS SAT AT the kitchen table and stared straight ahead. Marlon waved his hand in front of his face. Snapped his fingers a couple of times and got no response.

"Do you think we broke him?" asked Reese. She sat at the other end of the table sipping her tea.

As her and Marlon had returned to the house after dealing with the man, they had found Chris staring out at them from the window. He had not spoken a word since then. Just sat and stared.

Marlon leaned against the counter. "Maybe." He cocked his head to one side. "Dinner?" He raised his eyes at her and tipped his head towards Chris.

Reese glared at him. "No. We need him. We just need to snap him out of whatever this is."

Marlon gave a bark of laughter. *"This* is seeing his house guest consume the life essence of another human being. *This* is the inability to accept what he has seen. That is what *this* is. This is not the first time you have dealt with this. Remember Roanoke?"

Again, Reese glared at him. "Why is it whenever you need to make a point, that is what you use. There have been many other times, many other instances where we have had *this* as you say, why do you always return to that one?"

Marlon pushed himself off the counter and placed his hands on the table, bringing his face level with hers.

"Because that is where you broke me." He said softly.

"Wha...." Chris stuttered.

Reese and Marlon both turned and looked at Chris. He was blinking and his mouth was moving like a fish out of water.

Marlon took a glass from the sideboard and filled it with water. He placed it in Chris's hand and looked at Reese.

"Drink." Reese said. Pushing her power at him.

Chris blinked again.

Reese pushed harder. "Drink."

Slowly Chris picked up the glass and drank the water. He closed his eyes and when he reopened them, they were no longer glazed. They had focus. He looked from Marlon to Reese.

"What are you?" he squeaked.

Penance

Reese settled back into her chair and picked up her tea again. "We need to get you some new varieties of tea if we are to stay here. This Tetley doesn't quite cut it."

Chris stared at her. "Tea? You want tea? You just sucked the life outta a guy and you want tea?"

Reese looked at him. "Of course, I'm nothing if not dignified."

Chris scrubbed his hands across his face. He stood from the table and began pacing the room. Reese sat silently and watched; Marlon was on guard. After about 15 minutes of pacing, he sat back down.

"Are you some kind of vampire?" he asked, "I can't even believe I am asking that, but I can't unsee what I saw. You sucked that dude dry! Nothing but dust. What did you do to his daughter Selena? She just walked away. Are you a witch? What are you? Where did you come from? How can...?"

"Enough." Reese said. Chris immediately fell silent, but not from any power that she may have had over him. "I can't explain it all tonight. I do not think I can even explain it all. I have been what you see for as long as I can remember. I don't remember anything before this age. Now, that being said, I have been this age, for a very, very, very, long time. I have seen many things, done many things, until I locked myself away in 1921 in the crypt on this property. Every night I set myself to be tormented and tortured for the sins I had committed. I was not the nice gentle person you see now. I hungered and I fed indiscriminately. Man, woman, child, it did not matter to me. I traveled alone for a very long time. Until I met Marlon. Then I was cursed. Each soul I took a slash on my own. A wound I could not heal,

21

and a torment I had to carry every day. It did not stop me, but I became a little more choosy in my prey. Which is what you all were. Prey. To be fed on and discarded. Nothing more." She sipped her tea, watching Chris's face.

He sat staring at her, processing what she had said.

"How do you feed?" he asked.

"I pull the life force, the essence, out of the person. Like breathing in fresh air on a crisp spring morning." She said.

"Do you always kill them?" he asked.

"No, some I have only fed a little, and then returned once the essence had built back up. It's like a reservoir of water, you drain a little and it fills back up. I can feed off someone for a very long time before it begins to take a toll."

"What kind of toll?"

"Their mind begins to deteriorate. Madness sets in." Marlon replied.

Chris had forgotten he was there and jumped when he spoke.

"Why did you hide?" he asked, keeping an eye on Marlon now.

"The weight of all the souls I had destroyed became too much for me to carry." She said quietly.

Chris nodded as if he understood. He looked at Marlon. "You like her?"

Marlon again barked out a harsh laugh. "No. I was just a mortal man before I met her."

"What are you now?" Chris asked.

"Still mortal, but my mortality is tied to her immortality.

PENANCE

She dies, I die." he said.

"And if you die?" Chris looked at Reese with new eyes.

"She gets herself a new lackey." Marlon answered sardonically.

Reese glared at him.

"You do that a lot." Chris said.

Reese looked back at Chris, "What?"

"Glare at Marlon."

Marlon laughed again. "That isn't the worse thing she has done to me."

Chris's eyes widened. "What can you tell me?"

Marlon sat down and looked at Reese. She stood from the table angrily. "Fine. Tell him. If it will make you feel better, tell him. Just get on with it." She walked to the sink and turned on the water, rinsing her mug. "I don't have to stay and listen to it, again." She walked out the back door, across the yard and disappeared into the woods.

Chris got up from the table and grabbed two beers from the fridge. He twisted the top off both and handed one to Marlon.

Marlon took a swig and looked at the bottle. "My how things have changed." He mused. He set the bottle on the table and steepled his hands.

"I met Reese in a small village in North Carolina. She had been suspected of witchcraft and was a prisoner in my jailhouse." Marlon sat back picking at the paper label on his beer bottle. "She was as you see her now, petite, beautiful. She begged me nightly to help her escape, but I believed what the Priests said. I was a good, obedient colonist and my job was to guard her until her hanging."

He fell silent and stared at the table, not really seeing it.

"How did she escape?" Chris prodded.

Marlon swallowed a few times and spoke in a low hushed voice. "I swore to protect her from the Witchfinder. That last night, he had used tools that should never be in existence and seeing her broken was more than I could bare. That was also the night she broke me. She took a little piece of my will, my ability to stop her, and threw the jailhouse doors open with a tremendous thrust of energy. The jailhouse had remained standing, but all the glass had been blown inwards and shattered. Dust swirled and spiraled around it and around the few bodies that lay on the ground. The bodies looked strange, some like they were sleeping, some looked old and wrinkled. Screams came from every house, every shop, every corner of the village. All at once. People dropped and writhed in pain but there was nothing visible causing it. The screaming continued until there was nothing left but swirling dust and the dead. She left a body here and there, in the hopes of making a statement to anyone who found the village. They found the village, but they did not find any bodies. The colony was failing anyway. Just like the first had. We were cursed. We took land that did not belong to us, forced out the ones who were there before and killed those who opposed. You cannot take something with blood and violence and expect to prosper and thrive. People became sick, babies died, crops failed, just like the first group before us. Reese was blamed because she was unmarried, beautiful and every man wanted her. The wives accused her of witchcraft. I cannot even tell you where she came from. She just showed up one day in the village and lived among us like she had always been there."

Chris sat and digested the information for a moment. Then something struck him. 'Are you telling me you are from Roanoke?"

Marlon nodded. Not willing to put that into words.

Chris sat back in his chair with a thud. "Holy shit. You are a living legend dude! History books say no one survived! Yet here you sit. A survivor! Wait…how did you survive?"

"I spared him." Reese said from the door.

"If that's what you want to call it." Muttered Marlon.

"It is." She walked to the table, took Marlon's beer, drew a long swig, and sat down beside him. Chris sat very still, afraid to draw attention.

"He was kind to me. Over my many years I have been feared, revered, honored, beaten, used, abused, and placed on a pedestal. Marlon is the only person who ever treated me like a person. Normal. Albeit one accused of witchcraft, but normal just the same. He was kind. Back then, I rewarded kindness with life. Which means I would not take it. The townsfolk were not so kind. The men came to me, pawing and begging, the women came to me to rid themselves of the indiscretions they carried out and when the repercussions of their own sins fell upon them, they blamed me. Turned on me. So, I showed them just how powerful I was. I left most as dust beneath my feet. A few I left to be found by the next colony to come and try to live on that land. I destroyed the first colony, and I destroyed the second. For a long time, no one else came."

"No one was ever found in the village." Said Chris.

Reese grimaced. "That was Marlon's doing. He felt it was too disturbing to leave the bodies as I had. So, he burned them. I offered to drain the last of the essence and turn them to dust, but for some reason he felt a burial by fire was more honorable. His choice."

Marlon glared at her. "They did not all deserved to die the way they did. Withered and decayed to dust. The screams of agony were unbearable. These were people I had lived side by side with for many years. Crossed an ocean with. I could do no less for them."

Reese ignored Marlon's outburst and continued. "I stood at the gate; he surveyed my work. He did not seem scared, he was calm, which I later came to understand is a reaction to extreme shock. But it intrigued me. He had seen me at my worst. At my most furious, and he remained standing, facing it all. He even offered me the dog that was running the streets trying to find shelter. It made me laugh. I knew I had been alone too long and wanted a companion. One who would keep me from getting to far into my power. It can be a heady thing. He refused the offer. I took the choice away from him. Once I deem you mine, you lose the will to say no. You do as I bid, whether you want to or not. My will is his command. He can still do as he pleases, come, and go as he pleases, but we have found over the years that being apart causes each of us physical pain. If I want something he has to do it, mind you he grumbles about it most of the time. We have also found that I cannot die. We have tried. Others have tried. Marlon remains human. Heals human slow. But he continues to live, and either doesn't age, or ages very slowly. He hasn't changed in appearance that I have noticed. We have assumed that if I do die, he will die, but if he dies, I will remain."

PENANCE

Chris again pondered what he had been told. "What about Croatoan?"

Reese looked at Marlon in disbelief. "After all I have said to you, all that you now know, you are asking about some silly word?"

"It's kinda been a mystery since the village was found." Chris shrugged his shoulders.

Marlon laid a hand on Reese's arm. He could sense her frustration with Chris rising and calmed her.

"We carved the word ourselves. There was a small native tribe nearby, we felt that if anyone came looking it would like that the savages had killed them or taken them in. It depended on what they chose to believe. We also left stones with cryptic messages on them. Detailing deaths and Indian attacks. I could not spend every day worrying that someone was hunting us. I didn't want anyone pursuing us and I wanted those concerned to think the entire town had perished. It was the best we could do. Over the years we have seen the sensation that the word has caused, and the mystery that surrounds the colony. We remain vigilant and quiet, but we know they will never come for us. Not then, not now."

Chris folded his arms angrily. "So, you passed the buck?"

Reese furrowed her brow. "We what?"

"You blamed someone else." Chris replied.

"Yes. Humans have been doing it since the dawn of time. Why the outrage?" Marlon looked at Chris quizzically.

"Because I just lost fifty bucks dude! I swore the word meant something mystical and your telling me it means

27

nothing." Chris got up and pulled a strange device out of his pocket. Pushing some buttons, he put it to his ear.

"Dan, buddy, I owe ya 50. You're never going to believe what I just found out." Marlon snatched the phone from Chris's hand and threw it across the room. It smashed against the wall.

"What the hell man! That was an iPhone 11! Do you know how much those cost?" Chris was furious. He picked up his phone and looked at the shattered screen.

Marlon walked over to him and grabbed him by the front of his shirt. "You tell no one what we have told you. Understand?" he ground out angrily.

Chris struggled to get free of Marlon, but his grip was too strong. "Let me go man."

Marlon gave Chris a bit of a shake, "I asked if you understood."

Reese had come to stand behind Marlon and held Chris's gaze. She took a small breath in, and Chris felt an odd sensation in his chest. It rose until he felt his breath being pulled from him. Slowly it felt like he was suffocating. Frantically he began to nod his head. Reese breathed out and Chris took big gulping breaths in. Marlon released him. "No one will ever hear what we have just told you. Not from your lips. Understood?"

Chris nodded. "Understood." He croaked.

He had crumpled to the ground on his knees and Reese knelt until she was face to face with him.

"I let you live only because we need you to help us navigate this new world. Do not for one minute think you are not replaceable."

PENANCE

She stood and stretched. "I am tired."

Chris pointed towards the stairs. "Rooms up at the top of the stairs. Help yourself." He was rubbing his chest like it hurt but it was more of a burning feeling like indigestion.

Marlon and Reese headed upstairs to bed and Chris picked himself up off the floor. He retrieved his phone and examined it closely. It looked like it only needed a screen replacement. He would get that done tomorrow and meet Dan for coffee.

He had to tell someone, and he was pretty sure if Reese couldn't hear him, she couldn't hurt him.

Chapter Four

Best Kept Secrets

CHRIS SLID INTO the seat of his car. It still gave him the same rush it had when he had bought it fresh off the line in 1980. He turned the key and the engine roared to life. The 301 Turbo rumbled happily as he pulled out of his drive onto the street. His car always got noticed. It had since the day he bought it. He kept the 1980's Trans Am shined to a mirror sheen. It was his pride and joy. More so than any woman he had ever dated. Relationships had ended over this car.

He drove down the street a bit and pulled into the coffee shop parking lot. He could see Dan standing beside his car drinking his coffee. He gave Chris a nod as Chris backed into the spot beside him. Chris never just pulled in. The

Firebird must always be on display. It was a thing with Chris. Always on. He had never really given up the band persona as he had gotten older. He no longer traveled with the groups he used to, and was no longer a roadie, but he still maintained the lifestyle like he was. Still wore the ripped jeans and the band t-shirts, still drove the car, still had the long hair. Even though he was just over 50, he had never really grown up.

"Hey Bud, what's the emergency." Said Dan as Chris shut the car off and got out. He turned the key one click more, and his tape deck clicked on. Anthrax poured from the speakers and Dan leaned in the passenger side and turned the volume down. Chris shot him a dirty look.

Dan handed Chris his coffee as he leaned against his car.

"Man do I have some shit to tell you!" Chris said.

Dan nodded. He was a man of few words. Unless it was on conspiracy theories. Then he had a lot to say.

Chris took another sip of his coffee, lit a cigarette, and began his tale. Dan stood silently and listened. When Chris had finished speaking, he pushed himself off the car and pulled his phone from his back pocket.

Chris went to speak but Dan raised his hand, silencing him.

"Freddie, whatcha doing?" he asked the voice on the other end of the phone. There was a mumbled response.

"Good, tell the wife you are going out and meet me and Chris at the Top Spot. Grab Denny on your way." He pushed the button and hung up the phone.

Chris just stared at him.

Penance

"Did you not hear me say that she would kill me if she knew I told you?" Chris was a bit apoplectic at the thought of his other two friends being in the know.

Dan looked at Chris, blinked once, and crossed his arms.

"Dude, you just told me that not only do you have survivors of Roanoke in your cousins B&B, but that she and possibly he, are vampires. Either you've slipped a gear and we need to take you to the nuthouse, or you need us to protect that stupid ass of yours. Your mouth will get you killed if this is all true."

"Screw you, it's all true. I don't need your *protection* either. She likes me." Said Chris, with just the slightest of whine to his tone.

"Uh huh." Said Dan. He climbed into his car. "Get in."

Chris locked his car and the two drove down the street to the local bar. The inside was dark, and the jukebox played some old tune in the corner. A bar always looked sad and worn during the day, but the emptiness was what Dan was counting on. He took a table at the back by the pool table and ordered two beers.

"We can't tell them." Whined Chris. "I wasn't supposed to tell you."

"Well, that cat can't be stuffed back into that particular bag so suck it up. This is the best bit of information you have shared in a long time." Dan spied Freddie and Denny entering. The whole front of the bar lit up as sunlight streamed in the open door. He waved at them, and they both grabbed a beer from the bar and headed over to the table.

Freddie folded his tall frame into the chair across from

33

Chris and Denny sat across from Dan. Denny and Dan were brothers but if you didn't know, you wouldn't be able to tell. Denny was very much peace love and happiness. A true child of the 60's who never changed. Dan was full of anger, conspiracy theories and the odd need to punch something. Freddie was the quiet one. He watched people, listened to what they said, and could anticipate trouble before it happened. Many years spent as a bouncer for some of the rowdier bars in the city, he had learned to watch the body language. It often said more than words ever did.

"I don't have long. I promised the wife we would watch that new show tonight. She wasn't impressed I left her with dinner dishes." Said Freddie. He liked to portray that his wife Vickie ruled the relationship. It gave him an easy out.

Dan prodded Chris.

Chris downed the rest of his beer and told the other two what he had shared with Dan. The four sat in silence drinking their beer.

"Well." Was all Freddie said. He got up and got four more beers.

"Where are they now?" he asked as he sat back down.

"The B&B." replied Chris.

"Do they know you were coming here?" Freddie sat back and watched Chris.

"No. I told them I was going to get my phone fixed."

Freddie sat forward, leaned his arms on the table and stared directly at Chris.

"Don't tell them. Not one word. Don't mention our names, or that you even know us. We need some time to figure this out and the less interaction we have with them for now, the better. This will also buy you some time. You said she threatened you if you told anyone. I'm pretty sure telling three people would make her follow through."

Freddie then turned to Denny. "You still got all that old hiking equipment?" Denny nodded.

"What are you thinking Freddie?" asked Dan. He was very into the whole Roanoke side of it and was desperate to talk to Reese and Marlon. But if Freddie said wait, it was for a good reason, and you waited.

"I will get the wife's camping gear and we will set up base in the woods by the crypt you said you found them at. We will watch from a distance, when they come and go, where they go, what they do. I want to see if there is any truth to what you said. If there is, then we need to know exactly what we are dealing with. This is movie level shit. Not real life. If she has been eating your cooking then garlic is a myth, and they are wandering around in the day so that whole crispy critter by sunlight is bull too."

Chris furrowed his brow. "I'm not sure if they will be able to sense you there. She is kinda weird about some things and completely oblivious about others. The mailman wasn't even at the end of the drive, and she knew he was coming, Marlon had to restrain her, but when the satellite guy came with his truck it took her by surprise."

Dan scratched his chin. 'Maybe all the radioactive waves coming off the truck jammed her frequency?"

Denny rolled his eyes. "You and your theories. Satellite tv doesn't make you sterile, it won't give you cancer and they can't read your mind. There are no radioactive waves coming of repair men trucks."

Dan glared at his brother. "You don't know that." Denny threw his hands up and conceded defeat. There was no point in arguing with Dan when he was like this.

Freddie looked thoughtful. "It is something worth exploring. If we can dampen her abilities, shield ourselves somehow, it would be better for us."

"Create something like a Faraday cage around us?" Dan asked.

The other three looked at him. "What? I watch those paranormal shows. Nothing gets in or out."

Freddie nodded. "Something like that."

The four sat and discussed how they were going to pull this off. Freddie made a few calls home and soon they had a plan. They ordered some food and sat back rather pleased with themselves.

They got up after their meal and began to shoot some pool.

Chris bent over the table and an uneasy wave passed through him. He spun around and the back door opened blinding the four. When the door finally closed. Reese and Marlon were walking towards Chris.

"Wha...wha...what are you doing here? I'm just here playing pool with my buddies. How did you find me?" he asked in rapid fire succession.

Freddie groaned and put his hand on Chris's arm. He looked at Reese and Marlon, sized them up and pasted a friendly smile on his lips.

"You guys' friends of Chris's? He didn't mention he was meeting anyone but us here." He said.

PENANCE

Reese walked over to Freddie and lightly touched his arm. His face went slack and his eyes blank. She did the same with Denny and Dan.

"I told you not to speak to anyone." She hissed.

"I didn't!" stammered Chris.

Marlon snarled under his breath and took a step toward Chris.

Reese raised her hand and Marlon stopped. She walked over to Denny and sniffed the air around him.

"He smells yummy." She purred. With a few deep breaths, Denny was lying on the floor literally half the man he was a moment before. His expression was still blank. He had no idea his life was being ripped from him one breath at a time.

Chris was speechless. He had brought this on. He had involved his friends and now they had to pay the price.

Reese proceeded to drain every last drop from Denny until all that was left was a small pile of dust that she gingerly stepped over.

Wiping the corners of her lips, like she had just eaten something juicy, she slid her hands over Chris's back. He tensed at her touch.

"I warned you what would happen. We need you; we don't need them."

She turned to Marlon and nodded. He gathered the other three and brought them to her. She whispered into each of their ears and in turn they each left the bar.

She turned back to Chris. "Now we go back to the house. We need to have a talk."

Marlon grabbed Chris by the arm and walked him to the waiting cab out back.

Chris was shaking inside, and Reese just smiled at him.

"The rules are simple. Just follow them. The best kept secrets are the ones that will keep you alive."

Chapter Five

Reese

THE RIDE BACK to the house was silent save for the radio. Reese had made Chris turn off his music and just let the radio play in the background.

She stared out the window and watched the tree's whip by in a blur of green. She was angry at Chris, at the thought that he had actually disobeyed her. She had no mind control over him, and that caused her concern. If she could not control him with fear, then he would have to be eliminated and another guide would have to be chosen. The fact that she could not control him intrigued her, but she was beyond the mild curiosity it stirred at the moment. Reese needed to calm her anger and quiet her mind. She let herself actually listen to the words that the woman on the radio was singing. The beat had caught her attention.

"Blurring and stirring the truth and the lies (So I don't know what's real)

(So I don't know what's real and what's not)

(Don't know what's real and what's not)

Always confusing the thoughts in my head

So I can't trust myself anymore"

The words hit her like a wave, crashing into the last of her defenses. She took a deep breath and fought the images that raced behind her eyes.

She let her hair fall forward hiding her face from Chris. Although, he was totally focused on the road and doing his best to not look at Reese or meet Marlon's eyes in the rear-view mirror. Marlon on the other hand had caught the sudden change in Reese's energy. It was darker, colder. He knew where the song was taking her.

"So go on and scream, scream at me

I'm so far away (So far away)

I won't be broken again (Again)

I've got to breathe

I can't keep going under

I'm dying again

I'm going under (Going under)

Drowning in you (Drowning in you)

I'm falling forever (Falling forever)

I've got to break through

I'm going under (Going under)

PENANCE

Going under (Drowning in you)

I'm going under."

He watched the side mirror. He had realized that he could see Reese's face in the mirror on the door. He watched her eyes close and knew she was reliving the pain. He didn't know the full scope of what she had endured before she had come to him, but he knew what she had suffered since. He was amazed that she had managed to hold onto any shred of her humanity. He pushed his energy at her, trying to surround her, to let her know she was not alone, but the song had done its damage. She was too far to reach now and all he could do was wait for her to come back.

They arrived at the house and the three entered.

"How do I make the little box in my room play that song?" she asked Chris, not meeting his eyes.

"You can't." he said simply.

Her eyes flashed with anger. "Make it play that song."

Chris swallowed hard and turned into the living room, he took his iPod out, punched a few buttons, and handed it to her along with headphones.

"It's on repeat. If you want to turn it off, just push this button." He turned and went to his room leaving Marlon and Reese alone.

Marlon moved towards her, and she recoiled.

"I only want to help." He said quietly.

"You can't. Not right now. I just need to be alone, with this song. These words have taken me to a time that I had long forgotten, a pain I no longer wished to feel." She

41

replied. She had turned her back on him, which she didn't do unless she was hiding her feelings. He was always able to read her eyes. They never lied to him. He touched her shoulder and she jerked away.

"Don't." was all she managed before she fled.

Marlon stood riveted to his spot. The heat, the rage he had felt in that one touch had rocked him. The absolute despair that had overwhelmed the rage had almost brought him to his knees. He heard her door upstairs close and knew he would not see her again until morning. If even, then. She had never fled from him. She had never had that wild frightened look in her eyes before. Had never felt so broken.

Reese collapsed against the door as she shut it softly. Her heart still raced and that long ago fear coursed through her. She swallowed a few times before attempting to move. It had consumed her with a few simple lines of a song. That had never happened before. Not in any of the time she had been listening to music. The words had never touched her, never made her feel, never made her remember.

She sat on the bed and looked at the little square device in her hand. Faintly she could hear sound coming from the pieces she had seen Chris put in his ears when he wanted to block out her and Marlon. She placed one in her ear and the music poured into her. She put the other one in and lay back on her bed.

She stared at the ceiling and listened.

The urge to scream welled up inside her and she knew she had to get out of the house. She grabbed her coat, pulled on the boots that Chris had picked up for her and headed down the stairs. Marlon was sitting in a chair by the

PENANCE

fire and immediately stood.

"Where are you going?" he asked nervously.

"Out." Was all she said before she bolted out the back door. She had reached a full run by the time she reached the tree line and when Marlon reached the kitchen she was nowhere to be seen.

She ran until she ran out of ground to run on. She stopped just short of the edge of the cliff. The wind whipped her hair around her face and buffeted against her. The song, that damnable song, still played in her ears.

She opened her mouth and what she thought was going to be a scream came out as a wounded wail. She drew a breath and again the sound came. Over and over until she fell to her knees. She clawed the ground, she pounded her legs and howled at the powers that be. Every pain she had ever felt, every hurt, every piece that had been ripped from her escaped in that wail. She had put sound to the broken pieces inside her.

Her voice had gone hoarse, and her face was streaked with dirt and tears. She sat, legs hanging over the edge of the cliff, hair still blowing about her face. Her soul felt a bit calmer now. She looked at the sky above her, the land below her and spoke.

"How? How could you let me survive? Have I been so bad, so evil, so ugly, that I must continue to pay the penance you have laid out for me?"

No answer came, only the shriek of an eagle as it flew over.

She could think rationally now, the pain had been pushed back down. Think back to the worst of the pain.

43

The night had been like any other, and it was unlike any before. For she had no recollection of anything before that night. She had been walking, along a riverbank, but her memory tended to cloud that part so it could have been the shores of a lake. She had felt a hand, on her shoulder, maybe on her arm, and she had fallen.

When she had come too, she had been laid out on a marble table, hand and feet tied so she was spread eagle. Naked. She was surrounded by cloaks. By ominous faceless black holes. All chanting and moving around her.

The Mother of All Creatures they had called her. She had screamed that they were wrong, that she was nothing, nobody. They didn't listen.

The cloaks had parted and 6 had stepped forward. One wore the head of a wolf, one had blood smeared across his face, another wore the skin of a human, knit with the skin of an animal. A woman stepped for with strange symbols carved into her skin. Another carried fire, and the last was painted with blue designs.

Each carried a curved blade. They glistened in the firelight. Hands caressed her body, and she begged them to stop. Her pleas fell on deaf ears as they no longer saw her as human but as a means to further their own power. She was the catalyst they needed, the unhuman sacrifice that would appease their Master and grant them the powers of the immortals they had only heard whispers about.

Werewolf, Vampire, Shapeshifter, Witch, Phoenix, and Jinn. Each held certain powers, and each was desired by one of the six. They had hoped to retain all the powers within themselves but knew that one could not hold such greatness without succumbing to madness. They had researched and knew that little pieces would allow them a small taste of that magic. If ingested correctly, then they would become immortal and that which they sought.

Reese writhed and strained against the ties that bound her. She begged, bargained, and pleaded but to no avail.

The men took their turn with her, marking her with their seed, bruising her flesh in their intensity. The woman stood at Reese's head and stroked her hair the entire time. Encouraging the men, kissing Reese from time to time, laughing at her pain. Eventually Reese had just shut down. Mentally she was broken, her body having been broken long before that. When she no longer fought, no longer pulled at the ropes, they stopped. They needed her complete surrender.

They needed the absolute breaking of her spirit. The loss of her faith was the last piece, the remaining ingredient that they needed.

The woman turned Reese's face to look up at her.

"Open your eyes." She demanded.

Reese did as she was told. She looked up at the woman but didn't see her. She was no longer there.

The woman looked up at the men. "She is ready."

Each of the six removed their blades and each, in unison, cut a piece of Reese's flesh. Perfect circles about the size of a cherry.

Reese shrieked in pain. Her blood ran and dripped off the edge of the marble slab. She fought again. This time she knew she was fighting for her life. Her body began to glow and burn as they touched her. Each fell back, A shock wave blasted out from her as she screamed.

45

The ropes broke and she rose above them all. The wounds slowly reknit themselves and the blood that poured from them stopped. She lay, in the air, above them all, floating.

Gently she was laid back onto the slab as if invisible arms had held her. She opened her eyes and sat up.

Most off the cloaks had fled when she began to glow. Only the 6 remained.

She slid off the altar and walked around each of them.

She stopped in front of the one with the wolf head.

"You will retain the power, the strength of the wolf, you will carry his speed, his strength, but you will also retain his hunger. That hunger will haunt you, but you may only feed that hunger on the full of the moon." She touched the snout of the wolf, and the man immediately began to writhe, and his bones began to break and reshape into the form of a giant wolf. Fur flowed at a speed faster than the eye could see.

"The transformation will be absolute, but it will be excruciating. You will forever bare the pain you have caused me, on every moon that rises in its fullness, shall you feel the agony that you marked my body with."

She walked to the one with blood smeared on his face. Some of it was now hers. She smiled, but it did not reach her eyes.

"You will hunger for that which you cannot have. Blood will feed your body, but your soul will forever yearn for the one you will never find. You will seek me, you will hunger for me, but you will never have that again. That taste in your mouth, that feeling coursing through your veins, will

PENANCE

never come again. You will succumb to the hunger, to the ravenous ache for it, and you will destroy all that you hold dear trying to find it. You will be weakened by the sun that you worship, you will be sickened by the food you love, and you will never know the flush of heat from a life coursing through you. You will remain dead to all who know you. You will remain dead to yourself."

She looked at the shapeshifter. She sniffed in disdain. "You will have nothing but the ability to change your outer appearance. You may be a mouse, you may be a lion, but you will possess nothing more than what they carry. You will shed your skin and carry the skin of another and shed that to retain your own. Like the snake you are, you will be nothing but a husk, a shell, a pitiful duplicate of the real thing."

She then turned to the Witch and the Jinn. "You have the ultimate power, but you will remain in human form. Weak and vulnerable. You will also bear the marks of your choice. The scars will identify you to others and you will pay the price for that. You will burn, you will drown, and you will break. Only to be reborn again to suffer as you have caused me to suffer."

She paused at the one holding the fire. "You will have it worst of all. You, with your thrusting and your bruising. You will remain human; you will remain weak. You will die, and you will burn. Only to be reborn from the ashes. To rise and repeat the torment again."

She walked back to the altar and with a thought she stood upon it. Looking down at the 6 she laughed.

"You thought you would break me? You thought you could destroy me? You freed me. I am forever, I am

47

unending. You have taken the last of the human ties that bound me, that kept me small, and broke them. I will forever be here. Forever hunting you. Never rest my children, for yes, that is what you are. My children. You were created by and from my flesh. The Master you sought did not come for you, he came for me. I am your Master now, and you will never run far enough where I cannot find you."

Reese opened her mouth and let an inhuman sound resonate from deep within her. The 6 shattered, and their pieces scattered with the four winds that blew through the cavern. When she was alone again, she gathered her clothes, bathed the blood from her body and left the dim cave. She came back to the water's edge and collapsed.

Reese's thoughts came back to her, and she stared up at the sky. She remembered now. She had never remembered fully the moment she had become what she is now. Never knew fully what had caused this unquenchable anger inside of her. Now she knew.

Again, she stared at the sky.

"You were there." She said accusingly. "You spoke to me. You lied."

She stood and turned her back to the cliff and the ever-expansive sky.

"You said I wasn't alone."

She headed back towards the house.

"You are not." The wind whispered back.

Chapter Six

Marlon

MARLON STOOD AT the back door staring at the tree line. He knew she had gone into the woods, and he hoped if he stood there long enough, stared long enough she would reappear. That she would come back and talk to him. Not shut him out this time. She didn't. He pulled himself away, which was agony for him, as he could still feel every emotion, every pain, that she was feeling. He wanted to run after her, to comfort her, to avenge whatever hell she was tormenting herself with. He wanted to tear the ones who hurt her, limb from limb. But he didn't know who they were, or what they had done, just that they had put that look into her eyes, that fear into her heart.

He hadn't always felt such violence. Such anger. It had

only been since he had met her that he had felt this overwhelming protectiveness for a woman who could manage just fine without him. They had been together a long time. The first few decades had been against his will, or so he told her. If he was honest, he had begun to care for her long before she had ever made it mandatory. He still told her almost daily that he didn't care that the power she held over him was the only reason he stayed, but they both knew that wasn't true. He loved her. As deeply as any man could, as fully as any captive could of their captor. Stockholm syndrome. That was the description in a book a college kid had left on the tomb stairs. Marlon had read that book cover to cover. Trying to understand why Reese did what she did, why he felt like he did. It didn't explain much.

Marlon settled himself on the couch in front of the fire and let his mind wander back. Back to when he was just a man, mortal, free, and very much alone. He had fled England and come to Roanoke to start his life over. The woman he had wanted to marry had chosen another and although his heart wasn't broken, his pride was dented more than he cared to admit. He had taken the job at the jail which for the most part had been fairly easy. Most of the people of the colony were very pious and tended to keep their indiscretions quiet. Until she had walked into the village.

The people had been flourishing, happy to be settling into a new land. They had come to an uneasy peace with the local natives. If they stayed within their lands, no harm would come to them. They lived that way for a while and then she had arrived.

Reese had just walked into the village one day, with

nothing more than a bag and a few clothes. She had said that she had escaped from a tribe of Indians to the north, but she looked unharmed. She also looked very well fed. The townsfolk, being the good God-fearing Christians they were, took her in. They set her up with a small cottage on the edge of town, and many would frequent her home for remedies as she had away with wildflowers that grew around her yard.

Marlon would watch her walk by the jail, just following the sway of her hips with his eyes. He wasn't overt about it, but he was a man after all. One who lived alone and had not seen any prospects as of yet, to change that. He had entertained the thought that she may be one that could alleviate that, but when the rumors of the men of the village making late night visits to her home began to circulate, he quickly dashed that idea. He wasn't sure how much stock he put into those rumors. But pretty or not, he wasn't about to saddle himself with a woman he had to throw fists over every night, just to keep her honor. She was small of waist and fair of face and in a town of unpleasant looking women, that was a threat. He could hear them gossiping at the mercantile, adding to the rumors.

Then the small animals started disappearing. First it was a stray dog here or there, then a beloved house cat. Then larger animals. A goat, two sheep and a calf. Gone. No traces of where could be found, No blood, no bone, not even a slight disturbance in the dirt. It was like they had just vanished. The rumors of Reese being a harlot quickly changed to whispers of witchcraft. A harlot was bad, but one could live with that. Albeit with a red letter, but witch? That carried the threat of death. The women, when angered, could be vicious. Marlon would do his best at the town meetings to try and change the popular opinion, but his voice fell on deaf ears. So, he just stopped and listened instead. He knew what was coming.

He had approached Reese one night, as she made her nightly walk about the town.

"You know they are accusing you of witchery?" he said.

She had stopped, turned, and looked directly at him. He had never seen her eyes before, and he was taken aback at the myriad of colors. Gold, green, brown, and black, all played within the perfectly outlined circle. She cocked an eyebrow at him.

"And what say you?" she asked with a small grin playing about her lips.

Marlon shrugged. "I don't judge."

Reese laughed. It was raw, throaty, and real. Not like the twitter of the woman of the town. Reese didn't hold herself back. She embraced the laugh as one should. He grinned just listening to it.

He made a point from that moment on, to speak to her each night as she passed by the jail. He would sit in his chair, leaned back, looking like he was snoozing and watch from beneath his hat. She would slow her pace as she approached, almost as if she too were looking forward to the encounter.

They talked about anything and everything. He found out she liked the sound of the rain on the tin of her roof and hated the smell of rose water. He told her about his childhood, his almost engagement and how he came to Roanoke. They were becoming friends when the *event* happened.

A baby died, and a small child vanished. The milk began to curdle straight from the cow and the chickens had stopped laying. The rumor mill exploded. The word witch became louder and louder.

Until one night they left the town meeting and descended on Reese's home. Marlon was tasked with taking her into custody. She had begged him to let her go, that he was mistaken. He couldn't look her in the eye as the guilt of his actions weighed heavy on him.

He had locked her in the only cell they had. They had sent word to the proper authorities that they had a witch they needed to set for trial and were waiting to hear back on how to proceed. It had been weeks since the missive had been dispatched, and the whole time Reese had maintained her innocence. Then the witch finder had arrived. Marlon watched him with curiosity, as he set up in the town meeting hall. He erected a large wooden X, laid out all sorts of metal tools and instruments, many of which Marlon had no idea what they were. One looked like a pear, but it had a handle that seemed to twist, and the sides opened up like a flower.

Each day, they would bring Reese through the town and to the hall. Each day Marlon was dismissed and sent for when it was time to bring her back. Each day she was weaker, more bruised, and more blood dripped from wounds she didn't have that morning. Her eyes had become dead, and she just shuffled along. Her long, beautiful hair was now matted, and patches of scalp showed where it seemed hair had been ripped out. Her hands, which Marlon had always found elegant and dainty, were broken and curled into something resembling a claw. The fire and the fight in her had died. She no longer spoke to Marlon willingly, but only answered when he asked her a direct question, and only with as few words as possible. He felt awful, but he didn't know what he could have done to stop it. There was no explanation for the events that had transpired. When they had searched Reese's home, they had found the small child's shirt and a lock of the baby's hair.

One night she came back particularly beaten down. Marlon carried her into her cell and gently laid her on her cot.

"They will pay for this." She whispered.

"Who will?" asked Marlon.

"All of them. Every woman, every man, every child. Until there is nothing left but the dust they began as."

Marlon pulled the small, tattered blanket over her and left the cell. They had finally broken her mind. Or so he thought.

The next morning, he decided to stay and watch what they were doing to her.

They had strapped her to the large wooden X and the Witch Finder had ripped her blouse open. He was taking a long needle and was systematically stabbing each of her breasts then giving the spot a squeeze.

"No milk!" he exclaimed triumphantly.

The mayor, a bit confused, asked, 'What does that mean?"

The witch finder turned to him, a look of disgust on his face. A bride of Satan cannot sustain life, she cannot suckle a child. Her breast is dry, and her womb will be barren."

PENANCE

He motioned for the few townswomen that he had enlisted to come forth with the large sheet they held.

"Search her." He commanded. The women poked and prodded every inch of skin until one squealed with pleasure. "I have found it!"

The witch finder approached and examined the spot that the woman pointed too.

"It is in fact the mark of Satan! She bears the witches mark." He pointed to a small birth mark located just under her left buttock. He walked to the side of the wooden apparatus and turned the crank. It slowly flattened until Reese was lying down. He pulled her skirts up to her waist and ripped her bloomers off. He returned to the table and the woman again raised the sheet to cover her upper body and face. He returned to Reese with the pear-shaped object.

Marlon's blood ran cold when he realized just what the witch finder was going to do with that object. Just where he was going to put it. Which he did, with an almost angry vengeance. Reese screamed and writhed as much as the restraints would allow.

Marlon moved to stop him but the men standing by grabbed him and dragged him from the room. He fought them but there were too many. They pushed him out into the street and locked the door.

Marlon paced outside until it was time to collect Reese and take her back to the jail. The doors finally opened, and the women ushered him in. Reese lay on the floor in a heap. Blood coated the inside of both other legs, and her face was black and swollen. Her ripped clothes lay in a heap beside her. He carefully wrapped her in the material from skirt and lifted her into his arms. The rage he felt inside made his body shake. He didn't speak the entire walk back to the jail. He couldn't. The woman he had come to care about, strongly, was broken in his arms. Her eyes closed, barely breathing. She let out a soft moan as he laid, he on the cot. He left the cell, filled a basin with water, and grabbed a cloth. He gently washed the blood from her legs, her face, and her hands. He had found an old night shirt and eased it over her head. It fell to her knees, and she looked even more fragile.

"I am so sorry Reese." He said. "I will find a way to get you out of here. I won't let him hurt you anymore."

"Do you promise?" she asked softly.

"Yes." He said.

"Will you protect me no matter what?" she asked.

"Yes." He said but a bit more hesitantly this time.

"Would you give your life for mine?" she asked her voice stronger now.

Against his better judgment and almost against his will, he answered. "Yes."

The air around Marlon cracked and snapped as if lightening had shot through the room. A strong wind spun around Reese and Marlon scrambled back from her.

Her hair smoothed and softened to the luxurious locks they were. The bruising on her face faded and her skin once again appeared perfect. Her twisted gnarled hands cracked and popped as they returned to their original state. Within minutes, Reese, the woman he had known for almost a year, unbroken, and perfect, stood before him. Her hair spun and twisted in a wind that only seemed to engulf her. He had moved himself back far enough that his back was against the door of the jail. She padded over to him on bare feet, her hair swaying around those hips that had first caught his attention. His eyes were wide, and his breath came quick and harsh.

She leaned down as close as she could, her face inches from his. She captured his eyes and try as he might he could not pull them away.

"You will serve me. Until I deem you no more use to me." She said in barely a whisper.

"You will care for me; you will have the need to protect me above all other needs." She placed a hand on the side of his face and all the tension left it. 'You will be mine, until you are not. The choice will be mine and mine alone. Your mind will be yours, but your body will be mine."

She removed her hand and he blinked.

"What did you do to me?"

"I made you mine." She said. "You will protect me, until I decide I no longer need you." She stood and the nightshirt fell around her.

'Now, like I said before. They must pay." Flicked her hand and Marlon was slid across the floor, knocking him unconscious, and the door opened with a crash. The windows shattered and an unearthly wind surrounded her. She walked out into the street. As Marlon regained consciousness, he could hear the screams.

He wanted to help them. But he also knew they had brought on the hell they were about to experience.

Marlon's eyes refocused on the fire in front of him. For

the next few decades, he had cleaned up her messes, moved them from town to town, city to city, country to country. Until she had met a witch descended from the one, she had been searching for. He shook his head and stood up. He didn't want to relive that particular memory tonight. He had relived enough for now.

He again went to the back door and stared out. He heard her wailing, felt her screaming and releasing some of the pain she carried. Then he felt something he hadn't in over 100 years.

Peace.

It was faint and was gone as quickly as it had come. But it had been there.

Marlon saw her coming across the yard and schooled his features and prepared to greet her. She carried storm clouds and fury, but he loved her. For all it was worth, he had loved her before she had deemed him hers, and he loved her still and would after she was done with him.

Chapter Seven

Trouble Shared

THE NEXT MORNING and Marlon sat at the table as Chris came in. He stopped in his tracks because he could feel the tension. Reese turned to look at him and he actually took a step back.

"Just came for coffee." He said quietly. He knew from his mother that when a woman looked at you with fire in her eyes, you better tread softly. Reese had that fire.

Marlon waved absently over to the counter. "I followed the directives, but I make no promises."

"You cannot be serious Marlon. We haven't been back there since I freed those poor girls!" Reese exclaimed.

Marlon rolled his eyes. "You didn't free them. You

encouraged a rebellion. They were still married. They still had to tend to those men after they got their houses and their gardens. They still had to lie beneath them. They still sent girls from France. You just wound them up."

Reese glared at Marlon and snorted her disgust. "The Rebellion wasn't just about preventing those boorish pigs from bedding the women. It was about teaching the women that they have rights, but they must use what tools they are afforded in the time they live."

She rose and poured herself more tea. "Unfortunately, the tools they had were their bodies. But men being men, being denied the right to their beds and to the bodies of their wives did eventually bring them around."

"Regardless, we must go back." Said Marlon, dismissing what was shaping up to be another rant on women's rights. He had been listening to her go on about it for more time than he cared to remember. He agreed with most of what she said, and had always had a great respect for women, but for the most part she would complain, talk about taking action, then maybe rile up a woman or two and kill the offending man. If she did more than feed, he would be more supportive.

Reese stared at Marlon. She knew how he felt about her ire towards the rights of women and how she had watched them fight for every inch they had. When she had locked them away, women were just starting to have a voice, and to be heard. She didn't know the climate today as she hadn't bothered to ask, but from what she had seen of the scantily clad women they had passed on the way to the pub to get Chris, she was sure that they still had to use their bodies to get anything of value.

PENANCE

"How can you be sure your source is correct. You do not know anyone in this time." Said Reese.

A smug look came across Marlon's face. "While you were out screaming to the wind, Chris showed me how to use The Google."

"Uh…it's just Google." Said Chris. Marlon shot Chris a look and he promptly shut up and sat down at the table.

"Where you off too?" he asked. He had a sneaky suspicion that he would be driving.

"Louisiana." The two said in unison.

"New Orleans?" asked Chris excitedly. He had always wanted to go see Mardi Gras. It was still too early for that, but New Orleans was great any time of year.

"No." said Reese with an air of finality. "I will not go back there."

"You are being unreasonable!" Marlon argued.

"They issued a command for my death. For yours as well, if I remember correctly. You think that has changed? You think that they will have forgotten what we did, who we killed, after all this time?" she asked.

"Um…" Chris raised his hand. Both Marlon and Reese turned their eyes to him.

"What?" Reese ground out.

"History, historically, has been forgotten over time. I will be the first to admit that this new generation is all about forgetting what happened and erasing the mistakes of the past. Canceling the bad and uncomfortable. So, whatever you did a zillion years ago, I can promise, is forgotten."

Marlon cocked an eyebrow at Reese. "Excuse removed."

She huffed, crossed her arms, and sat back almost petulantly, in her chair. "Fine. The trip will not kill me, spending time in the French Quarter will not kill me, "she leaned forward and stared at Marlon, "but it just may kill you." She whispered that last part sending chills down Chris's spine. Marlon seemed unaffected.

"I will pack." He said almost cheerfully. He had enjoyed his time when last they were there. Before the unfortunate incident with a Governor's son, Reese had seemed relaxed, happy even. She had laughed, and danced, her eyes had sparkled with life. No one had died. Well, no one until the son. Frankly, he was nothing but a disgrace to his family and Reese had done them a service. Unfortunately, the Governor had not seen it that way and had issued warrants for all at the party that night. But the ones for Reese and Marlon were to be shot on sight. Deemed dangerous and do not approach. The town had formed a lynch mob and the two had fled to Canada.

Reese continued to sit at the table while Marlon left to pack. Chris stared at his coffee cup. He could still feel the anger rolling off Reese and he didn't want to make any sudden moves.

"Oh, for heaven's sake would you move or something?" she snapped. "You're annoying me."

"Why don't you want to go back?" he asked.

"Straight to the point, aren't you?" she placed her teacup on the table and steepled her fingers. "I killed someone who, although useless, was still the first and only born son and heir. His father was not pleased."

"Ah."

PENANCE

The silence stretched out between the two of them. After a time, Reese got up and rinsed her cup.

"Who is that?" she said in a voice so low Chris wasn't sure she had actually spoken. A man was walking around the back, spraying a liquid on the plants that grew wild. Chris stood and joined her at the window.

"Oh, that's my cousin." Said Chris. He looked over at Reese's face and it was as pale as a sheet. Fear began to uncoil low in his stomach.

"Your.... cousin? You are family to that monster?" she squeezed out. Chris was confused. He was pretty sure that Reese and Kyle had never met before.

"Monster?" he asked. "Maybe I should get Marlon?" he walked to the bottom of the stairs and hollered up for the man. Marlon appeared at the top of the stairs.

"You need to come down man. Reese is wigging out over my cousin."

Marlon walked into the kitchen and there before him stood a man. Reese was frozen in her spot at the sink, staring at him. He could feel the faint whisper of a breeze starting to stir around her.

"Hey Chris, just came to put some weed killer on the back. Didn't know you had company. You need to tell me these things man. I'm running a business here." The man spoke.

Reese sniffed the air like a wolf scenting her prey. Marlon moved the same time she did, and they both reached the man.

"Reese no!" he yelled. "It's not him. You killed him. Remember Reese, remember." He pleaded with her while

63

he tried to pull her away.

Her eyes were wild. "You found me." She hissed. The man paled. Fear had spread throughout the room and Reese could taste it like a fine wine. She rolled it around on her tongue. She could feel Marlon pulling at her and she turned her gaze to him. The minute he saw her eyes he let go and backed away.

She began circling Kyle, sniffing the air, and running her hands gently along his back. Chris watched as Marlon left the room.

"Where are you going?" he screeched. Reese spun to face him. She grabbed his face and looked directly into his eyes. "Leave." She said. Fear gripped Chris so tight that all he could do was stand and shake. She pushed him away and he landed on the other side of the kitchen, smashing into the wall.

Marlon returned with the suitcases, sat them down and then sat himself at the table. He knew there was no stopping her when she was like this.

"It's not him Reese. You destroyed him. All of him." He said quietly. She had returned to the man and was running her tongue along the back of his neck. Kyle wasn't a tall man, so it was an easy reach for Reese. Kyle shuddered involuntarily. Whether from pleasure or fear, it no longer mattered to Reese.

"You have haunted my dreams for decades Witch Finder." She nipped at his ear, and he yelped. "I have killed you so many times, in my dreams. Each time Marlon wakes me, tells me you are dead and gone, and each time I believe him." She drew a breath and a sound akin to a wounded puppy escaped Kyle's lips.

PENANCE

She came to stand in front of him, running her hands up his arms like a lover about to embrace her beloved. "Yet, as dead as he says you are, here you stand. Before me, tasting of fear, regret, and something dark."

Kyle whimpered.

"I have not lied to you." Marlon said. "I was there when you drew the life from him. The bottle with his ash is in the tomb. Shall I get it for you?"

Reese reacted to the mild disinterest in Marlon's tone. She turned her gaze to him. "He is a descendant then."

He had reached her. "That may be, but he is not the man who hurt you."

She stepped back from him and cocked her head sideways, looking at him like he was some kind of specimen. "Maybe not."

"Let us leave this place. Leave this Kyle to whatever life he has left." Marlon stood and walked towards Reese.

"He is hiding something." She said curiously.

At that moment, a completely unexpected thing happened. As Reese touched Kyle, Marlon placed his hand on Reece's arm.

Every dark though Kyle had, every mistake, every evil deed he had done since he first discovered that drowning a kitten gave him a feeling like no other, flashed in Marlon and Reese's mind. The screams of the innocent and the not so innocent. The faces of each one buried in the gardens, in the woods behind the house. In the basement. Reese saw them all.

Marlon tore his hand from Reece and backed away. That

had never happened before. He had felt what Reese had felt. The anger, the rage, the hunger. He wanted to see this man suffer and die at her hand. It was an almost all-consuming desire.

Reese had control now. She was what she was created to be. To some, she was a Goddess, to others, she was a Nightmare. To Kyle, she was judge, jury, and executioner.

"You may not be my devil, but you have been the devil to many others." She began circling him again, now with a distinct predatory walk.

"Your face has been the last many have seen in the terror of their last moments." She stopped in front of him again and drew another small breath. Kyle fell to his knees clawing at his throat. She had taken his air. The lungs in his chest were nothing but dust. His eyes bulged as he tried to draw a breath. She ran a finger down his cheek and the skin split like a ripe plum. Blood poured from the wound, and she licked it from her fingers. She bent and licked the wound, and it opened the beast inside of her. She tore at Kyle's chest, shredding the skin until all that was left were ribbons of meat. She drank the blood like it was water. Her pale face was now covered, her arms were thick with blood up to her biceps, like she had shoved both arms into a bucket of it. She paused and took a deep breath. The body before her shrunk.

Marlon had moved to stand behind her, he didn't know how he had got there, but he couldn't move away. He reached out and touched her shoulder and again he felt what she felt. The overwhelming need to feed brought him to his knees behind Reese. She pulled his arms around her and continued to feed. Marlon's head fell forward, and his forehead rested on the back of her head. As she fed with him at her back, she also fed him. He drew on her energy like he never had before. It filled him. When there was nothing left of Kyle, he spun Reese around to face him. Both were on their knees, she was covered in blood, he was vibrating with her energy. She reached up to touch his face and he turned away. No matter how much he was caught in the energy he still couldn't stomach the blood.

"What is this?" he said breathless.

Reese shook her head. She couldn't speak yet. He left her on her knees and got a cloth from the sink. Wetting it, he returned to her. He wiped her face clean and then kissed her. He devoured her mouth, and she kissed him with just as much passion. The energy between the two was crackling in the air around them and the smell of blood permeated everything.

Marlon tore his mouth from hers and stared into her eyes. It was Reese, but something else danced there as well.

Chris's garbled screams brought them both back to their senses.

"We better deal with this." Reese said, a small smile playing across her mouth.

"Can't I just knock him out?" Marlon asked teasingly.

"No." she replied.

They both heard a thud as Chris fainted.

"Well, that works." Said Reese.

Marlon laughed and hugged her tight to him. "Let's get this cleaned up. It will be easier for him to accept if he doesn't have to look at it."

Reese agreed. The two worked side by side until there

was no trace of Kyle.

They would talk about what happened eventually, but for tonight, trouble shared was enough.

Chapter Eight

Love Obsessive

CHRIS WAS SAFELY tucked into his bed; a strong sleeping pill and a few shots were needed to convince him that the carnage he had witnessed was just a nightmare. Not being able to cloud his mind or bend his will was starting to frustrate Reese. She was thinking that maybe it was time to move on. Find another guide. She sighed heavily and put the kettle on the stove for tea.

Marlon stood in the door of the kitchen wiping his hands on a bloody rag. He watched her move about the room. Graceful, effortlessly. They had worked tirelessly and because of her ever-building abilities, faster than a normal human, and had returned the kitchen to the way it was before she had bathed it in the blood of the Witch Finder.

Her ever-building abilities. That was something neither had acknowledged yet. They seemed to be getting stronger since they had left the crypt. New ones had started appearing as well. Like tonight, with the exchange of metaphysical energy. That had never happened before. Never had Marlon been able to feel *exactly* what Reese felt, the heat of the blood, how it had tasted, the surge of adrenaline and power it gave her. He had felt her hands plunge into the man's chest, felt his life ebb from his body and into hers. He had always been able to feel her human-like emotions, but never her non-human ones. He wasn't sure how he felt about that. He was human. A very old one, who never aged, but human none the less. He wasn't an overly violent man in his life before, he fought when he had too, even killed, but all out of necessity. Reese killed for more than that. She enjoyed it.

Reese could feel Marlon watching her. She always could. She felt every emotion that ran through him. She had since the first moment they had met. Which is why she had bound him to her. There was something about him that she still couldn't figure out. He held his free will, but his body did as she bade it. She knew he balked at a lot of what she had made him do, and she also knew that over the years, his feelings for her had grown. He cared for her when he was her jailor, but they had become something more as the years together had passed. She knew he had grown frustrated with her during her darker days. Always cleaning up after her, moving them to a safe place. It was his moral high ground that had brought her back to her senses, and had allowed her guilt to set in. It was that guilt that pushed her into the crypt. It was his ethical fiber that had given her the idea to have him rend her to pieces every night. She knew he would never take pleasure in it, that he would never do more than what was required. She had grown to care for him as well. Tonight, with the exchange of energy, she realized just how much. She couldn't see him hurt. She wouldn't see him in harm's way. The decision had been made.

She sat at the table with her tea and Marlon pushed himself off the door frame, walking towards her. "You look so serious. What is racing around in that head of yours?" he asked leaning on the chair across from her.

She looked up at him but found it hard to meet his eyes. "I'm fine, just tired." She said. He knew she was lying. She knew, he knew she was lying, but he let her be. He didn't push. They could talk in the morning.

"I am off to bed. Since we left the crypt, I have found myself sleeping again. It's a strange sensation after all this time, but not one I am objecting too." He gave her a half grin and came around the table. She jumped to her feet and quickly moved to the sink, under the pretense of placing her cup in it. "I think I will turn in as well." She mumbled. She moved quickly past him and up the stairs to her room.

Marlon watched after her. He knew something was wrong, but he didn't want to push her. Pushing her never ended well. There was plenty of time on the drive to Louisiana to talk about it all. The research he had done, and the contacts Chris had helped him make had confirmed what he had suspected. One of her "children" were in New Orleans. Possibly one of the original ones created. Stories of witchcraft had woven its way out of the city for what seemed like forever. Occult shops had begun to pop up and now it was something that was practiced out in the open. Rumors of a powerful sorcerer had spread across the internet and Chris had pointed him to all the right websites.

He had made a few calls and the leads had proven fruitful. There was one who seemed to possess some of the qualities that Reese had said transferred to the one called Witch. The Djinn also shared similar qualities but with all the occult shops in the area witchcraft seemed more likely. If they found one, they could find the rest. This new age of instant information had opened doors that would have otherwise been closed to them. Provided knowledge in moments that would have taken weeks to hunt down in newspapers and libraries. He had more in a few days than they had in the decades before their isolation. He had tried to get her to New Orleans before, but she had always refused. She had an almost fearful look in her eyes when Louisiana came up. He had asked what scared her so, but she refused to answer.

He clicked off the light and headed upstairs. He paused at her door for a moment but heard no movement, so he continued down the hall to his room. As he closed his door, a wave of aching sadness swept over him. It took his breath away and almost buckled his knees at the intensity of the emotion. He sat on the edge of the bed and collected himself. It wasn't his emotion. It was hers, but he couldn't figure out what could have created such despair. She had been distracted and anxious when she had left the kitchen but there was no indication that there was any heartbreak. He stood and walked to his door but as he reached for the knob the feeling disappeared. She had shut him out. He knew that feeling. The one of emptiness. She had done it before, when she had been deep in her darker times, so he wouldn't feel the pleasure she drew from taking a life. He didn't understand it now, as he had understood it then, but he knew when she reached that point it was best to let her heal whatever wound she had inflicted on herself and wait for her to open up to him again. He turned back to his bed and settled for the night. It was a long drive, and he would make her talk.

Reese stood at her window and looked out at the forest just beyond the backyard. Marlon had opened that door again. The one she kept sealed tight. She knew the research he had been doing. There wasn't much she didn't know. With nothing more than a breath she could read his every thought, see what passed before his eyes as if she were looking with her own. She knew he had found someone. A strong possibility. She could feel the pull. She had opened herself up to the energy around her and had felt a slight tug. Like a magnet. Fear had immediately settled in the pit of her stomach on the heels of that energy. Something dark was at the other end. Dark and familiar. She had felt something similar every time New Orleans had been brought into a conversation. That knot of fear. The cold ball in her stomach. She pushed it down every time and shut her mind down to that channel. But now it was back. It had started the day at the cliff. She had felt it chase her back from the edge, thought she had heard it whisper to her. She hadn't been able to shake it. When Marlon had started investigating the trail of her children, she had felt it reach for him. Visions of his death had raced before her eyes. No matter what she did to alter the course it always ended the same. Marlon dead, and her hands covered in his blood. When they had connected over the Witch Finder, she had seen it even clearer but this time there was a way to change it.

She pulled her suitcase from under the bed and began to pack. She had to make this trip without him. She now knew, he would die in New Orleans. If he came with her, she would be the death of him. She would not let that happen, so she had made the decision to do this alone. Once she had, a calm had settled over her. The fear was still there, but knowing that Marlon would be safe, would live out the rest of his life unharmed, gave her a sense of peace. Somehow, she knew that she would not come back from this trip. She knew that she would never see Marlon again and that had sent an ache through her so painful she had fallen to her knees. She had clamped her hands over her mouth to prevent the anguished whimper from escaping. She couldn't stop the tears from rolling down her cheeks, but she could do it in silence. Living without him was almost unbearable but living in a world where he was no longer was not even an option.

Her phone vibrated on the desk, and she picked it up. She had gotten quite adept at the "new to her" technology. The message was from her Uber, it was waiting down the road like she had requested. She sent a reply and picked up her suitcase. She stepped out into the hallway and looked towards Marlon's room. She had to look upon him one more time. She sat the suitcase down and moved silently towards his door. She opened it without a sound and walked inside. He was lying on his back, his face turned towards her. It was relaxed in sleep, and he looked so vulnerable and human. The tears started again as her heart tore in two. She gently traced her finger down the side of his face, taking in every curve, the line of his jaw, how the lines on his forehead smoothed as he slept. She inhaled the rhythmic cadence of his breathing. She let her emotions take her for a moment and placed the palm of her hand against his cheek. She needed to feel his warmth, his life. He nuzzled his face into her hand, and it almost broke her. For a moment she considered staying. Facing this with him. She gazed down at him and saw the pulse in his neck. The vision of his blood on her hands flashed before her eyes and she pulled her hand back. Her breath caught as the tears continued. She turned and walked to his door, with a final look back, she closed it. She had to move quickly. She could only hold the sobs back for so long, and it was becoming overwhelming. She could let go in the cab. She just needed to get out of the house.

She reached the Uber and got in. She gave the driver instructions, and they were off. They reached the train station, she paid the driver, gave him a healthy tip, clouded his mind, and got out. She knew eventually Marlon would figure out how she had traveled and where she had gone, but she wanted to put as much distance between them before he did. She wanted this over before he found her. Days ago, while Marlon and Chris had been busy at that computer, she had taken a trip into town. When she had locked them away, she had dissolved all their assets and put the money into an account at the bank. She had found out that now the bank had branches all over the country and that money could be accessed from anywhere. It was quite easy for her to gain access after all these decades, a few forged documents, a bit of mind bending, and voila, access to her "great grandmothers account". Now she had funds and could travel without having to use her powers. Marlon had learned what signs to look for when she had disappeared before. She had gone on a spree of sorts and had left him in a hotel in Chicago. It had taken a few weeks, but he had found her. If she used her power, it left a metaphysical residue that he could feel. With her abilities growing and getting stronger, she didn't want to take the chance that he may be gaining abilities too and find her sooner than was safe. Paying by cash was the easiest and best way to avoid detection.

She had booked a sleeper car so that she could have some privacy. She settled herself and looked out the window. Within moments the train started moving and the darkness began to fly by the window. She let herself relax and let the emotion come. Her forehead touched the glass and she allowed herself to cry, really cry. Her heart broke into a million pieces with each tear that fell, each mile that gathered between her and Marlon. Slowly the tears began to ebb, the sobs stopped, and she could think again. She opened her eyes and looked out the window once more. Dawn was approaching and the trees were black outlines against the lightening sky. She watched them race by.

A face, snarled in rage, flew at her, at the window and she recoiled with a scream. As quickly as it had appeared it was gone. She moved away from the window but didn't take her eyes off of it. Scanning everywhere for that face. She had physically felt the rage that it had carried with it. She didn't know where she had seen that face before, but it felt strangely familiar. She knew that face, but didn't know how, and she feared it. She was not one to fear anything, but she knew fear with that face. It was connected to where she was headed. Of that she was sure, and she now also understood that the man behind that face was the fear behind New Orleans. It wasn't the place it was a person.

She reached out and found what she was looking for. He was reaching for her. He took her breath and she clawed at her throat for a moment as she gasped. She had never encountered another with power like hers, or any power at all, but this man seemed to be able to draw breath, draw life from another as she could, but he could do it from a distance. The rage she felt from him began to subside and

PENANCE

she was suddenly awash in a new emotion. Possession. She belonged to him. She shut down the connection. She had no idea who this man was, and how he knew her, or why he was familiar to her, but she knew one thing. She belonged to no one.

As the last tendrils of his energy faded away and she sealed the connection closed, she heard a name. More of a whisper in her memory that words in her ears.

Adrian.

Chapter Nine

Unremembered Memories

THE TRAIN SLOWLY rolled into Union Passenger Terminal. Reese gathered her suitcase and made her way off. The city was different since the last time she had been here, but it also felt very much the same.

She wove her way between the people and out onto Loyola Street. She took a breath and exhaled slowly. New Orleans has a smell, a taste to it. You could feel it caress your cheek as a slight breeze blew by or run it's fingers through your hair. It had a feeling of life, older than anything. She felt at home here, but also had an overwhelming desire to run as far and as fast as she could away from this place. It was here that Marlon had finally found her and where she had made the decision to return to the property she knew so well and lock the two of them away.

It was where she had lost her senses, her sanity, and her heart. There was very little that she remembered of her time here, but as she stood in the warm humid air, with the city humming around her, a small blues group playing on the corner, the memories slowly filtered through. The band started to play something slow and bluesy, and a couple had started to dance on the sidewalk. She smiled at them and watched for a moment. She walked over, tossed a few bills into the open case at their feet and hailed a cab.

She got into the cab as the driver put her luggage into the trunk.

"Where to darlin'" he drawled as he climbed in the front. She had missed that wonderful accent and she smiled at him.

"The Monteleone, if you please."

The driver let out a slow whistle. "Livin' it high!" he said.

Reese laughed, "I suppose so, it has always been a favorite of mine."

It was a short ride and soon the cabbie was pulling up out front. The hotel loomed high above them, and Reese stepped from the cab and looked up at the building. It was decorated with ornate carvings and pretty little balconies. She had always loved this hotel and was happy to see that it hadn't lost any of its charm over the years. So many older buildings fell into disrepair or were redesigned for a newer more modern look. The Hotel Monteleone was still family owned and they had spent a considerable amount of money to retain that classic architecture.

The doorman came quickly over, motioning for the bellhop who was just inside the door.

"Good afternoon, Madam, welcome to the Hotel Monteleone."

Reese smiled at him. "Good afternoon." He held the door for her as she walked into the lobby. She checked in, gave the bellhop her room number and walked into the lounge. She wasn't a drinker, but she needed something stronger than tea to bolster her nerve before she went up to her suite.

When she had booked the room, she couldn't put her finger on why she had to have that particular suite. As the train had raced closer and closer to New Orleans, the meaning had become clearer and clearer. Then she had seen his face, remembered his name, and it had come back. At least the memories of that suite, and the time spent in it.

Adrian. She allowed his name to whisper through her mind. She dared not let it be more than that. She had felt the incredible power he now wielded and suspected that it was just a small taste of what he could now do. He had been a practitioner of the arts. The darker arts. She had been drawn to him for that reason. He was wild, untamed, and dangerous. He was also very, very human. That she knew now, was no longer the case.

She sat at the bar and ordered a whiskey, neat. The bartender raised an eyebrow at her but didn't say a word.

She took a sip and felt the push of power. She shook it off, took a much larger drink and the power pushed at her again. She sat the glass on the coaster, very carefully, very slowly, so that he could not see her handshake.

"Hello Adrian." She said as she turned.

Before her stood a boy no more than 15. He was dressed in a tank top and jeans. His mouth was smiling like he knew her, but his eyes were blank. Dead.

"Hello Catrina." Said the boy.

Reese smiled. That was the name she had used then. She had forgotten.

"This is not the body I remember." She said.

The boy laughed. "No, I suppose it is not." He came and sat beside her. Reese looked at the bartender and he seemed to not even see the boy.

"He isn't aware that I am here. To him, I look like a middle-aged businessman." Adrian laughed. "I appear to you as a child. I felt it was safer."

"Safer?" asked Reese.

"We did not part on the best of terms my darlin'. You did threaten to rip my throat out the next time you happened to put your hands on it, so I felt it safer to keep my throat away from said hands."

Reese furrowed her brow, she didn't remember.

The boy's face grew serious. "You really don't remember do you?"

Reese sighed in frustration. "No, I don't."

Adrian laughed. It was harsh and far deeper than the boy's throat should be able to make.

"Aw honey, well then, I will leave you to what you do remember. I am sure the rest will come back in time. When it does, I will be waiting. We have much to discuss, you and I." He blew her a kiss and suddenly the boys eyes held light again. A frightened light as he looked around.

Reese leaned over, touched his arm lightly and whispered to him softly. "Go child, remember nothing of this. You wandered a little too far, lost in your thoughts. Think happy tales and wander on home."

The boy got up and left. Reese downed the rest of her drink and headed up to her suite. The encounter had unnerved her. Adrian had seemed so smug, so excited that she had not remembered. What had happened that had made him afraid enough of her to inhabit the body of another to speak with her?

Her phone vibrated in her purse. She had been ignoring it for the last few hours but knew eventually she would have to answer it.

She pulled it out of her purse and swiped her finger across the screen.

"Where in that arrogant one-track mind of yours did you possibly think that this was a good idea!?" Marlon shouted on the other end of the line.

"Hello Marlon, how are you? Me? Oh, I'm fine, thank you for asking." She said sarcastically.

"I'm sorry but you know this is a bad idea." Marlon spoke a little softer now. "I didn't mean to yell. You know how I get when you aren't here. The physical pain I can deal with, the mental pain can be a bit much."

Reese sighed. She knew that a physical separation was hard on Marlon, but he had survived it before, he could do it again. She had tried making him hate her, but the effects of a physical distance were always the same.

"You knew it had to be this way. You can die, I cannot. If we are to find out information from here it has to be me. Only me."

"NO!" he hollered. 'You promised. No more running. You obviously lied." Marlon took a breath to calm himself. Reese felt his frustration level. She also felt a sharp pain in her hand. She looked down and a red circular welt appeared in the center.

"OW!" she said.

"You felt that!" Marlon exclaimed. Reese was silent. She was standing outside of her suite door looking at the scar on her palm. It was a quarter.

"Yes, I felt that. What the hell?" she whispered.

"That is what I have been trying to tell you, before you ran off in the night. The connection between us has deepened to a physical one. I hurt, you hurt, I feel you feel, and vice versa. It's only the beginning. There is more that is happening too."

She unlocked her door and stepped into the cool quiet. "Like what?" she asked.

"Who is Adrian?" Marlon asked. "And why is he a 15-year-old boy with the power of someone much older?"

Reese froze. "How?"

"I closed my eyes, thought of you and suddenly I could see and hear what you did." He replied. "What is happening Reese?"

She walked, a little unsteadily, to the settee and all but fell onto it. "I don't know."

PENANCE

"I am leaving tonight. Tell me where you are." He said.

"No. There are things I don't remember. Things I need to remember. Until I do, I need you as far away from me as possible. I need to know you are safe."

"Reese please. I remember what you were like when I found you. The blood lust, the viciousness. It took all I had to bring you back. You know it's not safe there." Marlon argued but Reese remained firm.

"I need to do this alone. Adrian is more powerful than what I remember. I do know that. He should be long dead, and yet he lives. His power was one of reanimation, not inhabitation. What he did today he shouldn't be able to do. The details that came back to me of the ritual spoke of such power bestowed on the one they called Jinn. If he is of that line, then I need to know. I need to know how dangerous he is before I bring you near him."

Marlon knew he could not change her mind. He clicked the button to book his flight and decided that she could be mad at him in person. It was better to ask for forgiveness than to ask permission.

"Fine, but until you know the full scope of his power, stay away from him." He said.

Reese agreed and hung up. She knew he was on his way. There were powers that had developed for her as well. She knew he was coming. She knew that he was already on his way to the airport. She also knew that the plane wouldn't leave the ground. Not with him on it.

The airport switchboard answered the phone. Reese pushed all the power she could at each person she got on the phone. Marlon would not be getting on that plane. Not tonight, or any night soon.

She hung up her phone again and switched it off. She would know when he found out. She would feel it, she didn't need to hear him yelling at her on the phone as well.

She took her suitcase into her bedroom and laid it on the bed. A hot soak in the huge tub was just what she needed. She may be an immortal, with powers beyond her comprehension at the moment, but she was also still a woman. A hot bath soothed more than just the body.

She grabbed a small bottle of champagne from the mini bar, turned the radio on to a blues station and sunk into the hot steamy water.

Half an hour later she was wrapped in a robe and curled on the couch. A knock on her door pulled her from her thoughts.

"Come in." she said. She had ordered dinner from room service.

That was not what walked through the door.

A man, about 30ish walked in. He was trim, his beard neat and he smelled like chocolate.

"Hello, I am a gift from Adrian." He said. His voice, like his eyes, held no emotion, No awareness. He reached into his pocket and pulled out a note.

My darling Catrina,

This is Darius. I wanted to give you a gift as a welcome home, and he seemed perfect. If I remember correctly, you do like them this age and well kept. I know your moral code is something you MUST live by, so this one likes young boys. Very young boys.

Bon appetite!

PENANCE

Adrian.

Panic fluttered in Reese's throat. She moved away from Darius, but he followed her. She bolted for the bathroom and again he followed her. She could feel the hunger rising in her. She had been fighting it since she stepped off the train. Pushing those memories back, refusing to remember them. But with a meal so perfect, so sweet standing right in front of her, it was becoming harder.

She closed her eyes and tried to breath slowly. All she could smell was him. She could hear his heart beating, the blood moving through his veins. The last kill, the witch finder, had awakened that beast in her. It had long been dormant, and she had been able to keep it satiated with animal blood. The witch finder had awakened that need, that craving for blood. She needed more than just a sip of energy from time to time to keep her hunger at bay.

She opened her eyes and Darius had moved right in front of her. All she had to do was push herself off the wall and she would be touching him. He stood staring at her. She reached up and touched his face. The blankness faded and his eyes awoke. He stared at her.

"Who are you?" he asked. She stroked his face again. With a thought the door shut and locked. An invisible buffer surrounded the room. No one outside of that room would hear a thing.

"I am the last thing you will ever see darlin'" she drawled. He squinted his eyes in confusion.

"You're such a small thing." He laughed. "And not my type."

"Oh, I know." She smiled at him. She elongated one fingernail and opened the skin in his cheek. "But you are mine."

Fear leapt to his face, and he began to scream. She so loved it when they screamed. Fear made the blood taste like candy. Fear made the energy come faster when she breathed it out of them.

Fear made the unremembered memories come back. His fear.

She licked her finger and smiled at Darius again. "Scream for me again." She whispered as she opened the skin on his other cheek.

And he did.

Chapter Ten

Fall into Me

REESE STRETCHED UNDER the silkiness of the sheet. Her body felt heavy limbed and satiated. A smile curved her lips as she remembered the previous night's meal. Darius had been all that he had promised he would be. His fear, his screams had awakened that put away part of her. His blood had filled her mouth like water. She had drank like a woman dying of thirst. Bathed her body in it. When she had finally breathed the last bit of life from his body and he was nothing more than dust on the floor, she had stumbled to the bed. She hadn't slept that well or that soundly in over 100 years. Not since Adrian.

That thought brought her back to consciousness a little more. He had known that she would not have been able to resist. He knew her better than anyone else. That side of her. The wild, uncontrolled chaotic savagery. He had fed it well. They had fed each other well. New Orleans was a good place to live if one wanted to remain anonymous, feed unnoticed. But unlike today's fictional depictions of the perfect hunting grounds for those like her, the French Quarter was not it. Faubourg Tremé or as it was known today, the Tremé, held the best, darkest corners. Adrian had lived in the Tremé and was rumored to have come from a long line of those who practiced witchcraft. Reese had sought him out when she was looking for more like herself. She had encountered many a charlatan and was expecting no less. He was the real deal. His magic tasted familiar but far enough removed from her to be unique and new. She had been drawn to him. A moth to a flame. She had burned at his touch. Ached with every sound of his voice. He had opened a part in her she didn't know she had. Pure predator. They had hunted, they had loved, and they had lived.

She pushed those thoughts back into the corners of her memory and rolled over burying her face in the pillow. The scent of blood filled her nostrils. She pulled her face back and cracked open an eye. It felt crusted with something. Wiping a hand across her face she could feel the remnants of the night before dried on her cheeks and caked in her hair. She almost giggled and she pulled the sheet from her naked body. It stuck in places and that did make her laugh out loud.

"I have missed that sound, cher." Drawled a deep voice from within the room. Reese scrambled up the bed and drew the sheet back around her. She scanned the room and found him. Sitting in a wing back chair just inside the

PENANCE

French doors of the bedchamber. The breeze from the balcony ruffled his hair and fluttered the sleeve of his cotton shirt.

"Adrian." She said flatly. "How did you get in? You were bound."

He laughed and a shiver went down her spine and settled low in her belly.

"My love, you bound me from places I did not own. Places I did not live. This Hotel, this whole block, most of the city, in one way or another, is mine." He stood and walked to the small table and lifted the receiver on the phone.

"Hello ma petite, could you please have Carla send up a recovery crew and my special breakfast?" he paused for a moment then continued. "Yes, utmost privacy please. Use the service elevator...No, not that one...yes, the special one." He hung up and walked towards the bed. Reese slid farther away from him.

He laughed again, a deep throaty very male laugh. Heat exploded in her. He paused and sniffed the air, like a dog scenting after his prey.

"I see I still entice you." He sat on the edge of the bed and tugged at the sheet. Reese held tight and her eyes slid to slits.

"You have not changed, so yes, I still find you physically appealing, but do not mistake my biological response for one of acceptance or forgiveness." She tried to look as menacing and as indignant as she could wrapped in nothing but a silk sheet and caked in dried blood.

A breeze wafted through the doors again and Adrian

curled his lip. "You need a shower. You smell like death." He stood and walked into the sitting room. He pushed on a wooden panel in the wall and a keypad popped out. He punched in some numbers and the wall beside the bed slid aside.

"You will find all you need in there. My staff must clean the mess you left in the bathroom, and you must shower. Both cannot be done in the same room. So, you will use my private suite." He turned as a knock rang out.

"Go. I do not want my staff to see you like this. Some images are harder to fade from the mind than others. I will have breakfast laid out when you are finished. We need to talk." He dismissed her like he always had. When Adrian was done with a conversation and had moved on, you knew. You no longer existed in that moment.

Reese slipped into the hidden doorway and found a full luxurious bathroom. She caught her reflection in the mirror that covered the wall above the double sinks. Her eyes seemed large and round in a sea of dried blood. Her hair was caked to her head and stuck to her back in places. Dried blood trailed down between her breasts and over her stomach. The trail continued down both legs and ended just above her feet. Strangely her feet were perfectly clean. It made her giggle again and she realized that she was in mild shock. Seeing Adrian, being that vulnerable, had shaken her. So had her response to him. She still wanted him, craved him almost as much as she had so many years ago. She was not giving in this time. Not falling for that sweet drawl and those dark eyes. His skin the color of coffee and cream. He had tasted as good as he looked. She shook her head and walked to the shower. She adjusted the temperature to be just slightly cooler than warm. Something

Penance

had to chase the desire from her, and she hoped cold water would do it. He was a dangerous man. She was dangerous when she was with him. She had no control over her predatory nature when he was around. Had she been paying more attention the previous night she would have sensed the spell on Darius. Adrian's magic was all over the young man. She could still feel it in the dried blood on her body. The spell had weakened her control over that nature. She stepped into the shower and the water fell around her. Reese hung her head and watched the water drip from her hair. Red, then pink, then clear. With each scrub, each lather, she felt more in control of herself. When she smelled of nothing more than honeysuckle, she turned the temperature up and let the heat seep into her. For a moment she let those emotions come. Tears mingled with the water and ran down her cheeks unabashed. She clamped a hand over her mouth as the swell of pain became almost overwhelming. A small whimper escaped before she could pull herself back. She drew a breath and gave into it. No one could hear her when she put up her walls. She let every wound, every pain, every scar Adrian ever left on her, every crack in her heart, pour out of her and down the drain. Soon the room was steamy and misty. The mirrors had fogged over, and the steam moved in waves from the stall. She had stopped crying and just felt drained. She lathered up the puff one last time and let the soap run down her body. She had her back to the door when she felt a cool wind reach for her. That wind brought a dark magic and her knee's almost buckled at the intensity. She spun around and Adrian stood on the other side of the glass doors. He had a robe in his hand, but it seemed forgotten. He had witnessed her breakdown. The look in his eyes told her as much. He stood staring at her.

93

She moved toward the glass door and put her hand up to hold it closed as he moved toward it at the same time. He saw her reaching up and thought she was reaching for him and before Reese could stop him, he was in the shower with her. He had her pinned against the cold tile wall, his mouth devouring hers.

She pushed with all she had against him. He didn't budge. She tried to turn her head away from him, but his hands held her firm. She pushed against him again, this time using metaphysical force along with physical. It moved him back just enough so he could see her face.

"Get out." She hissed, fury etching every angle of her face. He looked down at her and smiled.

"Ah cher, you don't mean that. I can feel the heat rising off you. Smell it on you." He leaned in again to kiss her, and she took a quick breath in. He wasn't expecting that, and he backed up gasping as she pulled the air from his lungs.

"I said, get out." She ground out. He stepped out of the stall and slowly began to remove his shirt. Panic began to flutter in her stomach. "What are you doing?"

This time when he smiled, there was nothing gentle in it. He was the hunter and this time; she was the hunted. "I cannot go out there soaking wet. It would make such a mess." He dropped the shirt on to the floor and reached for the button on his slacks. Fear mixed with need raced through Reese and she turned away from him. Once she broke eye contact, she could think a bit more clearly.

"I won't say it again Adrian. Get the hell out!" her voice had risen a few octaves. The air around her started to stir and it took her a moment to recognize her own magic. Once she did, she wrapped it around herself. She was in control again. She turned to face Adrian and found him standing barefoot with his slacks unbuttoned. Water glistened on his chest, and she wanted nothing more than to lick the drops from him, but she pushed that down and pulled her magic up tighter. She turned the water off and stepped out of the stall.

"If you won't leave, I will. I've had enough of these petty games. My body may want you Adrian, but I have no other interest than that, and have no interest in pursuing it any further than acknowledging that fact." She raised her head and strode confidently past him. "You are nothing to me. You were nothing to me then and you are nothing to me now. Nothing more than food." She pulled a towel from the rack and wrapped it around her body. Just as she was almost out of the room, she heard the growl.

"I was more than nothing!" Adrian roared. The room shook slightly. Reese trembled inside but turned to look at him. Disdain all over her face. "Please. You are nothing more than a magic man. A weak one at that. You claim to own half the city? How small minded of you. I own the world. There is no place I cannot go that I am not welcome. You are bound to places you must possess. I am the one who bound you. You dare to think you are better than I am? Stronger? You are NOTHING!" Anger had replaced any fear she may have felt. She had created him; she could destroy him. "I made you. I taught you how to increase your power, I taught you how to live beyond the one trick pony you were when I found you. Then you became a bore to me. Do not ever forget that. I made you and I can unmake you." Her eyes blazed and her hair spun around her in the wind her magic created. Her skin shimmered and heat rose off her in waves.

Adrian stared at her for a moment, then burst out laughing. "Sweet Catrina, it has been many years since you fled from me in fear. Yes, fear. I have learned much in that time."

The anger that had swelled in Reese exploded into rage. Emotional control was not something that she had a good grip on when she was around him, time had not changed that. Something close to a screech burst from her mouth and she lunged at him. Her nails had lengthened into her claws, and she swiped at him.

He was almost as fast as she was and was able to grab her wrists as she came at him. The momentum of her crashing into him propelled the two of them back into the glass walls of the shower stall. They shook but held. Adrian pulled her close, pinning her arms behind her.

"No one attacks me in my house. You do not control me anymore." He snarled. He yanked hard on Reese's arms almost pulling them from their sockets, just to prove his point. Rage flared in her eyes, and she leaned her head forward. She clamped her teeth onto his shoulder, and he roared in pain, throwing her off him. She crashed into the mirror above the sink and landed on the counter. The mirror cracked where her body had struck, and a small trail of blood wove its way down the broken glass. The smell hit Reese and it opened that primal place in her that she kept so tightly sealed. The blood in her mouth from the bite snapped something inside her. She bounced into a crouch on the counter and watched Adrian with eyes that were no longer human. No longer capable of rational thought.

Adrian knew that look and countered with one of his own. He pushed himself off the glass wall and stalked toward her. A low rumble coming from him.

PENANCE

"You know how this is going to play out Catrina. One of two things are going to happen." A musk had begun to rise from his skin. A scent. Purely male.

Need made Reese tremble slightly, the smell of blood made her growl. She licked her lips, and the taste of Adrian's blood filled her mouth. That was the last straw. Any humanity left; any semblance of control broke.

"My name is Reese." She purred. A scent of her own now rising from her skin. She leapt at Adrian, all teeth, and claws. She wrapped her legs around his waist, bringing one hand to this throat, claws just piercing his skin.

Fire blazed in Adrian's eyes. He swallowed so he could feel the claws dig in a bit deeper. His hands had come up to grip her hips as she had landed on him. He pulled down hard so she could feel just how aroused he was before he flung her into the glass of the shower.

"Reese my darlin', we are either going to fuck, or fight." He walked towards her lying on the shower floor. The glass had shattered, and her back was sliced and bleeding. She healed fairly quickly but not quick enough to stop the blood. The room was filled with the smell of it and pheromones. Reese regained her feet, in a crouch again, and looked up at Adrian.

"Fight!" She again pounced on him but this time she tore his throat open. He dropped to his knees but his grip on her never loosened. As he gasped for air, he ground himself into her. She moaned and breathed into him. His throat reknit and he got to his feet, carrying her into the bedroom. She struggled to get free, but he tightened his grip.

"Oh no love, not this time." He grabbed a handful of her hair and pulled her head back, stretching her neck to the

97

limit. He ran his tongue across her jawline, down her neck and across her collarbone. Then he bit her, taking a piece. The blood ran down her naked breasts pooling between them where their bodies touched. She raked her nails down his back, tearing it to ribbons, letting the blood flow over her hands before she healed him. He threw her onto the bed and tore at his pants. With one swipe she had them off. He fell on her like a man starving. He licked the blood from her, following the trail until it ended. He flicked his tongue over her, and she moaned. He continued his exploration until Reese's legs began to tremble and her hands scrambled in the sheets for something to hang on too. He brought her to climax over and over with his tongue until she could barely breath. Blood and sweat mixed and limbs slid over bodies. The fight was over. Now it was a race. Adrian kissed Reese again and this time she kissed him back, just as hard, just as hungry as he was. That broke any control Adrian had and he dragged her until she was flat on the bed. He pushed her legs apart and plunged into her. A scream tore from Reese as her back arched. He didn't relent. As if he was trying to erase the years, they had been apart. She clung to him at first, then, as the pleasure continued to build in her, she brought her hips up to meet him, thrust for thrust. Reese screamed again as orgasm hit her. As the waves crashed through her, it sent Adrian over that edge. His movements lost pace and his breathing became erratic. He wove one hand under her gripping her hip, and the other hand tangled in her hair. His own orgasm hit him drawing a guttural primal sound from him. Sending Reese into another wave of pleasure.

When it was over, Adrian collapsed beside her. The two lay still for a long time, catching their breath. Reese was the first to speak.

PENANCE

"Get out." Her voice was flat and devoid of emotion. Adrian pushed himself up and looked at her. Their eyes met.

"Did I stutter?" she asked.

"No ma cher." He said. Adrian climbed off the bed and looked at the destruction in the two rooms. The bed was covered in blood and the bathroom was torn apart. Glass was everywhere.

"You will need to find other accommodation. This room is no longer suitable." He walked naked to the hidden room, pulled a robe from the rack, and flipped open another panel full of buttons. He punched in another code and a door at the back of the hidden bathroom opened. "I do not care where you go, but if you plan to keep me away from you, you best be sure I do not own it. Because I will not be kept from you again. You still want me Catrina, Reese, whatever you choose to call yourself now. You still love me. Fight it all you want. I will win." He turned and disappeared into the door and was gone.

Reese lay on the bed staring at the ceiling for a very long time after he had gone. The room had gone from light to dark at some point. She sat up and wiped at her cheeks. They were covered in tears. She would never say the words out loud. Not ever again, but her heart knew. She had never stopped loving him. If that is what you could call what they had between them. She was pretty sure Freud had told her it was more obsession than love, but she had ignored him then. Now she wasn't so sure. No good had ever come from a relationship with Adrian. He hadn't changed. She knew that for fact. She had. She had found a love, so pure, so gentle it had scared her into hiding for a century. It had caused her to run away out of a need to protect him. What she had with Adrian was wild. Dangerous, and oh so addicting.

And she was afraid she was addicted, again. Adrian was one to fall on too, Marlon was one to fall in to.

And she wasn't sure she didn't need both.

Chapter Eleven

Desperate Measures

REESE HAD CLEANED herself up and somewhere between washing her shame down the shower drain and calling around to find another hotel, a crew of silent workers had entered the suite and put things back to rights.

"I'm sorry Ma'am Mr. DeMorte owns the entire chain." Said the flustered voice on the other end of the phone.

Reese wasn't one to give into cursing but there was a particularly offensive word dancing on the end of her tongue. She hit the end button and threw the phone onto the bed. She needed a new place to stay, and she refused to be at Adrian's mercy again. She had wanted him, there was no question there. He was her weakness. She couldn't think straight when he was around. Every primal instinct she had rose to the surface and the cool collected calm façade she carried, shattered to pieces. Much as the room had last night.

"Ma'am?" a soft voice said from behind her. Reese spun and glared at the young girl. She opened her mouth to snap something nasty at her and noticed the look in her eyes. It was clear, aware. Adrian hadn't clouded her mind like the rest of them.

"I keep my head down when Monsieur is about. He does not notice me, so he does not meddle with me." She knew what had caused Reese's confusion. She giggled slightly as Reese's confusion grew.

"I have a gift, he does not know, and by telling you I am trusting you with my life." Reese heard the words, but the girls lips never moved. They whispered through her mind like a soft wind. She opened her mouth to speak, and the girl raised her finger to her lips.

"We must be cautious. They may seem mindless, but he hears all through them." She handed Reese a piece of paper with an address in the French Quarter. "I will meet you there and explain."

Reese gathered her things and left the room. Adrian was sitting at the hotel bar when she reached the lobby. She could feel his eyes on her, but she refused to look his way. The pull became almost unbearable, but she pushed back at him, and he stopped. She was stronger than he was, she had just needed a reminder. No one controlled her, no one commanded her. She was the start of what had created him. All his power came from her, and with a breath, she could call it all back. She focused her mind, calmed her nerves, and took a small quick breath. Not enough for the woman behind the counter to notice, but enough that Adrian withdrew his power immediately and she could hear him start coughing. She smiled to herself, paid her bill, and left.

The thick night air hit her as she left the coolness of the hotel lobby. The air in New Orleans was something tangible. You could feel it on your skin, taste the sweetness on your tongue and almost hold it in your hand. She took a deep breath. She had missed this city.

She hailed a cab and headed to the address on the slip of paper. She pulled up in front of the large brick building. 837 Royal it said over the stark white double doors. The building itself hadn't changed much over the century. She paid the cabby and stepped out into the heat once more. It engulfed her like a hot wet blanket. There was a man standing off to the side watching her. She could feel the slight ripple of power roll off him, but he made no outward advance. She took her bags from the cabby and stood on the street looking up at the building. The young girl was a chamber maid at the hotel, how she could afford a place in this building she didn't know.

"Follow me."

Reese jumped and turned toward the man. His voice had floated through her mind like a soft touch. He was just rounding the corner onto Dumaine, and she hurried after him. Neither spoke. She followed him down the street a bit and into a small driveway tucked into the building. They wove their way through until they came out into a small courtyard in the center of the building. A pool was set against the one wall, with three large lion heads feeding water into it. The rest of the courtyard was lush with trees and flowers. The fragrance was almost overwhelming. The building rose three stories above them. People wandered the balconies or sat sipping wine. Blues music wafted from one open doorway and laughter from another. The man motioned to a small wrought iron table and told her to sit. Reese was a little taken aback but remembered that she had cloaked herself so that Adrian could not track her. This man had no idea of the power she held. She sat, placed her purse on the table and crossed her ankles under her chair. She reached in her bag and turned on her phone. She might as well check the multitude of messages Marlon had surely left since the last time; she had turned her phone on. He was not pleased. This new connection between them was a problem. Last night was not something he should have had to experience. She didn't know what to say to him. They had no formal arrangement. They had barely even admitted they had feelings for each other. Yet, she felt guilty, as if she had betrayed him somehow. She was avoiding him, and he knew it. Which is why he kept calling. He had stopped reaching out metaphysically. That was cut off abruptly last night. About the time her restraint had snapped. It had left a hole inside of her. When she focused on it, she was almost overwhelmed by the pain of it, so, she did what she did best, she hid. Closed herself off to it. Ignored it. As the phone came on it began vibrating. She was going to have to talk to him, or he was just going to show up, like the last time.

She clicked his name from her contacts list and put the phone to her ear.

"WHAT IN THE BLOODY HELL DO YOU THINK YOU ARE DOING?"

She removed the phone from her ear, sat it on the table and hit the speaker button.

"Hello Marlon." She said dryly.

PENANCE

She heard what she thought sounded like a roar and then Chris's voice came out of the phone.

"Uh Reese?" he said tentatively.

"Hello Chris." She said, again, dryly.

"Uh...What happened? I have a Marlon sized hole in the wall upstairs and several Marlon fist sized holes throughout the downstairs. I can't afford to fix any more damage. I have sent him outside to whack at the weeds, but they are only going to last for so long."

Reese sighed. She knew Marlon had a temper, which he usually kept in check. "Let me talk to him."

"Oh no!! You tell me how to fix this and then I will consider even letting him back in the house!" shrieked Chris. "Do you have any idea how strong that dude is?"

Before Reese could answer the phone was snatched from Chris's hand.

"Why? Just tell me that." Growled Marlon.

"I don't know." Reese said quietly.

Marlon grew quiet. "Did he hurt you?"

She knew that lying would be useless. He was still connected to her at that point. "Yes." She said.

She felt some of his anger leak out. "Did you hurt him?" he ground out.

"Yes." She said again.

"Are you with him?"

"No."

She could feel Marlon's confusion. "Then what was last night?" he asked quietly.

"I told you. I don't know. I was angry, I wanted to hurt him, and his power was so strong."

Marlon was silent for a bit and Reese could feel the battle inside him. He was hurt, and angry but he was hiding it from her. She could feel the weight of his feelings for her and the war he was having with his own beliefs on that. He had always been the jailer. He had never shown her any affection until recently. They had an understanding of sorts, which may have looked like a friendship but was more of a business relationship. She had developed an affection for him when he had been resistant to hurt her as much as she had felt she deserved. He had showed her compassion when she hadn't wanted it or felt entitled to it. Now he was hurt as a lover scorned and it was confusing him and that was angering him. She didn't push.

"I felt that. How did it get so strong?" She could feel Marlon again, faintly.

Deciding that for now, focusing on the new developments was best, she answered him. "I don't know. But he isn't the only one. There is a girl. I met her today, which is why I am on Royal Street. There is a boy too. They both have this power, the ability to talk in my mind. Like the power between us."

Marlon didn't say anything. She sat quietly but this time because she knew he was thinking. "The original power taken from you has mutated. Not one of the others has that, or anything close to that. The witch and the Djinn were the only one that you can remember that was given the ability to cloud the mind, but not speak directly to it. Do you think they are one of Adrian's?" He said the name like it was something vile tasting on his tongue.

Penance

"It didn't feel like his power. His carries a darkness, a heaviness, theirs was lighter, more at peace with the elements around them. His fights the elements, he bends the natural order to his will, while theirs felt like it came from the natural order."

"You know I am coming to you right?"

She sighed heavily. "Yes. I do. As soon as I know where I will be staying, I will text you the address."

"I thought you were staying at the hotel?" Marlon was confused.

"Adrian owns every hotel, motel, B&B, and roach infested rat hole in this city. In order to keep him out with the binding, I must stay in a place he does not own."

"Ah." Was all he said.

"Ah?" she asked.

"Yes. Ah. It makes perfect sense. The city you two once controlled and terrorized for years would be a perfect trap. He had to know you would once again return. Do not for a second think that he hasn't had a hand in your return. By owning all the hotels, he could ensure access to you whenever he chose. You are not the same girl you were then, and he didn't know that. Leave it with me, Chris and I will discuss suitable arrangements with a banker he knows in the Quarter. You may have to actually buy your own piece of paradise my love."

She drew a breath at the moniker. That was very personal and very unlike Marlon.

Reese saw the young girl exit a door in the courtyard and walk towards her. "The girl is coming. I will call you back." She flipped off the phone before Marlon could object.

The girl approached with the boy not too far behind.

"I should introduce myself; I am Cynthiana, and this is my brother Ash. We are Westmoorlanders." She said that like it meant something. She sat across from Reese and Ash stood behind her.

"I see you have no idea what that means." She raised her hand and a plate of beignets appeared with glasses of frosty sweet tea.

"You are the beginning of it all, but we are the end. Let me explain."

She sat back and light began to shimmer around her. "We are flesh of your flesh, bone of your bone, but we are so much more. We have the power of the elements at our command because we do NOT command, we ask. What was taken from you, at first was disgraced, used for ill and for power, then, to balance the energy, Nature created us. From the earth of the west moors of Ireland we appeared. Over the centuries we have learned to integrate like you.

Where you are dark, we are pure light."

Reese took a sip of her tea and sat back. She opened her mouth to speak but before she could get a word out, a strange feeling came over her. Her limbs felt heavy and full of lead, her head, fuzzy and she couldn't focus her eyes. She had read about this type of thing; she had been drugged. She tried to reach for her phone to call Marlon, but everything went blank.

Cynthiana looked at Ash, her face no longer peaceful and welcoming. "Take her down to Mother. Be sure to chain her with the special chains, the ones made for her. We can't

PENANCE

risk her getting out."

Chapter Twelve

Mother of All

THE SMELL OF decay surrounded Reese as she lay as still as she could. It felt so familiar but the cotton that filled her head made it hard to sort memory from reality. She lay on what felt like a small cot. That helped clear her mind. The smell of decay receded into memory. The cold damp of the basement and the fogginess had pulled the memory from her. Marlon was not coming to rend her to pieces, she was not paying penance for her sins. She had been drugged. The anger at that cleared the rest of the ketamine away. She sat up and looked around. The walls were a plain cinder block, painted black, a small window sat high on the far wall, covered in a dark cloth. The cell that held her was large enough for her to take a step or two from the cot, but not much else. She swung her legs over the side and as the cold cement floor touched her skin, she realized she was barefoot.

And shackled. Large iron bands encircled both ankles. She lifted one small foot and waggled the heavy chain that disappeared under the cot. She peered underneath and saw the chain attached to a large ring embedded into the floor. Her fingers brushed the shackles and sparks flew off them.

"OUCH!" she exclaimed. Magical runes glowed where her fingers had touched. They had spelled the iron to hold her. She almost laughed out loud.

"I have waited a long time for you." A voice, soft and comforting, drifted from the dark recesses of the room.

Reese sat back on the cot, still, but her energy was scanning every part of the room. It took only a moment before she found the small figure sitting in the corner directly across from her cell.

"You can release yourself. Ash was confident you couldn't, but he doesn't know what or who you are." The woman stood and walked into the dim light of the bulb hanging from the center of the room.

Reese immediately recognized the one she branded Witch. Rage boiled in her blood and a cold wind began to blow around her.

The woman smiled. "There is the fearsome creature that I knew so long ago."

Reese tried to step forward but stopped. She could hear footsteps. Two. One lighter than the other. Her power was leaching power from the magical runes, and all her senses, all her powers were charging up. The hearing of the vampire and the wolf were hers and she used them.

Cynthiana and Ash were approaching, their voices getting louder.

"Mother should have siphoned off the power that the runes haven't, and she should be close to human now." Ash said with confidence. Cynthiana looked at him, mild guilt on her face.

"I feel bad tricking her. She was so vulnerable at the hotel. I don't think she is the same person Mother knew. I saw no evil, felt no ill intent. The flowers I placed near her didn't wither or turn black.

Ash laughed, "She is supposed to be some super all-powerful force, don't you think she could see our little spells and counter them? You can be so naïve sometimes. I'm older, I know better. Which is why Mother put me in charge of the magical stuff."

Cynthiana grimaced. "You are only older by 13 seconds. She put you in charge of carving the runes into the iron because you have brute strength not the brains to cast the spells."

Reese looked at the Witch.

"You had children."

The Witch smiled softly. "Yes, twins. The only time I ever conceived. I have taught them to be light and love. To work with the elements and the natural energy. They are good, pure. Something I never was."

Reese looked at the woman thoughtfully. "Why were you there that night? Why did you take of my flesh?"

The woman laughed sardonically. "A man. Isn't it always

a man?" She sat back in her chair. "I was in love. It was wild, and crazy, and violent and all consuming. He was everything I wanted and everything I feared. When he told me we could have untold power, I believed him. I almost backed out when I entered the cave and saw you on the altar. But he convinced me it was alright. Then you cursed me. I was angry for a long time. I put a spell on him and refused to lift it. His brother begged and begged, and finally I relented, but it was too late. He was too far gone. I left. I left him in the forest, staring back at me with those grey wolf eyes of his. Three months later I realized I was pregnant. I became pregnant the night we did the ritual. They look young. Their aging is slowed. I am assuming because of the curse."

"They claim they came from Ireland, that they sprang from the Earth." Reese said.

The woman laughed. "I told them a story when they were small, of fairies and magic and good and evil. They chose to believe it and I never discouraged them. They have lived by a creed that no amount of love or teaching could have ingrained in them. They are good."

The woman stood again and walked to Reese's cell.

"I know you are going to kill me, and I am ready. I have waited for this day for a long time. I ask that you do me one courtesy first."

Reese looked at the woman, shocked. She had a lot of nerve asking for favors. "Ask."

"Please let my children live. Teach them how to fight those that did this to you, teach them the ways of the real world, and show mercy. Give them, what I never gave you."

PENANCE

The door to the basement opened and those very children descended the stairs.

The woman walked over to Cynthiana and Ash and kissed them both on the cheek.

"Reese has a story to tell you, listen to her. She speaks the truth. Know that I love you, and I always have. You are the only good things I have ever done in my life."

Cynthiana looked at her mother, "Mother, what are you talking about?" she looked over at Reese, "What have you done to her?"

"I have done nothing. Ask what she, her lover, his brother, and their friends have done to me." She spat out.

The woman's head fell forward.

"That's right. I am not going to kill you, not just yet that would be to easy. To end your suffering now, would be a gift. One which you do not deserve. Tell them what you have done. Tell them the truth of their longevity, tell them the truth of their parentage. Tell them it all."

"Mother?" Ash's voice sounded small and scared. The woman took their hands and led them upstairs. Reese could hear everything. The shock, the disbelief and then the anger. The accusations. Reese had suspect that the Wolf had been their father, now, she was sure. The Vampire was his brother. She had names. Locations. Places to search for them, or their descendants. As she sat on the cot listening to the conversation upstairs and reveling in the waves of emotional pain emanating from the Mother, she picked up on another power. One she was very familiar with.

Marlon.

He was racing to her rescue like the white knight he was.

He didn't know that she was no longer in danger. She sent a calming wave to him as swiftly as she could. He was coming so fast she wasn't sure if he would even notice it.

She looked at the shackles and waggled her foot again. She wasn't going to slip out of them that way. She closed her eyes, took a small breath and faster than a blink she was a small mouse sitting inside the circle of one of the shackles. She climbed over it, scurried out of the cell, and resumed her human like form.

Using the speed, she had she raced upstairs just as Marlon burst through the door. Ash lunged at him. Reese flicked her hand and Ash smashed against the wall beside Marlon. Then she spun her finger and Marlon began to struggle like he was tied up.

"What the hell are you doing?" he asked.

"I'm fine. There is much to tell you and I didn't want you killing the witness's before they had all the details."

She unbound Marlon and he came and stood in front of her. He grabbed her by the arms and did a thorough examination before he gave her a good shake.

"You ever scare me like that again, you ever leave me out of the plan like that again, and you ever just leave without a word, and I will tear you to pieces." He said. Anger, fear, relief, and an emotion she wasn't ready to put into words were etched into his face.

She just nodded and he released her.

"You were just an innocent girl." Cynthiana said. Tears staining her cheeks.

Reese looked at her. "I was."

PENANCE

Ash began to rouse from the floor. The woman came over and helped him up. As his vision cleared, he snatched his arm from her grasp.

"Don't touch me." He said. The woman dropped her hand and sat in the chair at the large wooden table.

They were in a large kitchen and Cynthiana and Ash had been at one end of a very large, long table and the woman had been at the other when Marlon had busted the door.

Ash scowled at Marlon and Reese took a quick breath, he gasped, and his hand flew to his throat, along with Cynthiana's. Reese raised an eyebrow. "You are connected?"

The two gasped and Reese released her breath. Once they could breathe normally Cynthiana answered.

"We always have been. He hurts, I hurt and vice versa. Puberty was a bitch for both of us in more ways than one."

Reese laughed at that. "I bet!"

"How did you do that?" Ash asked. "How did you steal our breath?"

"It is my chosen way of killing and surviving. I must eat to live, much like you, but I can live off the life force of others. Mostly I take a little here or there, people think they are choking on their spit, or they swallowed air and can't breathe for a second. That is all it takes, and I can go months without feeding again. I also use it as a warning. At any moment I can end you. Don't ever forget that."

Marlon let out a small chuckle. "Out of all the monsters in this room, hell in the world, she is the scariest."

Reese glared at him.

117

The woman stood and bowed her head. "I am ready."

Cynthiana's brow furrowed in confusion. "Ready for what?"

Reese walked to the woman, and slowly took a deep breath. The woman collapsed to the floor; her lungs deflated like a balloon left in the sun too long. She clutched her chest, and her lips made a smacking sound as she tried to take a breath.

"NO!" screamed Cynthiana. "Please! I know what she did to you was horrible, but she isn't that person anymore. Please!"

Reese gave a small breath out. The woman took a rattling breath.

"I have no intention of killing her. She is useful. She has information that I want. You two have done nothing to me but follow your mother's misguided orders. I do not kill the innocent anymore."

"Anymore?" Ash asked.

"Another story, another time." Reese answered.

The woman slowly pulled herself up from the floor. She looked at Reese. "I thought you wanted me dead."

Reese turned towards the stove, located the kettle, and filled it with water, placed it on the stove and turned on the element. She looked at Cynthiana. "Please tell me you have some sort of tea."

Cynthiana retrieved the tea and some cups and handed them to Reese. Then she went and sat beside her brother at the table.

Reese looked at the woman. "You are going to help us. I

want to track down all of you. Each one who took of my flesh. There is a man, he is Vampire, he is here, and he has powers that I have never seen. They almost match mine, but they have been twisted somehow. He is not stronger than I, but he is close. I want to find the one who made him. I want to find you all."

The woman nodded. "I can help you. I know the man you speak of. Adrian DeMorte. He is an evil man. I have done my best to avoid him. What do you need me to do first?"

Reese removed the whistling kettle and poured two cups of tea. She handed one to the woman.

"What is your name?" she asked.

"Tiana."

"Well, Tiana, I need you to find a way to kill him."

The woman paled. "No. I will not. I cannot."

Reese flicked her hand and a large gash appeared on Ash's chest. His shirt immediately began to soak with blood, and he tried to hold his skin together with his hands. Blood poured over his fingers.

"He will bleed out in about 3 minutes." Reese said.

Tiana screamed. "Please! You said you didn't kill innocents anymore!"

Reese smiled. "He isn't as innocent as he would have you believe."

Cynthiana looked at her mother in shock. "Mother please, help her, don't let Ash die." She screamed in pain as Ash writhed on the floor.

Tiana looked at her children and back at Reese,

119

desperation emanating from her in waves.

"Two minutes." Reese said flatly.

She flicked her hand and a similar gash appeared on Cynthiana. She fell back and Ash contorted in pain. Their blood mixed on the floor between them.

"One minute."

"Fine, fine I'll do it." Tiana cried.

Reese took a deep breath and blew over the two wounds. They reknit as fast as they appeared. Cynthiana and Ash fainted from the shock to their bodies.

"You are a monster." Said Tiana.

"Told you." Said Marlon.

Reese walked up to Tiana and put her face as close to hers as possible. "I am what you made me."

Chapter Thirteen

Death Is Inevitable

THE GROUP SETTLED into an uneasy truce. There would be no peace until Reese had found the rest, but she was willing to put aside the desire to kill Tiana and use her powers and those of her children to find the others. Ash and Cynthiana had spent most of the last few weeks talking to everyone they knew who had any sort of magical or otherworldly power. Tiana had spent her time talking to Reese. There were so many painful memories, it was a long process. Tiana broke down. A lot.

"Look, we are getting nowhere." Marlon grumbled. Tiana was sobbing uncontrollably again, and they had barely gotten started.

Reese stood and walked from the room. Marlon

followed.

"Something doesn't feel right. Every time we circle back to that night, she loses it. I can feel the block, the energy, It begins to swirl around her, and it gets stronger the closer she gets. It has a familiar feel to it. I've felt it before, but I can't place it." Reese paced the hall, her brow furrowed in concentration. She was absorbing some of the energy from the room Tiana was in. Marlon knew that look on her face. She was tracing.

He leaned against the wall and just watched her. She had never scared him, not even when she was sucking the life out of the village. Not when she had bound him to her with nothing more than her desire and a thought. He never once feared her. Nor had he feared for her. This woman, Tiana, had brought a fear to him that he felt in his core. She was one of the first. One of Reese's children. If they had found one, they could find more, and that stirred a fear in him. He didn't know why but something told him that solving the mystery, finding all of Reese's missing pieces, would bring about the end of not just Reese's search, but of something else as well. Something important.

Reese turned and looked at Marlon and his breath caught in his throat. He had looked at that face for hundreds of years, and still, at times, she could steal his breath and make his heart beat a little faster. He loved her. He had never questioned that. It just was. He had never pursued it, but he had never pursued another either.

".... down to the river." She said. She squinted at Marlon. "Are you listening?"

Marlon blinked at her, trying to clear his thoughts. He had never had this much trouble before. She had never had this much power over him like this. She had tried, but they had found that even though she could command his body to follow her words, his will was always his own. Now it felt as if she was taking that.

"I...I.... what?" he stammered.

"Are you having a stroke?" she came and placed her hand on Marlon's arm. A current shot through the two of them almost knocking them to the ground. If Marlon had not been leaning against the wall, they would have ended up just there.

Tiana burst from the room and Ash and Cynthiana came running up the stairs.

"What have you done?" cried Tiana "Why would you call him?"

"Mama, who? Who did she summon?" asked Cynthiana trying to comfort her mother.

"Adrian." Tiana said flatly.

Reese untangled herself from Marlon's arms and looked at Tiana confused.

"I didn't call him." She said. "I was trying to figure out what was wrong with Marlon."

"I felt it. The call. The specific energy that summons him to you. It is full of lust, desire, longing, and anger." Tiana stalked towards Reese, no more the broken woman she was a moment before. "You told me you had a relationship with him, but no longer. Now you summon him to my home? To where my children are? You lied!" she turned, and Reese grabbed her arm.

As they made contact a sound like a wounded lion

shattered the air. A light blasted from the two and swirled about them. Tiana and Reese continued to screech as fast as they could draw breath. The ball of light grew in size and intensity until it almost consumed the whole of the hall. When the pressure seemed more than the two could stand, the ball smashed into Reese. The two fell to the floor and were silent.

Ash and Cynthiana raced to their mother's side and Marlon to Reese's. He gathered her onto his lap, brushing the hair from her face. She slowly opened her eyes and looked up at him. Relief coursed through him, and he smiled at her.

"Can you speak?" he asked gently.

"Shiiiiiiiit." She whispered. His laugh was so abrupt it sounded like a bark.

Three feet away, Tiana was sitting up. She was shaking her hands and muttering. Her children knelt beside her.

"NO!" exclaimed Tiana. "This can't be!"

Reese stood and watched as Tiana stood and turned towards her. "You stole it!"

Reese, sore and unamused now, glared at Tiana. Her eyes mere slits. "First you call me a liar, and now a thief. You better explain before the last of my good humor is gone."

"My power!" sobbed Tiana. "You stole it. It's gone."

The four others in the hall looked at Tiana, shocked.

Reese was the first to speak. She could feel the power, racing through her, it felt like her power, but it had much of Tiana in it. That would fade she was sure, as it rejoined her own.

"I stole nothing. Do NOT forget how you came to have that power. You ripped it from my body. What was mine in the beginning has merely returned to me. As for being a liar, Adrian and I have been over for more than a century. I would not ever lie about that man."

She turned towards the stairs when the realization slammed into her. The power. The block she felt. What she now assumed was Tiana's power, was not. It was Adrian's. Her gasp was barely audible, but Marlon heard it.

"Reese?" he asked.

Reese continued down the stairs. She had to be away from him to think. She would never tell him, she never had, but he was a distraction. She found it hard to concentrate when he was too close to her. Lately it had seemed to be stronger than she had ever allowed it to be. Since returning to New Orleans, the thought of kissing him, and tearing him apart at the same time, was almost overwhelming. Now that she knew it was Adrian's energy that had been blocking Tiana, she also knew it was he that was driving her passion. Marlon was a lot of things, but he was still very much human. If she were to let go, to lose herself with him, she would kill him. He could not withstand the power of her love. Which is why she had never allowed her feelings for him to be known. The last few metaphysical encounters they had had, let her know that he felt the same about her. She knew he would die for her, but she had always assumed it was her command. Now she knew. It was so much more.

She fled to the courtyard. The night had settled in like a dark damp blanket. A fine sheen of sweat broke out across her skin. She looked at her arm in wonderment. That was new. That was very much a human thing, and she was far from that.

"Bonjour ma cher." She could feel Adrian standing behind her.

"You cannot be here. You do not own this house." She snarled.

He laughed. "No, I do not. But the courtyard is public domain. So here, I can be."

"What do you want?" he had moved up behind her. She could feel his breath gently caressing her cheek.

"You." He answered.

"No."

He laughed and it felt like silk on her skin. "You say no now, but soon. Soon you will have no choice. It would be easier to come to me by your choosing, than by my force."

"You will never be strong enough to make that happen. You have become delusional Adrian." She pulled the breath from him until she could feel him gasping. She tore at his flesh, feeling it rip to ribbons. Although her hands never touched Adrian, her eyes never actually saw him, she could feel his blood, sticky on her fingers. Smell it, pungent in the air. Reese walked towards the door she had escaped out of moments before but stopped in her tracks. She could feel Marlon. He was screaming. It took a moment for the metaphysical to allow the physical to penetrate.

He was howling like he had never before. Behind her she felt Adrian laugh. This time it felt like a snake, sliding around her, tightening. Reese raced towards the sound.

PENANCE

Just under Marlon's screams, she could hear Tiana calling her name.

"Reese! Stop!" she screamed.

The courtyard faded, the hallway she thought she had fled, reappeared before her. The smell of blood and other things filled the small space. She blinked several times to clear her vision.

Marlon lay at her feet. His eyes staring up at her. Tiana was silent and stood holding Ash and Cynthiana. All three had a look of terror on their faces.

Reese's brain refused to let her eyes see what lay before her. She knelt slowly and the carpet made a soft squish sound under her knee's. That simple sound snapped everything back into hyper focus.

Blood splattered the walls and dripped from the ceiling. Marlon stared at Reese, but there was no life left in his eyes. The only spot on him that wasn't covered in blood or torn to shreds was his face. The rest was almost unrecognizable. Pieces of his body stretched from one end of the hall to the other. She looked up at Tiana in confusion.

"Who?" was all she could get out.

Cynthiana pointed at Reese. She looked around to see if someone else stood there.

"You did this." Ash whispered.

She stared down at Marlon's lifeless body. She began shaking her head, mouthing the word no, over, and over.

When the reality of it all finally broke that last shred of denial, she let out a sound that shook the walls.

Adrian had clouded her mind and she had killed

Marlon.

She had killed Marlon.

Chapter Fourteen

There is no life

CYNTHIANA TURNED FROM the window above the sink. She looked at Ash and Tiana sitting at the table. Her face bore a tormented confused look. They had spent the last three days cleaning the blood from the hall. The smell of death still lingered under the Pine Sol and bleach. Ash and a few of his friends had tried to remove the body from the house but Reese had become uncontrollable. The living room still bore the holes in the walls from her pain. So, he was lying on a table in the basement. Waiting. Tiana had wanted to clean the body and wrap him in a burial shroud but again, Reese had become frantic and refused to let anyone near Marlon.

When Tiana was learning to use her powers, she had

decided to incorporate a lot of different customs into her belief system. She had been raised Jewish before she had met her boyfriend and joined the cult and their burial customs appealed to her nature-based practice. She wanted to wrap Marlon in a hemp burial shroud and perform the Taharah. But it required a minimum of 4 people and Reese just wasn't there yet. So, Marlon lay, untouched. Reese sat alone in the courtyard, staring blankly.

"Momma, we need to snap her out of this. Marlon can't stay like that forever." Cynthiana turned back to the window and watched Reese. She hadn't moved since Marlon had been taken to the basement. She just sat, in the same clothes she had worn, blood now dried on her hands, her face, and her clothes. Her tears had left streaks on her face, giving her a macabre mask like appearance. She had finally stopped shaking and now sat still as a statue. Staring. Cynthiana knew the blank stare meant that Reese was locked inside her mind, reliving those moments.

"If she stays like this much longer, we will lose her." Ash spoke quietly. He knew the look. He had seen it on his sisters face once. The only time Cynthiana had ever allowed herself to love, to let her guard down, she had let her passion overtake her and her lover had been killed. She had crawled into herself. Refusing to eat, to sleep. She sat staring, and it was all Ash could do to bring her back. Not all of her had come back. She never let herself love again, never let herself feel any intense emotion again. Never let her guard down. The only people she was close to were her mother and her brother. Ash knew that Reese had made that choice long ago and Marlon was the only real friend she had. The loss of him could easily destroy her. They had to pull her out of the dark place she had gone in her mind before she never returned.

None had any allegiance or relationship with Reese, or Marlon for that matter. But Tiana felt a great guilt for what they had done to her. She had been a child, no older than her own daughter. To see her broken like this, shattered from the inside, tore at her heart. She was human after all. No one deserved to lose a loved one like that.

A gasp broke the heavy silence.

"Momma! He's back!" Cynthiana's voice shook slightly as she watched Adrian walk casually across the courtyard.

Tiana and Ash bolted up from the table and rushed to the window. They all held their breath.

Reese sat on the same wrought iron chair she had when she had first come to this house. Although this time she didn't see the beautiful flowers, the pool or the lion's heads flowing with water. She didn't hear the birds or the sounds of the street beyond. She didn't feel the warmth of the sun or feel the slight breeze that stirred her hair. All she saw was Marlon. Torn and bloody, lying at her feet. But in her mind, his eyes were accusing instead of blank, his mouth, which in reality had been slack, kept asking her why.

Adrian's face drifted into view. She closed her eyes, thinking it was an illusion.

"Ma cher." He said softly.

Reese blinked again. In her mind that voice had come from Marlon's mouth.

That wasn't right, she thought. The fog that had enveloped her lifted slightly.

Adrian sat across from Reese and cross his legs, leaning

131

back on the chair. "Come back cher."

Again, the voice came from Marlon's ruined mouth. Making Marlon look like a string puppet. A slight scowl creased Reese's forehead.

In the house Ash grabbed Tiana and Cynthiana's arms. They were heading out into the courtyard to do battle with Adrian. They looked at him confused.

"Look at her face. Her body stature. He is reaching her. Maybe it is her anger that needs to bring her back and not our kindness."

The women turned and looked a bit closer at Reese. They could see the subtle change in her posture, she was a bit straighter, more tense, her face was showing a slight expression of confusion. They agreed to let her be, for the time being.

Reese refocused and again she was back in the moment she saw Marlon. But again, Marlon's mouth moved at an odd angle and Adrian's voice filtered out.

"This is unlike you. You do not grieve the death of a piece of mortal meat. You relish it. Why the weeping widow act?" Adrian scoffed, anger lacing his words. She had never shown even a bit of emotion when they were together, other than anger and irritation. She never professed words of deep emotion, nor did she seem overly pained by living apart. She did all she could to remain apart.

"Was this *servant* that special?" Adrian sneered.

Rage is a funny thing. It can cloud your mind, or it can clear it as quick as lightening. Pain had clouded her, but Adrian's words, his casual dismissal of what Marlon meant to her, filled her with intensely mind clearing rage. She blinked twice, took a shuddering breath and her eyes and mind cleared.

"This *servant* as you call him, was more to me than you ever could dream of being. He was my friend, my conscious, and my savior. Do not cheapen his existence again." She stared at Adrian, her face blank. Her voice spoke to the emotion she felt, but her features gave away nothing.

In the house, Tiana gave a slight smile. "She is back."

Ash heaved a sigh of relief. "Thank freaking God, I could not face Adrian again. I still bare the marks of the last encounter." He rubbed his arm absently where two long scars ran from his elbow to his wrist. "He is unlike anything we have ever come across."

Tiana looked at Adrian through the window. He had always reminded her of someone, but she knew it couldn't be them. They looked totally different and possessed different powers. While some were the same, others were not. But something niggled at her memory. She was one of the originals, the First Ones, one of those who had stolen the power from Reese. Her lover had become the wolf, his brother the vampire. She had known the other three, but not very well. Jordan was the reason she was even in the cult. She would have followed him anywhere. It was an obsessive and possessive kind of love and as she watched Adrian and Reese, she realized that what Adrian felt for Reese was dangerously the same. She could see the darkness, the insanity, swirling around in his aura. He was a dangerous man on his own, blinded by emotion, she knew he could be deadly. The body in her basement was a testament to that.

133

She turned to her children. "We need to move Marlon from the basement. Before Adrian realizes he is still here."

Cynthiana chuckled nervously. "I don't know why you insist on calling the main floor a basement. Just because the entrance is on the second floor doesn't make it a basement."

Tiana shot her daughter an aggravated look. "I spent a long time in the Mid-west. We had basements. If it is below the main entrance, it is a basement to me. Regardless of what you want to call it, the body has to go. Adrian would do a whole manner of horrible things to Marlon to hurt Reese."

"How do you know that?" Cynthiana asked.

"I just know." She replied. She had refused to tell the children about their father. He was a cruel and violent man but what she had done to him was beyond unfair. She knew her children would never forgive her for such cruelty.

She sent Ash to make some calls. They couldn't bury him, not until Reese was ready, and bodies weren't buried in New Orleans, they would have to put him in a crypt. So, Ash would have to find one of those as well. But for now, they needed a safe place for Marlon, that Reese would accept, and Adrian would never be able to get too.

A scream from the courtyard made the three in the house run outside.

Reese stood in the middle of the yard, the pool behind her, arms thrown wide, screaming. Her hair flew about her face as if she was caught in a tornado and her clothes rippled around her body. The sound that came from her was guttural, almost inhuman, and full of rage and pain. It was directed at Adrian. He lay on the cobblestones beside

PENANCE

the small table, bleeding from various cuts on his face and hands. Tiana did a quick scan and saw no broken glass and knew that Reese had inflicted those marks.

Adrian began to rise to his feet and Reese slammed her energy forward and he tumbled back until he came to rest against the wall. More cuts appeared on him, and more blood ran down his face.

She screamed again and this time Adrian rose up the wall, pinned. His face contorted with the effort to pull himself free. With a roar he fell back to the cobblestones. Slowly he rose to his feet.

"You may eventually best me, ma cher, but it won't be today. You let emotion rule your actions. That makes you reckless. You have lost that cold blooded part of you, and it has made you weak." He brushed the dirt from his linen slacks and took a handkerchief from his pocket and dabbed at his face. "Marlon held you back and you know it. When you were with me, you were at your best, your fullest power. We ruled this city and could have gone so much farther if he had not interfered. Once you see that you will know that I did you a favor freeing you from him."

Cynthiana let out a gasp as it felt as if all the air from the courtyard had been sucked out. You could almost see it being drawn to Reese. She pulled it all into her, all the power she could, all the energy from around her, and sent it all at Adrian. Again, he ended up pinned to the wall and bleeding. But again, he pulled himself free.

He smiled coldly at Reese. "I will leave you for now cher, but you will come to me. You will be mine again. You know this. It is the only way it can be. It is the only way it has always been." With those words, he was gone.

135

Reese stood ramrod straight for a few minutes longer, then she collapsed to the ground. Tiana flew to her side.

"I am alright." Reese said slightly breathless.

"I will be the judge of that. You have been catatonic for the last few days. You are in no shape to know what is alright and what is not." Tiana was stern and motherly, and Reese smiled at her. She was a good woman, despite what she had done. She allowed Tiana to help her into the house.

Once they were seated in the living room, a cup of tea in Reese's hands, Tiana told her what they had decided about Marlon.

"If Adrian discovers he is not decaying, and that he is here, he will use that against you. If you are determined to defeat him and to find the others, you can't be distracted by the safety of his..." she paused..." of Marlon."

Reese sat silent for a few moments then rose and went to Marlon's side.

She looked at his face, so peaceful. Tiana had cleaned him up, and mended his wounds as best she could. He looked like he was sleeping. She touched his face gently, a tear slowly rolling down her cheek.

"I don't know how to do this without you. There is no life without you." She whispered. "You kept me grounded; you kept me sane." The tears were flowing freely now, and she let them come. "I never said this to you, and I wish I had. I can only say it to you now and hope that wherever you are, you hear me."

She kissed his forehead softly and leaned down until her lips were inches from his ear.

"I love you."

PENANCE

She straightened, turned towards Tiana, and gave her a nod.

"Have Ash do what needs to be done. We have a battle to prepare for."

As they returned to the living room, a harsh pounding came from the front door. Reese immediately went into combat mode and Tiana tried to cloak them in protection, but her magic wouldn't come. She grunted in frustration. Cynthiana waved her hand and the cloak fell onto the house. She then went and opened the door.

A man stood there, with an almost frantic look on his face. He was about 6'2, brown hair, green eyes, and a beard.

"Where's Tiana?" he barked at Cynthiana. A loud gasp came from behind her, and she turned to see her mother standing there, her eyes wide.

"Jordan?" she asked, her voice shaking.

He pushed passed Cynthiana and grabbed Tiana by the arms. Ash was immediately at his mother's side.

"Let my mother go!" he growled.

Jordan became very still. He looked at Ash, and then back at Tiana.

"Mother?" he asked her softly.

Tiana gulped a few times and looked from Cynthiana to Ash.

"Yes. They are my children." She said, fear lacing her words.

Reese came to Tiana's side and physically pried Jordan's hands from her arm. She took a small breath and Jordan stumbled back.

"Now that I have your attention, why don't we adjourn to the living room and talk like civilized adults."

Jordan gasped as his air came back and followed everyone.

Tiana paced nervously.

"Momma?" said Cynthiana.

Jordan's eyes widened, "You have two?"

Tiana nodded. "Twins."

Jordan's eyes grew small. "How old?" he asked.

"Old enough." She replied.

"Oh, for heaven's sake," snarled Reese. "Will you two quit dancing around the obvious? We don't have time for this."

Tiana took a breath. "Ash, Cynthiana, this is your father, Jordan." She turned to the man who sat stunned on the couch.

"Jordan, these are your children."

Reese clapped her hands together. "Fabulous, now that we have that out of the way, why are you here?"

"I have kids?" Jordan stammered.

Reese snapped her fingers in front of his face, "Focus, you can go all family man after, why are you here?"

Jordan blinked and cleared his throat.

"I felt a loss of power, for lack of a better phrase. So, I traced it to here."

"Explain." Reese said.

Jordan looked at Tiana questioningly. "She is always like

PENANCE

this, just answer her. She is *the one* You owe her answers."

Jordan's eyes got even wider. "With each death, I can feel the loss. From my calculations, there are only 3, but you are alive so that means there are still 4, but you are powerless."

"I tried a simple cloaking spell when you knocked, and I couldn't do it. I don't understand what happened to my power." Tiana said.

Reese gave Jordan a hard look. "Who are you? What form did you take?"

Jordan knew what she meant. He looked at her and saw the girl from so many years ago. She was tailored now, sophisticated, but her eyes, her face, were the same. "I am the werewolf."

"What do you mean 'with each death'?"

"Lloyd, who was Jinn, and Sarah, who was the shapeshifter, are dead. Jayden, my twin brother is the Vampire. He is still alive but in hiding. Aaron, the Phoenix vanished a century ago and I haven't been able to track him."

Anger rolled off Reese in waves and Jordan inched away from her.

He tried to speak but she silenced him.

"If it were not for our battle with Adrian, I would kill you where you sit. I have searched a long time for my *children* to exact my revenge for what you have done to me.

Jordan lowered his head. "My life has been hell. Your curse has been a torment for me." He said quietly.

Reese rose from her seat. "Good."

She told Cynthiana to go and get some paper and a pen.

They needed to make a graph of who everyone was, and what had happened to them. Where they were located and how they died. She needed to track it to find who was killing them.

"The power should have come back to me with each of the deaths, it did not. Someone has taken that power. We need to find out who that is."

The small group spent the rest of the night charting the tree of First Ones and their descendants.

"So, Adrian is a descendant of Jayden." Tiana said, looking at Jordan.

"Yes. We came across him in Pittsburgh. He had powers that seemed familiar, but we had never met someone like him and knew, or thought we knew that no one had made offspring. It was just after you had returned me to human form and Jay felt that I needed to be as far away from our hometown as possible. We took a road trip. I learned to control my wolf side and he made a family, of sorts. Adrian left us shortly after his change. I haven't seen him since."

Tiana shuddered. "He is here. He is the one we are going to war against."

Jordan laughed. "He is nothing but a vampire, with some other extra powers. Nothing you can't handle and definitely nothing Reese can't deal with."

Reese looked at Jordan. "He is so much more than that now."

Jordan made an o shape with his lips.

Cynthiana stretched in her chair. "Ok, now that we know all the players, can I ask a few questions? I suddenly have two parents and would like to talk about that."

PENANCE

Reese laughed. "Be my guest."

She walked out to the courtyard and left the little family to figure out how they were going to work. She took a deep breath, pulling in the fragrant New Orleans night air. A slight breeze picked up and ruffled the hair at her neck, sending goosebumps up and down her body.

"I love you too." The voice floated on that breeze and Reese froze for a moment then let her grief and pain come.

She sat at the little table and let the tears come. She finally let herself say goodbye.

Chapter Fifteen

The Road to Hell is Always Paved

ASH AND HIS friends had removed Marlon to a new location. No one spoke of it and Reese refused to know where he was, to protect him from Adrian. They spent the days after, going over the "Family Tree", or so Jordan called it. Tiana called it the Legend of The First Ones. Reese just called it The List. The more Jordan talked about his time with Adrian, the more familiar it began to sound. She had been drawn to him, from the start. He had been standing across the street, sunglasses in place, white linen suit moving slightly in the breeze that wove it's way seductively down Bourbon Street. It was midnight but he seemed to have a glow about him. Like the sun had kissed him before dipping below the horizon to sleep, leaving behind a piece of itself on his cheek. She felt what he was long before he walked, or more like sauntered, over to her.

"You smell new." He said with a delicious Cajun drawl. Reese scowled up at him and wrinkled her nose.

"You smell like death." She replied. "And you have blood and bits of your last meal on your collar." Her stomach fluttered and she had this overwhelming urge to pull him closer, but she turned on her heel and walked away.

He watched her go for a few feet then grinned.

"You know you don't want to go down there." He whispered into her mind. It stroked things deep within her and she stopped walking. She was taken off guard by his ability to mind speak. She could do it with Marlon but had never met someone else who could. When he spoke to her again, he was right behind her. His breath slithered down her neck and stirred the hair at her nape. She shivered slightly as if she were cold and leaned back against him. When her back touched his chest, she startled out of the spell he seemed to have her under.

"You feel it too don't you cher?" he said softly. She took a slight breath and heard him gasp. She smiled. She still had her power. Could still take what she wanted, no matter how he made her body feel.

She had control for a while, or so she thought. She clouded Marlon's mind to keep him away. Sent him on wild goose chases looking for her. She put up her shields so he could no longer feel her, but she kept tabs on him. She had hoped that he would eventually give up and find joy or at least some kind of peace of his own. But he didn't. He continued to pursue her.

Penance

Adrian and Reese tore up the city. Literally. They left body after body in their wake. They felt like Gods with no regard for human life. Young, old, it didn't matter. They relished in the blood. They drank their fill then bathed in it, had sex in it. The thrill of getting caught made them bolder and bolder. One particularly busy night in the Quarter, they strolled down the street, feeding at will, and dropping the empty vessels on the sidewalk. Only when the screams around them became deafening, did they stop. That was the night Marlon found them. He was enraged. He had spent eons protecting Reese, hiding her and her abilities. Cleaning up when she got a little too carried away. Adrian destroyed all that. He removed the last bits of humanity that Marlon had fought for Reese to hang on too. Reese was nothing but instinct and primal need. She laughed when she saw him.

"I told you to stay away; Even removed all trace of me to make it easier on you. Yet, here you stand, looking like I just ate your favorite puppy." She laughed.

Marlon stood his ground. "This is not you. Not the you, that you want to be."

Adrian chuckled and dropped the teenager he was feeding on. "She is a predator now. Top of the food chain. She is who she was meant to be." He dragged a passing tourist to himself and offered his wrist to Reese. She bit into it daintily, until the blood met her tongue. Sharp teeth came out and she tore the wrist open. The man stared at Adrian and didn't move. He had almost a half-smile on his face and Reese not only drank the blood from him but inhaled his life force. When she was done, she wiped her mouth on the man's sleeve, as that was all that was left. The dust that was the man drifted away on the breeze.

"Marlon, my faithful jailer, it is time we parted ways.

Adrian is right. I am much more than I was with you." She reached out to touch his cheek, in an attempt to give him a patronizing pat, but when her skin touched his, a jolt of electricity went through both of them. It brought her out of the daze she had been in since she met Adrian. She saw him, truly saw him, for the first time.

She was afraid.

Reese shook her head and brought herself back to the present. Dwelling on the past was not going to help her.

She had wandered back to the courtyard again. She looked around and nothing seemed as beautiful, as bright as it had when she first arrived. The gentle sound of the water flowing into the pool sounded harsh and mocking now. It was tainted. It was where she had thought she had killed Adrian, where she had grieved for Marlon, and where this nightmare had begun because of her relentless search for her children.

"Hello cher." Adrian sat casually at the little table.

"You have a lot of nerve coming here. I could kill you without a second thought." Reese ground the words out between her teeth.

Adrian laughed. "You won't kill me. Not today. There is too much you still don't know. Who am I Reese?"

Reese furrowed her brow. "You are Adrian. Vampire. With powers I don't quite understand, but a vampire none the less."

Again, Adrian laughed. "No Reese, Who. Am. I." he asked again. Emphasizing each word. "Think on it."

He turned to leave and looked back at her. She stood perfectly still with a blank expression on her face.

PENANCE

"Call Jayden."

She blinked and he was gone. She returned to the house and found everyone in the kitchen. Cynthiana was showing Jordan the family photos and Tiana was pounding, almost angrily, at a ball of dough. Ash just looked sullen and uncomfortable.

"Where is your brother?" she asked. The room fell silent except for the rhythmic pounding of Tiana's fists in the dough. Reese walked to the table and leaned down so that she was face to face with Jordan.

"Where is your brother?" she asked again, with a bit more force. He shrank a bit back from her.

"He is hiding."

Tiana spun around. "Hiding? After all he has done, he is hiding?" she stormed to the table and slammed her hands down. "He did this to us. He brought this hell upon us. Tormenting us with untold power, convincing us we would be Gods, rulers, unshakable. He destroyed Reese, he made you a monster, and destroyed what we had. Lloyd and Sarah were nothing after the ritual. A Djinn and a shapeshifter; both mortals, both vulnerable. He got the ultimate power, he got immortality, he got ageless beauty, and he is hiding?" She gave an exasperated sound and stomped out of the room. Cynthiana ran after her. Ash trailed behind slowly, but not before he shot Jordan one last sullen look.

Reese sat in the chair across from Jordan. "Where is he?" she asked again. He opened his mouth to speak, and she stopped him.

"Before you lie to me again, think very carefully. I was

there, remember? You are twins, you moved in sync with each other, finished each other's sentences, each other's thoughts. When one inhaled the other exhaled. So, I ask you again, where is he?"

Jordan closed his eyes, took a deep breath and a moment later, a knock came at the front door.

"He is here." He said.

Reese went to the door and opened it; Before her stood a much younger looking man, who bore a striking resemblance to Jordan. The minute she saw him, his face, the memory came flooding back. It was he who had lured her to the river. She was meeting him there, for a secret rendezvous. She was giddy with joy and anticipation as she strolled along the river's edge.

When he looked at Reese's face, his froze in fear. Any color the vampire may have had in his face drained away. Jordan rushed up behind her before Jayden could bolt.

"It's ok brother, she won't hurt you. Not yet at least." Jordan led Jayden into the house.

Jayden's eyes never left Reese. Tiana came back into the kitchen and as soon as she saw Jayden, she let out an aggravated scream and left the room again. Cynthiana brought her back a few minutes later.

"Hello Tiana, good to see you again." Said Jayden. Tiana just grunted angrily. Reese almost snickered.

Jayden turned to Jordan. "Why have you summoned me here brother? You know we aren't safe. Lloyd and Sarah proved that."

"We found Adrian." Said Jordan

PENANCE

Again, Jayden seemed to pale, which Reese found rather entertaining for a vampire. "You all need to leave. You need to be as far away from him as possible."

Reese sat in the chair beside Jordan, he leaned away from her slightly.

"That is not an option." She told Jayden. "He must be destroyed. He is far too dangerous to be left alone. I know this from experience."

Jayden stood and began to pace. "You don't understand. He isn't what you think. He can't be destroyed."

Jordan looked at his brother, "What do you mean? You created him. He isn't any more than what you gave him."

Jayden looked at his brother sadly. "No, he is so much more."

Tiana's eyes shot to Reese. "You said the same thing."

Jayden turned to Reese. "When we did the ritual and you cursed us, you didn't tell us everything did you?"

She smiled at him. "No. I didn't."

Jordan and Tiana looked at Jayden quizzically.

"You left out the part about knowing our victims. Those we take life from. Knowing their hopes and dreams. Seeing their joys and their regrets. Knowing all their secrets."

"I did." Replied Reese. "What did you learn from Adrian? What are you not telling us?"

Jayden sat back down at the table, a sad look crossing his face. "We were good people." Reese made a sound in her throat. "Once." Jayden continued.

"Lloyd, Sarah, Aaron, Jordan, Tiana, and me. We grew

149

up together. We went through everything together. We were best friends and then we were teenagers. Hormones do funny things to friendships. Where we used to all lie in a big pile watching the stars and talking about our dreams, was replaced by awkward glances and nervous giggles. Lloyd and Sarah became a thing, and it broke Aaron's heart. He was in love with Sarah, but she loved him like a brother. I thought he was weak, a sissy when he would leave the pile, tears glistening in his eyes, as the two snuggled. Until it happened to me." He looked at Tiana and she let out a gasp. "Yes, I was in love with you, but you loved Jordan. You always had. I suddenly felt like Aaron, and we bonded over it. We would spend nights talking about all the what if's. When I found the book, it looked like one of my what if's could come true. If I was stronger, better, you would love me; Then you got pregnant and I knew, it was never going to be."

"How did you know?" Tiana asked. "I didn't even know."

Jayden smiled softly. "You always got this furrowed brow when your cycles would come. You were snappy for a few days, face like thunder, then you got all soft and feminine around the edges. Almost three months passed and nothing,"

"This is all lovely and I really wish we had time to wander down memory lane and relive the night you tried to kill me, but I need to know about Adrian."

Jayden refocused is attention. "That night, I was angry. I wanted her to choose me. So, I chose what each would get. It was part of the spell that I didn't share with the others. I didn't know you were going to curse us, that was coincidence, but you cursed us being directed by the spell. I got vampire because that is what I chose, my brother, wolf, and so on. I wanted Tiana to love me, to need me. I had only the best intentions for her, for us."

He rubbed is hands over his face. "But you know what they say about good intentions. It didn't work out that way. Tiana became angry, Lloyd and Sarah fled together, and Aaron disappeared. We kept in touch, but after decades had passed and no one heard from him, we all assumed he was dead. Then Lloyd was killed, and shortly after, Sarah. When we met Adrian in Pittsburgh, we were running. We thought it was you." He looked at Reese. "We spent our whole supernatural lives covering our tracks and we had thought you had found us."

"What changed your mind?" asked Reese, she was getting impatient with Jayden's story.

"Adrian." Answered Jayden. "When I drank from him, I learned everything about him. I also realized that I could never tell anyone in case he found out."

Jayden fell silent. Reese rose angrily. "Will you finish the damn story!"

"Adrian isn't Adrian. That is a face he took from a meal he had. He has that ability because he killed Sarah and absorbed her abilities. He can cloud your thoughts and has the abilities of a Djinn because he did the same to Lloyd." Jordan looked at Jayden, fear and realization running across his face, one emotion chasing the other.

"Who is he Jayden?"

Jayden took a deep breath. "You can't kill him, not permanently, because Adrian is Aaron. The Phoenix. He will always rise. Since I made him vampire, he is as close to indestructible as one can get."

Tiana fell into the chair she had been standing beside.

"Fuck."

Reese sat down beside her and looked at Jayden.

"Yeah, what she said." She whispered.

Chapter Sixteen

Gone, but not

REESE WAS ANGRY. She was furious with herself. How could she not have known her own power? How had she not recognized it in Adrian? Yes, it was perverted and twisted and so far from what it originally was, but she should have known. She should have felt that part of her, squatting in him like a toad. The revelation that he was the Phoenix was not what she wanted to hear. When she had cursed Aaron with that particular power, her only thought had been of him burning over and over for eternity. She had been enraged and vibrating with power that night and didn't think beyond the immediate pain she was causing them.

She had been pacing the courtyard for hours. Table,

pool, repeat. She was trying to figure out how he had managed to get the current abilities that he had. She didn't remember him being able to speak mind to mind, or send an apparition, when they had been together.

The thought of the years she had spent loving him, believing in him, trusting him. The things she had allowed him to do to her, the things they had done together to others, caused her physical pain now. She had almost lost Marlon because of him.

"You will never lose me."

She froze.

The words whispered across her like a soft breeze. She could almost feel them touching her. She closed her eyes and Marlon's scent assailed her senses. The sharp musk of his cologne, the smell of his skin when he had been in the sun too long, his own natural scent. It was so strong she could almost taste it. Her heart skipped a beat and that familiar warmth that was Marlon's energy, began to uncoil from the place she had locked it. She tried to push it back and it grew stronger. She opened her eyes and paced faster.

"NO." she said out loud. All her instincts screamed this was a trap.

"It's not a trap love. I am still here." Marlon said.

She spun around until she had looked at every corner of the courtyard. It was empty. She stood very still and let her other senses search. A block away she heard a window open, and the lines of a song drifted out.

Because I'm broken

When I'm lonesome

PENANCE

And I don't feel right when your gone away.

You've gone away.

You don't feel me here anymore.

Reese fell to her knees. She thought she had cried all she had in her. She thought she had released all the pain she had carried from not only that night, but from losing Marlon. She had not. The pain, the torment, spilled from her lips in a sound akin to that of a wounded animal. She beat the ground with her fists as she let it all pour out.

The pain of that night.

The betrayal. The physical pain. The rage at the power they had taken from her.

The disillusionment of Adrian. The power he had over her once and her willingness to let him have it.

The love she carried for Marlon but would never speak aloud. The guilt she carried for the innocent she ripped from this world.

The loss of the only man who taught her what love truly was.

It all came out. It poured out of her mouth, with each scream and it seeped into the ground in the blood that ran from her fists as she pounded them on the stone.

Marlon's scent faded. She tried to hang onto it but the more she reached, the farther it got.

Then the laughter came. Soft, vicious, and full of power. It echoed through her head, it pounded on her body, and it bounced off the walls of the courtyard.

She immediately fell silent and sat very still, waiting. Adrian liked an entrance, and this was it. He was coming. She could now feel his power moving towards her.

Tiana had heard Reese's screams from inside and had ran to the kitchen window. She had learned that you didn't just run up on Reese when she was like this. That was more than just a mistake. It was a death sentence. Luckily, Jayden was immortal, so he had survived, but she wouldn't.

"Reese?" she called from the window. She had watched the grief and had also seen it stop suddenly. She could feel an electricity to the air, but not much more. The more time she spent with Reese, the more human she became. Ash and Cynthiana didn't seem to be affected and Jayden and Jordan's curses were physical ones. Hers was metaphysical. It was like Reese was absorbing that part of herself back. A thought struck her, but watching Reese now, she knew she would have to talk to her about it later. Reese was anything but rational.

"Reese?" she said again, a little louder. Reese waved a hand at her hushing her. Then Tiana felt it. That crackle, that niggle in the base of your spine. That pit of fear.

Adrian.

She turned to look behind her. He couldn't enter the house, she knew that, but she had to make sure he wasn't standing there. Waiting to kill her.

When she turned back, he was standing in front of Reese. She was still on her knees, and she now appeared to be bleeding. Blood dripped from her face.

"I said look at me!" Adrian snarled. Still Reese sat, motionless, looking at the ground in front of her. She could feel his pull. She knew if she looked him directly in the eyes, she would be momentarily lost to him and that would be all the time he needed. As of now, she honestly didn't know if he could kill her or not. He had made her do things she never thought possible, he could do things she never imagined anyone else doing.

He was the male version of her. He didn't have all her abilities, but he had honed the ones he did have razor sharp.

He pushed that energy at her, and she rose off the ground. She closed her eyes and focused her mind on anything she could. Marlon was the first thing that came to her.

Adrian screamed in rage. The windows of the house shook. Tiana and the others in the house had now come into the courtyard.

Jayden stepped forward and looked directly at Adrian. He was the only one who could. "What do you want?" he demanded. He had learned that if you showed Adrian weakness, he would exploit it, pull at it like a thread until you unraveled.

"I want her." He said. He flicked his eyes, and Reese flew 15 feet and slammed into the wall. A blood smear appeared on the brick as she fell to the ground. Tiana and Cynthiana raced to her. She was pulling herself up. The women thought Reese was hurt, but when they saw her face, her eyes, they backed away. Cynthiana hid a grin.

Reese's eyes had been pure fire. They had also been the color of Marlon's.

"Use me love." He had whispered to her when she had

been on her knees. What Adrian had taken as submission and inability to fight back, was really Reese drawing the metaphysical energy that was now Marlon. She had pulled it into herself and woven into her own power. He was a part of her, more than he had been when he had drawn breath.

She rose slowly. Building the power, letting it rise and fall like a wave. With each breath it pushed farther out from her. The intensity in the courtyard grew and those who were human had to leave. Jayden and Jordan shared a look and began to back away from Adrian.

Adrian looked at the motley crew for a moment. He watched Ash and the women retreat into the house, he watched the vampire and the wolf back away to the far corner. Then his eyes came to rest on Reese. Her back was to him, and she seemed to be inhaling and exhaling slowly, but deeply. He pushed his power at her, and it was shoved right back at him. Then his nose was filled with the scent of a man, a very masculine, angry man.

"Well, well, well." He laughed. "Had to hang onto what you could love?" he sneered at her. "You have become pathetic. It will be a service to kill you. Put you down like a lame horse."

A large cut appeared on Adrian's right cheek. The blood poured down his neck and soaked into the collar of his white shirt. His hand flew up and touched it. Almost immediately it healed over.

Another slash appeared across his chest ripping the shirt open and baring the muscle under the skin. Blood again poured down him. Again, it healed almost immediately.

"You think these little displays will hurt me?" he asked laughter bouncing between each word. Reese finally turned to look at him.

Her eyes burned with power. Her skin glowed almost translucent, and she hovered just a few inches off the ground. A breeze had appeared and moved her hair about her, giving her an ethereal look.

The laughter died in Adrian and caution crept into his face. More cuts and slashes appeared on his body and a pool of blood began to form at his feet. He healed them as fast as she inflicted them, but it took his concentration away from what he was projecting. He had to pull his power in to heal the wounds before he bled out.

"Oh no my darling. I know they won't hurt you." She said as she slowly moved towards him. Her eyes never left his. She reached out one hand and squeezed her fist closed tight. Adrian's hands flew to his throat. Reese pulled her hand back rapidly and Adrian's throat exploded into a torn mess of flesh and bone. He gurgled and sputtered as he healed the damage.

"None of this will be enough to kill you. Not permanently." She smiled at him. She now stood before him and gently traced her fingers across his cheek, opening a wound so deep you could see his teeth. "But it is enough to distract you."

Before Adrian could speak or turn, Jayden pulled his head from his body and Jordan plunged his fist into his back and pulled his heart out. It beat for a moment and then stopped. Adrian's eyes registered shock a second before his body fell to the ground. Everyone jumped into action.

They only had minutes before the body burst into flames and Adrian rose from the ashes. It was the ashes they wanted.

Each were armed. Whisk, broom, Tiana even had an old dust buster. They were going to collect the ash and keep it in separate jars until they could figure out a way to eliminate him permanently. They figured if they kept the ashes separated it would be harder for Adrian to resurrect. Jayden and Jordan would take a jar each and return to Pittsburgh, Ash and Cynthiana would take a jar and head farther south, and Tiana and Reese would keep the remaining jars here. They would keep in touch via email and text, never speaking out loud and certainly not in the presence of the ashes. They didn't know if Adrian still had some sort of consciousness and could hear them.

When the flames died down the group went to work. Jayden and Jordan left right away, Ash and Cynthiana left after dinner.

When it was only Tiana and Reese left, they went into the cold cellar. Tiana buried her jar in the Eastern corner, and Reese put hers into the brick and cemented it in.

They returned to the kitchen and Tiana put the kettle on. Tea was something her and Reese both enjoyed and had bonded over.

"Ok, now that the house is empty, talk. Tell me what happened before Adrian arrived." Tiana sat down and looked at Reese.

Reese sighed. "Marlon seems to be lingering." She said. "I had thought I had felt him just after he died, but I brushed it off as wishful thinking. Today he came back in force. Again, I tried to brush it off as a trick this time, but it was him," As she spoke his scent filled the kitchen and Tiana gasped.

"Wow, he really doesn't want to go does he?" she asked

jokingly.

"No, I don't." was his response.

Reese gave a 'see I told you' look to Tiana.

"Well." She said. "It's not like we have enough to deal with, now we have to figure out what we are going to do with him. He can't stay a ghost. They tend to get grumpy. We either have to put him back in his body or make him cross."

Reese looked at Tiana confused. "Put him back? Is that even possible?"

Tiana nodded. "Yes, if the body is still in good condition."

Reese pulled out her phone. She punched some numbers, and, in a few seconds, there was a voice on the other end of the phone.

"Ash, where is he?" Tiana couldn't make out Ash's reply, but it didn't sit well with Reese.

"I know what I said, but your mother just gave me information I didn't have when I made you promise." She shoved the phone at Tiana. "You explain it to him."

Tiana told Ash what she had told Reese. "Are you sure?" she asked after a few moments. "Ok, I'll tell her." She hung up the phone and Reese all but pounced on her.

"Well?"

"He is in perfect condition. Like otherworldly perfect. Ash said he looks like he is sleeping. That isn't normal. Something is keeping his body preserved. We need to think about this Reese. What if Adrian has already tampered with Marlon's body?"

Reese shook her head. "He couldn't have. Even if he did, we will deal with that when the time comes. I want him back. I need him back. Tiana please. We have to put him back." Her voice wavered slightly with the desperation she felt.

"Easy love." Marlon said. "I don't feel Adrian's power around me, or my body, but we need to be rational about this."

Reese opened her mouth to speak, and Marlon silenced her. "I want to come back as badly as you want me back. You and I have some unfinished business." He said softly. "There are things I want to tell you, face to face. Things I want to hear again, in person. But I won't risk your life, or anyone else's. It doesn't seem like I am going anywhere, as long as my body stays in good shape, we have time. This way I can get information for you that I can't in a physical body."

Tiana pointed out that he was right. He could eavesdrop easier than they could. Reese glared at her but realized that they were both right.

"Don't you leave me again. You hear me, Marlon? You stay with me, until I can put you back in your body."

Marlon's laughter filled the kitchen. "I promise."

"Pinky?" Reese asked.

"If I had them, yes. Pinky promise."

Chapter Seventeen

Just one night

THE VICTORY, HOWEVER small, had been short lived. It started with the jars at the house, they had broken first and the dust had swirled and danced through the house to an open window and were gone. Then Ash and Cynthiana called, their jars had broken. Then Jayden and Jordan. Whatever power Adrian had now, was strong enough to pull his ashes back together allowing him to reanimate.

The group returned to the house on Royal Street, cleared the last of the mundane from the whole building, and began working tirelessly, trying to find a weakness in Adrian. Marlon had been true to his word; he would go and spy on Adrian and then report what he saw back to Reese and Tiana. Which, sadly, wasn't much. Adrian just seemed to be growing in power. He chose those with any kind of magical or mystical showing of power and would drain them almost to death. Leaving them hovering on the brink. Then he would let them recover and do it again. Like he was topping up his reserves. Summer faded into Fall, and they were still no farther ahead. Once October hit, Tiana was busy with other things as well. October in New Orleans was a busy time for her. Reese had given her a small portion of her power back. She read tarot, gave aura readings, and worked many a love spell. So, Reese had been doing most of the work alone. Ash had been a help, but he wasn't much good at research.

The evenings were Reese's favorite time. She would walk the streets of the French Quarter, watching the revelers, listening to the music, which had always been one of the things that she enjoyed, no matter what the decade or what the season. The night seemed to have a life of its own. The air vibrated and hummed with energy.

Reese stopped on a corner near Bourbon Street. She tuned out the sound of the crowd and just focused on the music. A slow bluesy tune drifted out of a nearby bar, and it took her back.

It was almost Halloween and Reese and Marlon strolled down the street. Party goers jostled along the sidewalk, but no matter how inebriated they seemed to be, they never actually made contact with the couple. Reese had put a barrier around them so they could enjoy the life pulsing swirling and humming, but not be bounced around. A particularly drunk man lurched toward the two, leering at Reese.

"Hey darlin'" he slurred. Marlon took a protective step in front of Reese, but she laid her hand on his arm and stopped him. She dropped the barrier for just a moment, long enough for the man to enter their space and then slammed it back into place.

"Reese, what are you doing?" Marlon asked suspiciously. He had seen her do this particular trick before. It always ended bloody. Reese ignored him and began circling the man. He wobbled slightly on his feet, but his eyes never left Reese's.

"It's a party, all around us, I just want a party favor." Reese said. She grinned at the man. He smiled sloppily back. "He isn't a good man, Marlon. He has done some very bad things. Just two blocks over is a little girl who is still crying from his most recent visit."

"Reese..." Marlon said, his voice laced with caution. "We are on the main street. You can't do this here."

Reese looked at Marlon, then spun around, her arms wide. "No one can see us. No one can hear us." She slashed a hand toward the man, opening his left cheek, down to the bone. He still stood staring at Reese with a grin on his face. Blood poured out of the wound and Reese's nostrils flared like that of a predator scenting its prey. "He will look like any other drunk, falling on his feet in the street. They won't even move him until morning when the cleanup crew comes by."

She turned toward the man and stuck a finger in the wound. Licking her finger, she grinned at Marlon. "As bad as he is, his taste is divine."

Marlon just shook his head and turned his back. He had no need to watch. Reese turned back to the man, the pain of the wound in his cheek was starting to uncloud his mind. His brows squinted together in confusion. A hand came up to feel and felt the blood and the spell that Reese had cast on him broke. He began to whimper and worked up to a full-blown scream. Reese laughed at him.

"Scream all you want. No one can hear you." She purred. Her primal side was riding her completely now and hunger was taking over. She was careful how she fed so she would not be caught, but every now and then she almost needed a good blood bath. She needed the hunt, the kill. It was a drug for her, an aphrodisiac even. She walked to the man and ran her tongue up his neck and licked the edges of the wound. The man began pushing her away and she grabbed his face, stared into his eyes, and uttered two words. "Be still." The man stopped moving and absolute terror filled his eyes. Reese giggled. She drew her finger down his arm and more blood appeared. She raised his arm to her mouth and licked from elbow to wrist. Her mouth clamped down over the wrist and she drank. She released his arm and it fell limply to his side. Moving up close to him she pressed the length of her body against him and nuzzled his neck. Hollywood had created so many vampire myths, none of which were real, that every now and again, she liked to fully play the part. She elongated her canines, letting the man see them and then sunk them into his neck. She immediately retracted them, as they were not a requirement for feeding, and again drank deeply. Reese wrapped an arm around the man as his legs had begun to wobble from more than alcohol. The blood loss was getting to much to keep him standing. She lowered him gently onto the sidewalk against the brick front of a store. She knelt delicately beside him, trying to keep her skirt out of the blood and continued to drink. His wrist, his neck, his cheek, until he was pale and gray. She then stood, wiped her lips daintily with a lace kerchief and turned back to Marlon.

PENANCE

Before she could speak eyes so brilliant, so bright, caught her attention. She felt frozen in place. Her mind raced and she pushed hard back against the energy that was holding her. She broke the contact, turned back to the man on the street and took a quick breath. Within seconds he was nothing but dust drifting down the sidewalk in the breeze.

"What's wrong love?" asked Marlon. He knew the look on her face. It was one of fear. She always had that look when she felt they were close to being caught.

"There is someone in the crowd. He was able to see me." She enforced the barrier and tucked her arm into Marlon's. They continued strolling down the street like nothing had happened. She didn't see the man again, but later she realized that was the first time she had seen Adrian.

Her mind came back to the present. Heaving a sigh, she opened her eyes.

"Hello ma cher." Adrian stood before her.

Reese turned and began walking away from him. Her heart racing. She had been foolish to come out at night, to leave the safety of the house.

Adrian's laugh followed her down the street. "You can run from me, but I will catch you eventually. I could have had you now, as you stood remembering. The night we first set eyes on each other. The night I knew, you would be mine."

Reese wanted to stop, she wanted to face him, to scream at him, claw at him, but she knew it was useless, so she continued her pace until she was safely within the gates of the courtyard. They had recently purchased not just the building, but all the buildings that surrounded the courtyard. That was now a safe haven in which Adrian could no longer enter. She collapsed onto the wrought iron seat at the little table. She sat, with her head in her hands and just took deep breaths.

Tiana saw her from the window and came running out. "Where were you? What happened? Are you alright?" she fired the question at Reese.

Reese raised her head and looked at Tiana. "I went for a walk. Yes, I know it was stupid, Adrian found me, and yes, I am fine. Shaken but fine."

Tiana sputtered and grumbled for a few minutes, pacing back and forth, before she finally came and sat with Reese.

"I understand the need to be out. I really do. Especially this time of year. But you must show caution. We can't lose you, for emotional reasons, and for practical ones." Reese nodded and promised she wouldn't leave again.

Tiana's face quickly changed from consternation to joy. "I have a surprise for you!" she beamed.

Reese cocked an eyebrow. She was very rarely surprised. "Oh?"

"I've been looking through some of the books that Cynthiana has brought be from the voodoo practitioner she is friends with. As you know, the veil between the land of the living and the land of the dead is at its thinnest tonight."

Reese nodded. It has always been that way. The dead could walk among the living for 24 hours. It was why she never hunted on Halloween, or Samhain as those in the past had called it. She didn't need a fresh kill getting up off the ground to give her hell for ruining their day.

PENANCE

"Yes, that is where the practice of wearing costumes came from." Said Reese. "So, the dead couldn't tell the living from the other dead." Her voice trailed off.

"The dead can walk among the living..." she stammered, looking at Tiana.

Tiana nodded. "For 24 hours."

"We only have 8 hours left love."

Reese's eyes shot to the back door. There stood Marlon. Flesh and blood. She closed her eyes and listened. Air traveled in and out of his lungs, from habit, but his heart did not beat, there was no blood flowing through his veins. He was alive, but only by the magic of the night.

Which she decided was good enough. She flew into his arms, then immediately jumped back. They had never embraced as such. Both had kept their distance, both keeping their feelings hidden, until Marlon had inconveniently died.

Marlon's hand shot out, gripped Reese's arm, and pulled her back to him. He wrapped his arms around her and buried his face in her hair. He took deep breaths, inhaling her scent.

"I have missed the smell of you." He murmured.

Reese tightened her arms around him. "I have just missed you. All of you."

She looked up at him and smiled shyly. "I didn't realize you were so tall!" Marlon let out a laugh and stared down into her eyes. The smile slowly drifted from his face, replaced with one of longing, of wanting. Reese ran the tip of her tongue over her lips. She knew what he wanted, what he was thinking and if he didn't hurry, she was going to take matters into her own hands.

A moment later, Marlon's lips touched hers. A soft sigh escaped her lips and she melted into him. One hand crept up and tangled in her hair and held her head in place. The kiss deepened, passions rose, until Tiana cleared her throat uncomfortably.

"If you would just move to the side, I could get by and leave you two alone." She muttered. "By the way, surprise Reese!"

Reese spun around and hugged Tiana so tight she couldn't breathe. When Reese released her, Tiana stood in shock.

Reese laughed. "I'm sorry I have been such an ogre. You have given me something I can never repay you for. I cannot thank you enough."

Tiana smiled. "After what I was part of after what we did to you, this is but a small token of apology." She turned to enter the house. "Remember, he may appear to be of flesh and bone, but he is not of flesh and bone. You will be unable to do many things, and at the end of the night, when the clock strikes 12:01, he will return to the spirit realm and this body will return to the dust and twine we used to hold the spell together. He looks like a man, like Marlon, but he is not a living, breathing man." Blushing she moved quickly towards the door. She had not thought she would need to have that part of the conversation with Reese, but after witnessing the kiss she knew, it was required or there could be some very disappointed people.

As she reached the door, she turned back. "Oh, one more thing. Do not, under any circumstances, leave the safety of the compound. If Adrian were to get Marlon's spirit in this form, he could trap it in this body, essentially making a puppet out of him. You would have no control over Marlon. He would be a slave to Adrian."

Once they were alone in the courtyard, Marlon turned Reese back to look at him. He tipped her face up with is finger under her chin.

"Say it again." He whispered. Reese looked at him confused. "The words, say them again."

She smiled, "I love you." She said. Marlon closed his eyes. "One more time."

She cupped both sides of his face and he opened his eyes to look down at her. "I love you. I always have. From my cell as your prisoner, to the crypt as you tore me apart night after night. I have always loved you; I just haven't always been brave enough to tell you."

"I hated doing that to you." He said. "It took something from me every night, hearing your screams, knowing that in that moment, I was the terror that haunted you, that caused you such pain." He placed his hands on hers. "I love you too." He leaned down and kissed her again. This time neither showed any restraint. It was something both had longed for and denied themselves for so long.

When they came up for air, Marlon grumbled. Reese cocked an eyebrow at him. "Not good enough?"

He gave her a sarcastic look. "Hardly, it's just not enough period. It's beyond good, and I want more. Sadly, this body will not accommodate that."

Reese gave him a hug and then a playful shove. "You will have that soon enough." She laughed. "Once we figure out how to end Adrian, we can bring you back and spend the weekend wrapped in bed sheets if you want."

"A weekend?" he asked slyly. "I was thinking a few years, maybe a decade or two might appease me, for a bit." Again, Reese laughed. It was throaty and seductive and all women.

The two spent the next several hours talking and touching. They put all thoughts of Adrian and the current dilemma aside and just focused on the moment. Tiana had snuck a blanket outside and they had spread it on the ground by the pool. They two lay, arm in arm, watching the stars.

"Well, isn't this a nice romantic sight." The voice sent a shiver down Reese's spine. She sat up and looked behind them.

Adrian hovered just inches above the ground. "You can't be here." She hissed.

Adrian laughed. "I can't touch the earth that you own, but the air, ma cher, is free to all." He turned his sights to Marlon. "You are looking a lot better than the last time I saw you old friend."

Marlon sprung to his feet, pulling Reese behind him. "You have no business here, and I am not your friend."

Again, Adrian laughed. "But we have spent so much time together lately. You skulking around, listening to my conversations. Me feeding you nothing of use."

Adrian clapped his hands together. "I would love to stay and chat, but I have business elsewhere tonight, so I must do away with the small talk and get down to it."

He raised his arms and Reese could feel the sudden snap of energy.

Penance

"Ad hoc corpus

Tuus spiritus manere

Facere iubeo ultra hanc diem

Servus eris

Ad me solum serve

Dormi nunc in pace

Desiderium meum tibi placebit"

He spoke the Latin words over and over. Marlon's face began to show fear and Reese fought to hang on to him.

Tiana came running out of the house the minute she felt the magic begin. Adrian's voice got louder and stronger and Marlon slowly began to rise off the ground. Reese hung on with all she had, but it seemed that her strength had all but disappeared.

"Tiana what is happening?" Reese screamed. Tiana was muttering a counter spell of her own, but nothing seemed to work. Marlon's face went slack, and all life disappeared from his eyes.

"TIANA!" Reese screamed.

Within seconds, Adrian and Marlon were gone.

Reese collapsed on the ground. Tears raced down her cheeks and her fingers dug into the cement, leaving cracks. Her strength had returned.

"I'm so sorry. I didn't know. I didn't know." Tiana sat, rocking back and forth.

"Didn't know what?" Reese said through gritted teeth.

"The air. He has passage through the air." Tiana answered.

"What was he saying?" Reese asked flatly.

Tiana looked at her sadly. "It was Latin, loosely it translated too.

'To this body

Your spirit will stay

To do my bidding

Beyond this day

A slave you will be

To serve only me

Sleep now in peace

My desire you will please'

He has locked Marlon's spirit in that body. Like I warned, he will be a puppet. A spirit does not survive inside an artificial container. The consciousness goes mad. He is nothing but a killing machine for Adrian now. We can't bring him back, Not now."

Reese pounded the ground, sending cracks along the courtyard and up the one wall of the building behind her.

"I will not accept that." She stood, a look of tightly held determination laced with a cold rage, settled on her face.

"I will be back." She said.

Tiana sprang up. "Where are you going?"

"To either bring Marlon back or set him free for good. I will not let him be a slave to Adrian."

Tiana touched Reese's arm gently. "All I wanted was to give you just one night."

PENANCE

Reese looked at Tiana. "You did. Now I am taking it back. I am taking back all my nights, all my days and everything else that Adrian has stolen from me. I want what belongs to me. He is no longer allowed to have it."

She touched Tiana's face and took a small sip of air. The last of Tiana's magic flowed quickly back into Reese.

Both women's eyes grew large. Then they had an idea.

Chapter Eighteen

All Bets are Off

ADRIAN SAT IN his living room smoking a clove cigarette. He had developed a taste for them years earlier when he had encountered a bunch of spiritualists at a festival in Tennessee. The smoke had flavored their blood and he had enjoyed them ever since.

"You know she is going to kill you right?" ask a female voice from the other side of the room.

Adrian's eyes slid over and gazed at the woman. Coldly.

"She can try. She is no longer a match for me. She never really was. You see, love weakens a woman. While it will make a man fight, even kill, it makes a woman soft, gentle, hesitant."

The woman laughed. "She doesn't love you anymore. Why can't you see that?"

It was Adrian's turn to laugh. "I am not naïve ma petite. It was never me she loved. It was the kill. Now it is Marlon. For reasons that escape me. She loves the human. She has prolonged his life to keep him close. It is that love that I will use against her." He stood in one fluid movement, and it took the woman's breath away. She has always been fascinated with him and had followed his movements closely. What she could glean from the papers, local gossip, and on her own. Her mother had forbidden any contact, and Cynthiana could see why now. He was powerful. More powerful than even Reese had anticipated. Her curiosity was what had gotten her caught. She had wanted a closer look. She knew he had Marlon trapped and she had wanted to see if she could figure out where and get a closer look at the man himself. She had been foolish, and now, she sat, captured herself, in a cage, suspended from the ceiling of Adrian's living room.

Adrian had walked to his desk and was speaking into his phone.

"Yes, yes, bring her up please." He hit the end button and placed the phone back on the desk.

He turned towards Cynthiana. "Your mother has noticed that you are not with your ever-present brother. She is here to speak to me."

Cynthiana's heart leapt into her chest. "Please, don't hurt her!" she begged.

Adrian laughed. "I have no intentions of causing your mother harm ma petite. She is a messenger."

Penance

Tiana was escorted into the living room and Adrian waved to the settee and motioned for her to be seated. Her gaze never left Adrian and fear was etched clearly on her face. Adrian smirked and looked over at Cynthiana and winked. Tiana's gaze followed his and a small scream escaped her lips before she clamped her hand over her mouth.

Her eyes flew back to Adrian. "She is no threat to you. Please let her go! Take me instead!" she begged.

Adrian smiled at Tiana; his eyes glinting coldly. "Oh, I have use of you. You will take a message back to Reese for me."

His hand flicked slightly and a screamed ripped from Cynthiana. Blood spread across her shirt. His hand raised and the shirt tore open revealing a large gash across her chest. Bone gleamed in the afternoon light. Adrian stood and walked over to the cage, reached in, and ripped the shirt from Cynthiana's body. It dripped with blood. Cynthiana had now collapsed on the floor of the cage. Tiana stared as hard as she could to catch a glimpse of breath from her daughter. When she saw the slight rise of her shoulder, she breathed a small sigh of relief.

Adrian tossed the shirt at Tiana. "Take this to Reese. Tell her that it is just the first part of the message."

Two men came into the room and before Tiana could say a word, escorted her out.

Adrian went to a door, hidden in the wall, and opened it. Marlon stepped out. He looked over at Cynthiana and a small grimace creased his face. Adrian had been able to capture his essence, trap it in his body, but he had not been able to capture his soul. His thoughts and his feelings were still his own.

The two men returned with a small child of about 12 years old. She was dirty and her hair was matted. A sour smell emanated from her. Adrian crinkled his nose.

"Clean her up, feed her, and then return her to me." He ordered. The two men took the child and left.

"What need have you of a child?" Marlon asked.

Adrian just smiled. "Sit." He said. Marlon sat. He may have his own thoughts and feelings, but Adrian controlled everything else.

They sat in silence, Adrian gazing out the balcony doors and Marlon watching Adrian.

After about an hour, the two men returned with the child. They brought her over to the couch where Marlon sat. She sat beside him and looked around.

"Nice place ya got here." She said. "Thanks for the bath and the food."

Adrian smiled at her. "You are welcome child. Tell me, do you have family?"

She shook her head and the scent of honeysuckle rose off her still damp hair. "Nah, I was left at the crawdad stand in the market about a year ago. 'tole to stay put and me ma and pa never come back."

Adrian nodded with feigned concern. "How did you survive the streets?"

She sat up as straight as she could, trying to look as tough as she could, "I got me friends. They help me, I help them."

Adrian laughed. "You mean you steal for them, and they

protect you." The girl nodded.

Adrian stood and walked to the balcony doors and looked out. "Nothing happens in this town without me knowing. Nothing happens without my say so. Do you understand?"

The girl looked confused. "You run this place?" she asked.

"You could say that. You worked for me. I was the final say." He came and stood before the child. "You owe me."

She scampered back on the couch. Fear now working its way back into her eyes. "I did as I was s'pposed to every time. I never skimmed. I was an honest thief!"

Adrian nodded, "Yes, but do you not think that all the food, the protection, the place to sleep, was worth more than what you managed to pilfer off the tourists? Come now."

He returned to his seat and the cold blank stare returned. "I will now collect my debt."

He looked at Marlon, who, even though he knew it was useless, shook his head. "Please, don't make me do this."

"I must make my message clear." Adrian replied. He flicked his hand and suddenly Marlon was on the small child. Her screams lasted only a few seconds, as Marlon made her death as quick as possible. Adrian had only ordered her dead. He hadn't said how. He had torn her throat out, severing the jugular so she had bled out in a matter of moments.

"Take her to Reese. Deliver her only to Reese. Then return to me."

Marlon scooped up the girl in his arms gently and left the penthouse. He traveled in the shadows until he reached the back door to the courtyard.

"Reese." He said. He didn't have to yell. He knew she could hear him. Knew she could smell the blood on him, on the child. The gate flew open, and she stood before him. She stepped back allowing him entrance.

Marlon laid the child at her feet. "A gift. A message. From Adrian."

Reese knelt down and looked at the child. She bore such a resemblance to Cynthiana. Her heart stopped for a moment. Tiana had returned with Cynthiana's shirt, soaked in blood, and now this child, throat ripped to shreds, lay before her. The message was clear. Cynthiana was next.

"Who?" she asked.

Marlon stood silent. Reese stood and grabbed his arm. "WHO?" she demanded.

"Me." He said quietly. Her heart shattered.

The message was driven home with no more questions.

She was to return to him, to Adrian, if she wanted the carnage to stop. If she wanted Marlon set free, she had to give over to Adrian. Completely. He would accept no less. The child represented the innocence of her love for Marlon, the purity of their relationship. The bloody shirt, the ties she had formed. Adrian had destroyed both. He had made it clear he would continue until she gave up the foolish notion of happily ever after. He didn't care if she loved Marlon, all he wanted was to own her.

"What else has he made you do?" she asked.

PENANCE

"You don't want to know." Marlon replied. "But I would do far worse if it kept you from him."

This man, this beautiful, goodhearted, gentle man, was destroyed. He had always been the voice of reason for Reese, the calm to her chaos, and Adrian had taken that from him. Made him do unspeakable things, breaking something in him. Just as she had when she had him torture her for her deeds.

"NO!" Marlon snarled. He had heard her thoughts. Seen the torment on her face. "Don't you dare!" He came and stood in front of her. "I would do it all again. Every bit. The torture made you see the wrong in what you did, you paid the price that you felt was needed. Yes, it killed me inside, but it rebuilt you. You beat the hunger. You beat the primal instinct to kill. You can beat this."

Before Reese could speak, a cold wind whipped through the courtyard. The child, almost forgotten on the ground, stood to her feet, and faced Reese.

"Do you see what this monster has done to me?" she asked. "Do you see what he made him do?"

Blood began pouring from her mouth, wounds opened on her arms and legs. A pool of blood formed at her feet and began creeping towards Reese. The child began to scream, in a child's voice.

"Please make the bad man stop. Mommy! Daddy! Save me!" she begged. Before Reese could move, Marlon jumped on the child and within seconds had her head in his hands. His face was buried in the bloody hole that her spine had left in the base of the skull. Slurping noises escaped as he

183

gnawed at the hole like a terrier after a rat.

Rage exploded in Reese, and she tore the child from Marlon. The glazed look in his eyes told her that he was no longer in control.

"You listen to me you bastard. You think you can break me? You think using Marlon to perform acts of depravity will make me come back to you? Think again." She flung Marlon out of the courtyard and slammed the gate.

"Tiana! Now!" she yelled.

Tiana came out of the kitchen chanting a binding spell. Marlon could no longer enter the courtyard. She had locked both he and Adrian out.

"As above, so below!" Tiana finished. They had put a bubble of protection over the compound, air, and earth.

"You have taken the one thing that kept me grounded, the one thing that kept me from turning into the monster you are. All bets are off. Let the games begin."

Several miles away, Adrian collapsed on the floor, blood pouring from his eyes, ears, nose, and mouth. She had struck back. She had won this round.

Chapter Nineteen

What have you done?

AFTER THEIR ATTACK, Adrian grew quiet. He stopped sending messengers and Reese could no longer feel his energy hovering around the fringes of their boundaries. She desperately wanted to breathe a sigh of relief, but she knew better. The minute, the second she let her guard down, would be the instant he would strike. She didn't think for a moment that he wasn't keeping tabs on them; he was just a bit more cautious now. Licking his wounds and regrouping, she was sure.

She had been standing at the window looking out at the street for so long that the sun had set and the room behind her was bathed in shadow. The streetlights had started to flicker and come on, giving the street outside a movie set appearance. The soft amber always made things feel more like fantasy than reality, to Reese. She still hadn't gotten used to electricity. She had spent so many centuries by candlelight that she still preferred the glow it gave in the dark. She heard a click behind her, and light instantly filled the room. She gave a sigh and turned away from the window. Tiana was just settling herself on the couch with an armful of books.

"Some light reading?" Reese asked a smile playing across her lips. The two had scoured almost every book they could get their hands on in all of New Orleans. Anything on old magic, blood magic, ancient deities or things that go bump in the night, they read, looking for some way, some clue to take out Adrian. Maybe even a hint as to what he was. If they could figure out how he did what he did, how he even existed, then they would unravel his power.

"These just came into the library. Monica called me this afternoon to tell me they had arrived. You seemed lost in thought, staring out the window, so I let you be and went and picked them up. If I had of known you would still be at the window, I would have poked you before I left." She squinted at Reese, "You ok?"

Reese opened her mouth to give Tiana her standard answer, but when she saw the genuine concern in her eyes, she changed her mind.

"No. I'm angry. Beyond, angry. I'm frustrated that this is taking so long, and Marlon is suffering at Adrian's hand, I am angry at myself that I put him in that position because I just needed to be with him one more time, I'm angry that my emotion got the better of me, that I allowed it too. I...I... I miss him. More than I ever thought possible. I had always believed that I was better off alone, but that I kept him around because he was useful. When I locked us away, I told myself it was to serve a purpose, he would enact the punishment I chose for myself. I took his ability to refuse me away from him. He objected but he couldn't stop himself. It served my needs, and that was all that mattered. When we emerged this time, when he convinced me that I had paid enough, that I had suffered enough and to step out into the sunlight, I told myself I needed him as a go between to navigate this new world. The night I left him, I felt something I never had. My heart broke. The night he died; I knew. I loved him. I kept him with me for that reason. I also knew, he loved me. But somewhere, I already knew that."

Reese sat on the couch beside Tiana and put her head in her hands. She took a shaky breath and Tiana saw something on Reese's face when she lifted and looked at her, that broke her heart. It was a sadness so deep, so real, it radiated from her eyes, it trembled along the line of her lips and quivered in her chin, as she did all she could to hold back the tears she refused to shed.

As Reese looked at her friend, because that is what Tiana had become, she noticed a shiny bit of garland in her hair and her whole demeanor changed. Tiana pulled back just a bit, instantly wary. Reese's moods could be unpredictable and when she was feeling intense emotion, they could be downright scary.

Reese's lips began to twitch. "Um…." She reached up and plucked the garland from Tiana's hair. "You hugging tree's again?"

Tiana laughed and took the garland from Reese. "It's almost Christmas. Monica was having the kids decorate the library tree, so I helped out a bit. Maybe a bit too much."

The sadness crept back into Reese's face. "Christmas." She murmured. She got up and went back to the window. Tiana came and stood beside her. The houses that lined the streets began to turn on their Christmas lights, the garlands that hung across the streets started to light up and you could clearly see the season was in full swing now. Reese's eyes had been blind to it earlier as she had been so lost in thought.

"I forgot it was Christmas." She said sadly.

Tiana laid a hand on Reese's arm. "Did you and Marlon celebrate?" she asked tentatively. Marlon was a hot button topic, and she never knew if Reese was going to collapse in tears or tear up the room.

"We did. Once." She said. "It was shortly after we first met. He was my jailer. I was accused of witchcraft." Her eyes took on that faraway look again. "We were in North Carolina." Reese's mind drifted back to that night as she told Tiana about it.

**

Reese huddled on the small cot, trying to keep warm. She had tucked her feet up under her skirts and wrapped the poor excuse for a blanket around her shoulders. If she didn't move, it was almost bearable. Almost.

She heard the clank of the jail door and raised her head just a bit. She peaked out from under her hair and saw that the day jailor was leaving, and the night jailor was starting his shift. Marlon was his name. She had been talking to him for the past few weeks, every night, until dawn. He was nice and treated her with a respect she wasn't used too. One

PENANCE

that the town didn't feel she deserved. Once the day jailor was gone, she sat up straighter and brushed back her hair.

"Hi." She said. Her voice was raspy and hoarse. They only allowed her one tin cup of water every 4 hours. She had saved her one cup of water to help choke down the dry crust of bread they gave her for midday meal. The only meal she had each day.

"Hi." He answered.

"I wasn't expecting you tonight." She smiled.

"I offered to work so John could be with his family. It is Christmas." Marlon stoked up the old pot-bellied stove and the room got increasingly warmer. He grabbed a blanket from the wooden box at the end of the night jailors bed and took it over to Reese's cell. He handed it to her through the bars. She scrambled off the bed and wrapped it tightly around her. It almost touched the ground, but Marlon could see her bare feet sticking out. She looked so small and helpless. He knew what the townsfolk said about her, but the woman he had gotten to know over the past few weeks was the farthest thing from the evil they accused her of. Reese, a bit warmer now, slowly walked over to the small window in her cell. She peered out between the bars and saw people moving about the town. She could hear singing faintly and the shout of children as they ran around their parents.

"It's Christmas?" she asked. "I've been here that long?" she sat on the bed and tucked her feet up under her. She still shivered uncontrollably, but her teeth had stopped chattering together.

Marlon poured a cup of hot coffee from the pot on the stove and took it to her.

"Here." He said as he held it between the bars. She got up and took the cup, but she was shaking so hard that she spilled it all over her hands.

"OW!" she cried out. She immediately looked up at Marlon. "I'm sorry!" she exclaimed. The day jailor was free with his whip when she dropped something or didn't do things as fast as he would like. She knew Marlon would never hurt her, but it was habit.

Marlon let out a heavy sigh. He walked over to the door to the outside and locked it. He then grabbed the keys from the desk and came back to her cell.

"I'm going to let you come sit by the stove until you warm up. Don't make me regret it." He unlocked the door to her cell and opened it. She stared at him. He stood before her, nothing between them but air. Her heart sped up just a little and she stepped out of the cell. She could have overpowered him, she could have breathed the life right out of him, but she didn't. She walked slowly over to the chair he had pulled up beside the stove and sat down. Letting the warm envelope, her, she stretched out her feet towards the stove and wiggled her toes, getting the circulation flowing again. Marlon again handed her the cup of coffee and this time she held onto it. He pulled up a chair and sat across from her. He put his feet up on the desk and leaned the chair back on two legs.

"What did you used to do for Christmas, before…well, before here?" he asked. Reese looked at him blankly.

"I didn't even know what Christmas was until I came to this town. I have never celebrated it, or even heard of it. I knew nothing of this Savior you all speak of. I knew there was something much bigger, much more powerful than I, out there, I just never knew His name."

She sat the coffee cup down and folded her hands in her lap. "The women talked of him as if he were their father. They called him God the Father. When I asked them to tell me about him, they called me heathen, witch."

Reese pulled her feet back and crossed her legs on the chair. "I went to their church once. I could feel the energy, the power, swirling around them, but they seemed so unaware of it. They kept praying and asking for signs, from their Almighty, as proof of his existence, but they refused to see what He had already put in front of them. I pointed it out to the Preacher and was told to never come back. So, no, I have never celebrated Christmas. No one ever told me what it was about."

Marlon grumbled about the ignorance of the women in the town. They prided themselves on their piety and their Christian values but when it came time to put those values into action, they turned ugly instead. For the next hour, Marlon told Reese the story of Christmas. She listened to every word. When Marlon was done, she sat silently watching the flames in the stove.

"What do you believe?" she asked.

Marlon sat for a moment. He put real thought into her question. No one had ever asked him that. It was generally accepted that what the preacher preached, you believed without question, but the bible he read, which was the same one the Preacher used, inspired him to question, to seek knowledge, and to find truth.

"I believe in God. I believe in Christmas. I don't believe that just because a person is different, it makes them evil. That is all I have to say on that."

Reese laughed. "Always playing the middle ground." She got up and wandered around the small jailhouse. "So, we are celebrating Christmas together then?" she asked.

Marlon smiled. "I guess we are." He watched her walk over to the small tree that the day jailor had put up. It had decorations made by his children. It had small things from the jailhouse as well. A cell key, iron shackles, a misshapen star. She walked to the window and listened to the bustle of the people outside.

"Where are they all going at this time of night?" she asked.

"To church for midnight mass." Replied Marlon.

"Midnight what?" she asked.

"Mass. It's what they call the service every Sunday, but on Christmas Eve, they do a special mass at midnight, to welcome in Christmas. There are candles, the children dress up and act out the nativity, they sing, and then they go home."

"So, they welcome Christmas as a community before they do as a family?"

Marlon nodded.

"Interesting." She said. "What do they do when they get home?"

"The children go to bed, waiting for Father Christmas, the parents follow shortly after. Christmas morning, they exchange gifts, attend morning service at church and then go home for a meal of roast pheasant, and all the trimmings."

Reese gazed out the window. "Sounds decadent." The

PENANCE

sounds of the townsfolk had died down and all was silent.

"Oh Marlon!" Reese exclaimed. Marlon rushed to the window to see what had caused Reese's shock. Gently falling from the sky were big fluffy snowflakes. They settled on the ground and began to settle on the sill of the window. Reese stuck her hand out between the bars and caught some. When she pulled her hand in, they melted immediately, which caused her to giggle.

"It's snowing!" she said. Marlon laughed at her excitement. She was like a child. He hadn't really seen her smile the entire time he had known her; she hadn't really had much to smile about. But in this moment, as she caught snowflakes on her fingers, all that was forgotten. She was smiling, big as could be, her eyes twinkling. They returned to their chairs by the fire and Reese's face became thoughtful.

"Let's exchange gifts." She said.

"What?" Marlon asked.

"Let's do as best we can and make a real Christmas. This may be the first and last one I ever get. Let's do it the way you told me about."

Marlon smiled. For tonight, he was willing to indulge her in anything she asked for. For the next hour, the two searched the jailhouse for things they could wrap up as gifts. A deputy's badge, a roll of cotton, some kindling, and a beat-up bible they found in the bottom drawer of the desk. Marlon had packed more food in his lunchbox than he needed because he knew that they didn't feed Reese during the day, so they spread it out on the desk, which they had pulled closer to the stove. Reese found two candles in the cabinet and set them on the table. She stood back to look at her handiwork when the church bells began to ring.

"OH!" Reese exclaimed as she jumped in shock. Marlon laughed heartily. "Those are just the church bells. Mass is over. It is Christmas."

Reese ran back to the window and saw all the townsfolk, now quiet and solemn, returning to their homes. She could hear singing, soft and sweet. It was a perfect moment. The snow gently falling, the singing and the ringing of the church bells. She felt Marlon come up behind her. She turned around and didn't realize he was as close as he was. She stumbled into his chest and his arms came up to steady her. She looked up at him.

Marlon stared down at Reese. Her body ran the full length of his, her face upturned towards him, her cheeks flushed from joy and warmth. He wanted to kiss her, more than he had ever wanted anything. He knew he couldn't. He closed his eyes, reigned in his self-control, and gently set her back on her feet.

"Merry Christmas Reese." He said softly.

She wasn't about to let this perfect moment go. She put her small hands on his chest, got up on her tip toes and kissed his cheek.

"Merry Christmas Marlon." She replied. She settled back down on her feet and stepped back. "Let's eat!" she said and clapped her hands. The moment was gone, but the magic lingered.

**

"We talked until dawn, then he locked me back in my cell. I still have that bible, tucked away in my trunk." Tears gently rolled down Reese's cheeks as she refocused on the window in front of her. She was back in New Orleans, standing with Tiana.

"Did you ever celebrate Christmas again; in all the years you've been together?" Tiana asked quietly.

"No." Reese turned away from the window. "I think we both knew that it was a door that if opened, we could never close again. There was a connection between us, one that neither wanted to acknowledge. Now, it's too late."

Reese returned to the couch and picked up one of the books Tiana had brought back.

"The Malleus Maleficarum? Really?" she raised an eyebrow at Tiana.

Tiana sighed. The conversation was over. Reese wasn't going to discuss this anymore no matter how hard Tiana pushed.

"Sure, why not. Could be something in there." She said.

"I knew the man who wrote it. There is nothing of use in this trash." She tossed it on the table.

It landed beside the piece of garland she had pulled from Tiana's hair.

"Merry Christmas Marlon." She whispered. Her heart opening up for just a second, to allow herself to feel the connection they had.

Across town, Marlon looked up. "Merry Christmas Reese." He whispered back.

Chapter Twenty

There Will Be Blood

THE BODIES LITTERED the basement floor. Men, women, all dead. Tiana, stood at the bottom of the stairs, shock etched on her face. Reese stood in the middle of it all.

"Really?" Tiana asked, her voice quivering just a little. "All at once?"

Reese turned to face Tiana; a small trickle of blood ran down her chin. She wiped it with the back of her hand and smiled. Satisfied.

"That my darling friend, was just an appetizer." She gingerly stepped over the bodies, avoiding the pooling blood. Once she had reached her friend, she snapped her fingers. The pile of corpses disintegrated into dust. Reese blew out just a little and a wind whipped through the damp room and out the cracks round the windows taking the dead with it.

"Well. That was at least an easy clean up." Tiana grimaced. She didn't like the idea of killing people, but they had figured out that Reese needed to build her strength. Her magic. She needed to be as strong as Adrian, if not more.

Ash had done some research into the places Adrian had been after he had left Jayden. Tracking him before that was difficult as Jayden had only been able to glean impressions from Adrian's blood. Usually when a Vampire feeds from a human, they know all there is. Every secret, every step ever made, every word ever spoken. But by the time Adrian was turned, he had very little humanity left in him. When he turned, the last of it died with his human form.

They knew that Adrian had come from the north, they all had, so Ash had started there trying to retrace Adrian's steps when he was still Aaron. Cynthiana was with Jordan and Jayden, using her magic to pull any impression, any fleeting image she could, while Tiana and Reese had looked into Reese's magic. Adrian had released Cynthiana when things had gone quiet. Reese believed that Adrian had taken that as a sign of surrender and had grown bored. They still didn't know where Reese came from and who or what she was before they had taken her that night. The group had been watching her for a few weeks before they decided to do the ritual. She had just appeared in their small village one night. They knew she was different. Flowers would appear behind her as she walked if she was hot a breeze would suddenly appear. She seemed to breathe life in almost every move she made. A bird with a broken wing, in her hands, flew in hours. An animal born still; she breathed life into it. The group knew they could steal that power, take a piece, one to each. What they hadn't anticipated was the trauma, the brutality of the event, would pervert the power, cursing each, twisting her.

Now, she took life.

Now she used what she had almost forgotten she had known, to build her power. She had been mortal before, after that night she was immortal. Each had been created from her body, her essence, including Adrian. Each could be unmade. Including Adrian.

He had absorbed the power of the others he had killed, that is how he had become so strong, just as he had the night he had taken her flesh. Reese had constructed a plan using that premise. If she could absorb enough magic from others, she may be able to bolster her own and stand against Adrian. Her only thought was to see him dead. She needed all the magic she could get. A niggling thought kept creeping in. She had heard a voice the night she changed. It told her she wasn't alone. She had thought that meant that someone was with her. When she met Marlon, she had thought it was him. Now that voice was whispering to her again. You are not alone. That was all it said.

Reese pushed the thought aside and followed Tiana upstairs. They had more work to do before either could rest tonight.

Tiana had connections in the Quarter, she knew who was good magic, who was light, and who crept in the shadows. Those were the ones they sought. Reese would absorb their power and then feed on the life force left behind. Sometimes she made it quick, but the really dark ones, the ones you wouldn't leave your children with, you wouldn't turn your back on, she played with. One such group, a cult, was operating in the darkest parts of New Orleans, just past the Ninth Ward. Posters lined the poles up and down the streets, of children, some as young as three, who had disappeared. Many from their beds at night. Some in the few seconds that it took for their mother to turn her head.

Reese wanted to play with them. On the nights when Marlon tore her apart, it was the children she had taken, in her blood lust, that she made sure she paid for the most. Tonight, she would make several more pay.

Neither woman spoke but gathered the necessary items and headed out in Tiana's car. When they arrived at the address Tiana had been given, Reese laid her hand on her friends arm.

"I will call you when I am finished." She said softly.

Tiana looked at her confused. "You can't go in there alone. They don't know you."

Reese chuckled softly. "You forget my friend, what I am."

Tiana opened her mouth to speak again, and realized she was being foolish. Reese was stronger than any person in that building. She was the original. They were just descendants.

She reached into the back and pulled a bag up to the front. She handed it to Reese.

"Inside are the vials for the essence. Make sure you don't lose any of them. And don't mess up my bag. No blood on it. It's a bitch to get out." She said with a smile. She had that bag on that night many moons ago. Reese recognized it immediately. Reese giggled slightly at the inside joke. They had reached a place in their strange relationship that they could joke about what Tiana had been part of.

Reese stepped out of the car and the chill in the air swirled around her. The building sat before her. It was shaped like the letter U with apartments on both sides and a walkway between the two at the far end. A man sat in a wheelchair outside of a door on the ground floor, smoking a cigarette.

"Ya don't belong 'round 'ere" he said. "Bad gris gris."

Reese looked at him and drew up just a little power. She let it shine in her eyes, swirl the hair on her head and ruffle the scarf around his neck. His eyes grew wide, and he began backing up in his chair.

"Bad gris gris." He mumbled as he rolled away as fast as he could.

Once he was gone, Reese sent her power out, seeking the power that held this place. She found it quickly. The cult had built a reputation on fear, so they didn't take many precautions to stay hidden. She picked up Tiana's bag and entered the third door down. It opened to a small room with another door. That door led down a long dark flight of stairs. Halfway down she could hear crying, screaming, and laughing.

A smile curled her lips. She was going to enjoy this.

At the bottom of the stairs there was a long dark hallway, the sides traced with Voodoo markings. She could feel the energy seething just beyond those barriers. She closed her eyes and took a deep breath. Just as quick as a blink, the energy faded away. She heard slithering and slapping as whatever lurked in the darkness fell to the floor, dead.

She continued down the hallway and eventually it opened into a large cavern like room. It was lit by hundreds of candles. Cages and marble altars were placed around the room. In the far corner, a large pile of bones and wetter things rose up from the floor. It was festooned with beads, chains of cowry shells and candles. This was the main altar.

"Hey!" a male voice hollered. "What have we here? An unexpected visitor. Looks like the shadow man has brought us something to play with boys."

Very male laughter filtered through the room. Reese felt about 10 men scattered around.

"Hello boys." She said softly.

She flicked a wrist, and one was at her feet. She knelt down on her heels and placed a hand under his chin, lifting his face. She caught is eyes and where confidence and bravery was a moment before, was now replaced with fear. He knew.

She trailed her hand up his cheek, opening the skin as she did. The man tried to scream, she could see it in his eyes, but his mouth refused to allow any sound to come out. She stood, lifting him with her, nails dug into his throat.

She kept lifting until he was off his feet, then she swung her arm out to the side, gave a twist, and ripped his throat out with one move. He fell to the floor gurgling. Reese opened Tiana's bag and removed a bottle, uncapped it, and drew the power from the man. The vial filled up with an almost iridescent glow. She recapped it, placed it into the bag and knelt back down. This time she tore open the man's chest, reached in, pulled out his heart and stood back up. It had been so quick it still quivered in her hand. She brought it to her lips and took a large bite out of it. Blood ran down her chin and her hand. She tossed the heart to the floor, took a breath and the man, the heart, and the pool of blood, dried up into dust.

The remaining 9 men, who were originally moving towards her, now backed away. They backed all the way the altar. Reese was standing in the only way out.

She raised her hand again, flicked her wrist and the cages opened.

"Go." She said.

The captives ran. She flicked on her phone, called Tiana, and told her to expect a group of children and a few women to come out and to get them to safety.

She then turned back to the men.

"Now, where were we." She said with a smile.

Within moments, blood was spraying like mist. Men were screaming and Reese laughed and danced her way around the room. With each step she tore another wound into a man. She ripped the arm off of one and beat another with it. She pulled the legs off another like wings off a fly. She twirled and skipped, she danced with what parts of the men remained.

She passed a mirror at one point and her appearance caught her attention. Her once white pantsuit was now blood red. Her face and hair were drenched in blood. Bits of skin and internal organs clung to her face and hands. But it was her eyes. Her eyes burned a brilliant blue.

She was almost ready. Every ounce of power she claimed, every little bit of evil she eradicated from the world, was a blow to Adrian. She could feel his anger rising with each reaping of power. She reveled in it. She longed for the day to come when they would again meet face to face.

She returned to Tiana's bag and removed two other bags. One empty and one full. She removed all of her clothing and placed them in the empty bag, she then opened the full bag, and removed cleansing cloths, and fresh clothes. She wrapped her hair in the scarf that was in the bag. No cloth was going to clean that. Once she was presentable, she walked over to the altar. It hummed with power. She drew all she could into herself and placed the rest into the remaining bottles. Then she tipped all the candles over and set the whole place ablaze.

As she walked to Tiana's waiting car, she felt the evil finally let go of the place. She also heard Adrian scream in frustration.

She smiled.

Chapter Twenty-One

The Spoils of War

REESE HUMMED WITH power now. Her eyes a constant brilliant blue. Tiana wasn't afraid of her, per se, but she was a bit more cautious than she had been. Reese's moods weren't nearly as wild as they used to be, but she had seemed to settle into a cold, calculating, almost inhuman state. She showed neither fear, nor joy, happiness, nor sorrow. She just was. Tiana believed that this is what Reese had once been when she was in her full power. God like. Her abilities innumerable now. Secrets were no longer allowed as Reese knew them before they were even given sound.

Tiana sat at the table, in the stillness of the early morning and sipped her tea. She jumped slightly when a loud rumble shook the glass in the cabinet doors. She got up and went to the front window. A large RV rolled to a stop in front of the house. The door opened and Ash stepped out. A few seconds later, Cynthiana came around from the driver's side. Tiana opened the front door and scowled at them.

"What the hell is that?" she asked. "And why have you parked it in front of the house?"

Cynthiana laughed. "It's my new home."

Reese had joined Tiana at the door. "Your what?" she asked.

The twins reached the door and Ash raised an eyebrow at his mother. "You going to let us in, or leave us out here on the street?"

Tiana backed up and the two passed by her. She followed them into the kitchen. Cynthiana had started pulling can goods out of the pantry and Ash was raiding the fridge.

"What are you doing?" she demanded.

Reese sat down and just watched in amusement. She had heard the two discussing this idea a few weeks ago, and she had agreed, it had merit, but she wasn't sure it was going to work. But then again, she didn't know how a lot of things worked in this new world. She moved with confidence through it, but there was still a lot she had to learn.

"We are getting provisions." Ash said.

Cynthiana could feel her mother's frustration rising so she put the cans of soup down and sat at the table across from her. She took her mother's hands in hers and took a breath.

"We have an idea." She began.

Tiana opened her mouth to speak but Reese silenced her.

"Let her speak. It has merit." She said. Cynthiana looked at Reese surprised. She thought that her and Ash had been very careful and kept the secret.

"Heard it all huh?" she giggled. Reese smiled and nodded.

Cynthiana turned back to Tiana. "Adrian cannot enter a dwelling that he doesn't own. That vehicle parked outside is our new home. Ash and mine."

Tiana opened her mouth. Reese shot her a look and she closed it again.

Ash joined them at the table. "We own it. Outright. Paid cash. No loopholes. We are going to live in it. Which makes it our dwelling and by theory, Adrian can't enter. It gives Reese a way to travel around the city and still be safe. Taking her into the Tremé and the Ninth Ward was dangerous. Adrian could have come at any time. Traveling is where she is most vulnerable, so, we fixed that. Mobile home to the rescue!" he grinned at his mom. He was very proud of this idea as most of it was his.

Tiana considered it for a moment. "It just might work. No one knows how the laws of entering work and they are one of the few things that Hollywood did get right about vampires. But none of the lore, myth or otherwise, ever covered a home on wheels."

Reese laid her hands on the table and looked at the three.

"We need to test it." She said quietly.

Tiana jumped up. "And if it doesn't work? We are all dead."

Cynthiana and Tiana both started talking at once, and it was Ash who silenced them.

"If it doesn't work, we make sure we have an escape plan. Park it outside one of the places Reese now owns. If he gets in, Reese goes out the emergency hatch and into the house or building, depending on where we are. If we park it beside an empty lot she owns, it will only be a matter of steps."

The three women stared at Ash in silence.

"What?" he asked sarcastically. "I really am more than just a rockin' bod you know."

Reese stood up. "We need to know, because if it does work, then we have the last piece of our plan in place."

Tiana grunted in frustration. "I still think it's a stupid plan. RV or not."

Reese smiled slightly. "I know. But I need Marlon back in his own body. I can't fight Adrian if I am worried about what he is going to do to Marlon's spirit."

"For all we know, Marlon could be too far gone to be put back." Tiana said. "He has been in that puppet for a very long time now, been made do some very horrible things. No one's sanity can survive that."

"Marlon can." Said Reese. Her voice held conviction. "He isn't like anyone else. He survived centuries with me. He can survive Adrian."

She walked to the doorway of the kitchen. "Are we

doing this?" she asked. She headed to the front door and heard the other three follow.

Tiana put a hand on Reese's shoulder, stopping her. "Ash, bring it around to the drive. Down the side street. First, I don't want the neighbors to see me get into that contraption, and second, if Adrian makes a move while we are transferring here to there, then no one will see it."

Ash nodded and jogged out the door. The three women turned and headed for the courtyard. Reese paused at the door to the cellar. She laid her hand on it and closed her eyes. She sent her energy down into the small room. Marlon's body lay on the table, still as peaceful as he was the day he died. Tiana had done an amazing job fixing his wounds. He still looked like he was sleeping. They had decided to move his body back into the house to make sure it stayed safe. The reason for moving it was moot the minute Adrian took his spirit. Reese wasn't going to let him get Marlon's body.

And now, they were going after his spirit. They still didn't know how to defeat Adrian, but Reese couldn't focus on anything until Marlon was safe. She had tried and failed. She needed no distractions when facing Adrian, and Marlon was her biggest. As long as Adrian had him, he knew Reese wouldn't attack. She needed to remove that security from him.

The RV rumbled down the small side street and stopped at the end of the drive. The three women walked to the edge of the property line and Ash met them at the door of the RV. So far Adrian hadn't attacked when Reese had gone out. But she knew, each time was a risk. She was still vulnerable. She was also making him increasingly angry. Each cult she took out, each faction of evil she eliminated, took back a bit of his power. He lost his grip on that piece of property and Reese immediately bought it the minute his power was off of it before he could. She had several properties around the city now, almost encircling him. If the RV worked, then moving between those properties just became a lot easier.

Cynthiana and Tiana crossed the sidewalk and climbed into the RV. Reese stepped out of the safety of the building and onto the cement. She held her breath for a moment but sensed nothing. She crossed and climbed into the RV. It was a lot bigger inside than it looked. A leather couch lined one side, an island framed a small kitchen and across from that was a table with bench seating. A door at the back led to the beds and bathroom. Reese settled herself at the table.

She looked at Ash. "Let's go to the house just down from Adrian's hotel. He has been holed up there since I took out that major faction in the 9th ward. From what I have heard he feels safer there and it gives him access to food without having to leave the building."

Ash nodded and put the RV in gear. Not long after they pulled up to the house. The hotel was about half a block down. Ash turned to pull in the driveway and Reese stopped him.

"We can't test the theory if it is sitting on land I own." Reese pointed out.

"Oh yeah." Said Ash. He threw it in reverse and settled it along the curb out front of the house.

Everyone piled out and stood on the sidewalk.

Tiana looked around. "Now what?"

Reese smiled at her. "Now I bait the trap." She released

some of her energy and searched for Adrian's. He wasn't hard to find as he owned most of the block. She gently sent her energy out in waves and suddenly felt a hard tug.

"Everyone get back on the RV. He is coming." She said quietly.

"We aren't leaving you out here alone." Argued Tiana. Cynthiana tugged her mom's arm.

"We have too. We are no good to her if we are dead on the pavement." She said. Tiana followed her daughter and got back into the RV. Immediately the two went to work casting the protection spells around Reese.

Reese could feel the energy building and knew that Adrian could feel it too. He would know that she was expecting him, that this was a trap of sorts. You couldn't really trap a creature like Adrian.

Half a block down, Adrian screamed in anger.

Reese heard it.

Reese felt it.

The energy coming towards her picked up speed and she braced for impact. One minute she was standing on the sidewalk, prepared for battle, the next she was flat on her back staring up at the sky. She sat up slowly and sound slowly began to come back to her. She could hear Tiana screaming and Cynthiana and Ash calling to her.

As she sat up fully, her gaze fell on what hit her. Marlon stood, eyes blank, in the spot where she had stood just a moment before.

"Reese?" Tiana had stopped screaming and was a bit calmer now. None of the three dared step from the RV.

Reese waved her hand towards the RV and stood up. "I am ok." She brushed off her linen pants and walked towards Marlon.

"Hello ma cher." It was Marlon's mouth that moved, but Adrian's voice that came out.

Reese nodded. "Adrian." She said flatly.

Adrian, in the Marlon puppet, circled Reese, sniffing the air around her. "You smell delightful." He sneered at her.

"You smell dead." She replied. She didn't dare show any emotion to him. He used it as a weapon.

Adrian pranced a little, doing a pirouette. "Like the new outfit?" he asked. "Maybe this way we can resume our reign over this city. You seem to like this body better than the one I am in now."

Anger flared in Reese's eyes. "You will never be the man Marlon is. Not wearing this puppet, not ever." She started to walk towards the RV when something stopped her. She tried to move her legs and they refused.

"Adrian, let me go." She asked, quietly. She pulled all her energy into herself and prepared to release it. She knew it could blow the Marlon puppet apart, but it was a chance she was willing to take if need be.

Adrian continued to circle like a shark. "I could kill you right now if I chose to ma cher." He stopped in front of her. "You are powerless. You cannot move; you cannot fight." He reached up and tucked a piece of hair behind her ear and that is when Reese struck. Her hand flew up and grabbed the Marlon puppet's wrist.

"NOW!" she yelled. Immediately Tiana, Cynthiana and Ash began chanting. Tiana lit a stick of sage and cedarwood

PENANCE

and slowly began to descend from the RV. Cynthiana and Ash were armed with bottles of liquid, one amber, one red as blood. They raced towards Reese and Marlon/Adrian and began drawing symbols on his forehead, arms, and any other exposed skin.

The Marlon puppet began screeching and trying to pull away from Reese, but she had a tight grip on him. She couldn't pull the life from him, but she could follow the thread of energy from the puppet back to the source. She saw Adrian, sitting in his living room, in a crushed red velvet chair. He was holding his head and screaming, desperately trying to push his energy back at Reese. A small smile played along her lips. She took a look around the room and saw sigils and warding's drawn on all the walls, windows, and doors. Beside him, sitting on the table was a small wooden box. The crystal embedded in the top, glowed blue. Reese knew that was where Marlon's spirit was, where Adrian had contained it while he inhabited the puppet. She felt the spell that Tiana was weaving begin to tighten and pulled her vision back to her body.

"Now." Mouthed Tiana as the three got back onto the RV. Reese drew up all her power and shoved it into the puppet. She could feel more than hear Adrian exploding in rage. The puppet shook and convulsed. Reese, with her grip still on the wrist began walking it backwards to the RV entrance. When she reached the bottom of the stairs, she gave one final push, she added a bit of sharpness to it and Adrian's face, half a block down, suddenly began bleeding from a cut that appeared across his cheek. This distracted him long enough that his essence retreated from the puppet. When Reese felt the hold let up, she shoved the puppet onto the bus and Cynthiana and Ash pulled it up the stairs. Reese also leapt onto the bus, and they slammed the door shut.

The air shook around the RV. The windows rattled and the whole thing swayed. After a moment it stopped.

Reese's cell phone rang and all four jumped at the sound.

She swiped the screen and hit the speaker button.

"THIS IS NOT OVER!" raged Adrian. "You may have your little puppet back, but only because I willed it so. You are NOT stronger than I am."

Reese giggled just a little and that set Adrian off on a tirade. She hit the little red button and ended the call.

Tiana didn't really see the humor in the situation, but she had learned to let it go. Immortals could be a strange lot. "We need to dismantle the puppet." She said quietly.

Reese looked down at Marlon's face. It looked so peaceful. "I know."

She turned and walked to the back of the RV and opened the door to the sleeping quarters. "I know it is just twine and baling wire, but I still can't watch him, it, come apart." She closed the door softly.

Tiana and Cynthiana did the reversal spell and within moments, what was once a perfect replica of Marlon was reduced to the bits and pieces that Tiana used to craft the spell. they gathered up all the pieces and put them in a bag. They would be burned once they returned to the compound.

Tiana sat at the little kitchen table. "Let's go home." Without a word, Ash got behind the wheel and drove back to the compound and into the garage. As they all walked into the courtyard, Reese finally looked at the burlap bag that held the pieces of the Marlon puppet.

"To the victor go the spoils." She said quietly. She knew the puppet wasn't actually Marlon, but to see it walking and talking and being able to touch him, made his actual death seem unreal. To know his spirit was inside that puppet, that the emotion and love that she felt were real, made the loss of the puppet feel like the loss of Marlon all over again.

She walked over to the small fire pit that Ash had constructed and lit the wood. She motioned for Tiana to bring the bag over. She took it from her and gently laid it on the fire. The four stood around the flames and watched as every last bit burned.

In the orange glow of the flames, Tiana could see tears slowly running down Reese's face. She also saw the fire of anger burning in her eyes. Reese looked up and met Tiana's gaze.

"Now we bring Marlon home and prepare for battle."

An uneasy wind whipped through the courtyard, weaving around each person. Each shivered as it passed.

"You are not alone" it seemed to whisper.

Chapter Twenty-Two

Fear and Loathing

EVERYONE HAD HEARD the whisper, but no one dared speak of it to Reese. They assumed it was Adrian, but Reese knew better. She had been hearing that voice for as long as she could remember.

It had been a few weeks since the confrontation on the sidewalk and Adrian had been eerily quiet. Reese had spent several days, in silence herself, sitting with Marlon's body. He was still perfectly preserved.

She kept hoping that his spirit would find its way back to her, but she knew, the sigils she saw on the walls of Adrian's living room would be spread throughout the hotel. It was to keep things in and certain people out. Marlon was trapped.

Tiana stood at the stove stirring some awful smelling concoction when Reese walked into the kitchen.

"What the hell is that smell?" she wrinkled her nose.

Tiana laughed, "It's just weed killer. I don't like using chemicals on my vegetables and herbs, so I make my own. It repels bugs too."

"It would certainly repel me!" she teased. She plugged the kettle in and got some cups out for tea. She had developed an appreciation for the electric kettle over boiling water on the stove. Some modern conveniences were pleasures while some, she still shied away from.

Once the tea was made, she sat at the table and watched Tiana pour the rancid liquid into small spray bottles. "So why the happy homemaker routine?" she asked. "We have a war to fight and your protecting tomatoes?"

Tiana stilled her hands. "I think better when my hands are busy." She turned to face Reese; fear etched all over her face. "We are going up against one of the most powerful creatures I have ever seen. I was there when Aaron was created when we all were. I know the power he had then, and the power he has now absorbed. I'm not a stupid woman. I know that some of us will not survive this fight. My fear is that it will be my children." Her voice shook a little.

Tiana took a shuddering breath and sat at the table with Reese. "You are immortal, Adrian, virtually indestructible, Jayden, immortal, Jordan has superhuman strength. I am human, my children, although blessed with longevity, and powers like mine, are human as well. We don't stand a chance against all that power." Her shoulders slumped. "So, I do the *happy homemaker* routine, so I don't fall screaming on the floor."

Reese reached out and grabbed Tiana's hand. "You know I would never let anything happen to Ash or Cynthiana. Or you."

Tiana cast a skeptical look in Reese's direction. "I mean it. I know I was beyond angry when I found you. I wanted nothing more than to destroy you for what you did to me. But I have come to realize that you were just as much a victim as I was. Well, maybe not as much, but Jayden manipulated you, so did Aaron. You have lived in fear since your run in with Adrian. As others started to come up dead, you have lived in fear of me finding you. But you still helped me when I did find you. Knowing I could literally suck the life out of you, you brought me into your home, albeit against my will, but you let me stay, you worked with me to unravel the lineage of The First Ones, and you have become a friend."

Tiana just stared at Reese. She considered Reese a friend but didn't know it ran both ways.

Reese slapped her hand lightly on the table and stood up. "Yeah, yeah, enough girly bonding crap, we have a plan to formulate. We still don't know how to get Marlon's spirit back."

Reese walked into the living room and looked out onto Dumaine. It was slowly filling with wandering tourists. So innocent, enjoying their holiday, wandering the Quarter, unaware of the power they were walking by. Human's always intrigued her.

Their naivety.

When confronted with the supernatural, they tended to

panic, or became overly obsessed with proving it. They couldn't handle it in a matter-of-fact kind of way. They overreacted and it amused her.

If they only knew the amount of magic and power that swirled around them every day, none of them would be sane. The only one that seemed to roll with it was Chris.

Reese took a sharp breath in. Chris! This kind of thing didn't faze him, he just blustered a little, and then accepted what her and Marlon were.

Reese returned to the kitchen. "I have an idea." She said to Tiana. She sat at the table and pulled out her phone. Tiana shot her a look over her shoulder as she continued to ladle liquid into the bottles.

"Well, are you going to share with the class?" she asked. Reese shot her an aggravated look.

"Yes, smart ass. I'm calling Chris." Reese put the phone to her ear. She had a brief conversation and then hung up. "He will be here by the weekend. That gives us three days to perfect the plan."

Tiana put the ladle down, grabbed a tea towel and leaned her back against the counter. "Again, do you want to share with the class? We don't have a plan."

Reese pouted just a little. "We do. Not a very good one, but we have one."

Tiana laughed, "We have the outline of what could be a possibility of an idea of a plan. We do not have a plan."

Reese shot her a withering glare. "Fine, I have a plan."

Tiana sat down at the table waiting. Reese remained silent. "Reese, this is where you share with the class." Tiana said softly.

Reese settled a smug look on her face. "Since you keep using that class reference, I think I will wait until the rest of said class show up."

Tiana got up from the table in a huff. She knew that stubborn look on Reese's face. There was no point in pushing until Ash and Cynthiana arrived. She could be extremely stubborn. They chatted about random nothingness for about an hour while Tiana filled her bottles and started another tincture.

"All I'm saying is, you could at least pick up the socks. It's a small area, I want it clean." Cynthiana said as she and Ash walked into the kitchen. Cynthiana walked over to Tiana and kissed her cheek.

Ash slumped into a chair at the table and grumbled. "You're not my mother."

Tiana turned around, put her hands on her hips and glared at Ash. "But I am, pick up your damn socks. You don't need to live like a slob."

Ash opened and closed his mouth a few times before you could see the expression of defeat cross his face.

Cynthiana sat down at the table and looked at Reese. "So, what's going on? Mom said you needed to talk to all of us."

Before Reese could speak, someone knocked on the front door. Ash went to answer it and came back with Jordan and Jayden.

Reese stood and addressed all the people sitting at the table. "I have a plan. Somewhat, and it is going to take all of us to enact it."

She began to pace, almost nervously. "We need to get Marlon's spirit back from Adrian."

Cynthiana laughed harshly. "That's your plan? He has that hotel guarded six ways from Sunday. None of us can just walk in without getting noticed."

"I know. Which is why I called a...friend. He is human, in every sense of the word, and he doesn't get weirded out by things like this. He just rolls with the punches, so to speak."

Jayden leaned forward at the table. "If he is human, he will be nothing but food for Adrian. He will be destroyed within seconds."

"Adrian is holed up in his hotel. Surrounded by humans. Chris will blend right in. Adrian won't take the chance of exposing himself to the humans. It is something he was very strict on when we were together. He loved leaving a mess, for the human's to find, but he didn't want it traced back to us. So, he will have his select humans, that he uses for food, and they will be spelled to not be able to identify him. Chris can walk right in, book a room, and walk right out."

Jayden nodded. "Ok, I can see that working. But why can't one of us go with him? Both Tiana and I are experts at cloaking ourselves."

"That would work except I followed Adrian's energy back to the source when we rescued the Marlon puppet, I took a quick look around. He has the place covered in sigils and wards. There is no way anyone with any kind of supernatural anything is getting anywhere near that place. If you look, all the occult shops and crystal shops have closed up for 'holidays'. He has chased all the power out of the area."

Jordan stood and walked to the window.

He looked out over the backyard. "We can get him in. Do we even know if Marlon's spirit is still...alive, or whatever he is. And if he is, Adrian is going to be keeping him close. He isn't going to let your human just walk right in and take him."

"No, he isn't." replied Reese. "But we can guide him to where the box is that is holding Marlon. I also saw it when I was looking around."

Ash waved his hands in the air. "That's all fine and good. We have a plan. A shitty one, but a plan. With one major hole in it. How are we going to get Adrian away from the box so Chris can take it?"

Everyone began talking at once, throwing out idea's and spells that could be used. Tiana thought she could cloak Chris to make him invisible to Adrian, but Jayden shot that down. One of the powers that he acquired from Reese when he became vampire was to see the unseen.

Jordan thought maybe he could transfer some of his speed and strength, but Cynthiana pointed out that it would leave a magical mark that again, Adrian would sense.

"Stop." Reese said quietly. No one heard her.

"STOP!" she said loud enough to rattle the cups in the cupboard. Silence spread throughout the room.

"I have that figured out as well." Reese said.

Jordan walked towards her from the window. "You gonna tell us?"

Reese shook her head. "Not yet. It's better if no one knows until the time comes."

Tiana jumped up and grabbed Reese by the arm. Reese looked down at her hand in shock. "You can't expect us to just go into this blindly!" Tiana yelled. "You need to trust us Reese. We have done nothing but help you. We aren't going to hurt you again."

Reese smiled and patted Tiana's hand, gently prying the fingers from her forearm. "It's not that my friend. I am doing this to protect you. If you all know each detail of the plan, then we are at risk of Adrian finding out before we can put it in motion.

"You all know he is everywhere all the time. Just because he can't get in here, doesn't mean he isn't listening. He could be using any one of us to eavesdrop."

Tiana dropped her hand. She knew Reese was right. She smiled at Reese and turned towards the group. "Let's find beds for everyone. We might as well all stay under one roof. Makes it easier to keep shields and guards up."

Tiana headed upstairs to look for blankets. Reese stood in the doorway and watched the group chatter and joke among themselves. If they only knew what the final piece of the plan was, they wouldn't be so happy.

Her heart hurt for a moment with an emotion she couldn't quite understand. She had spent what she could remember of her life, loathing each person in this room, fearing what they had done to her. Her feelings had changed from fear and loathing to friendship and love.

What she did know was, if this didn't work, she would miss each and every one of these people.

PENANCE

A lot.

Chapter Twenty-Three

Best laid plans

CHRIS ARRIVED FRIDAY afternoon with Freddie in tow. The two stood outside on the sidewalk and looked up at the building. Freddie played cautiously with the knife on his belt and Chris laughed at him.

"You chickenin' out buddy?" he asked.

Freddie shot Chris a glare. "No, you idiot. It doesn't feel right. Remember those nights at the Brookside? Right before trouble broke out? That's how this feels."

Chris looked up and down the street and then back at the front door. "I don't feel anything."

Freddie patted Chris on the shoulder. "You never were good at sensing a fight, just getting in them."

Ash opened the door and stared at the two of them. "Reese!" he hollered. "You said there would be only one."

Reese let the curtain fall and stepped back from the window she had been watching them from.

"I did." She sighed heavily. "But Chris doesn't always listen to instructions. He has this idea that he knows better." She walked to the door that Ash was blocking.

"Let them in. Chris and his friend are no threat." Ash moved aside and the two men passed by him.

Tiana came running. "Stop right there!" she shouted.

Freddie looked at Chris, "She gonna break out in song?" Chris shushed him and the two stopped walking. Tiana threw water at both of them and then a handful of salt.

Ash walked around the two, sniffing the air. Freddie reached for his knife. "Be still." Reese said and Freddie stopped moving. Chris looked at his friend and shook his head. "I warned you." He whispered.

After a few moments, Ash stepped back and looked at Tiana. "They are clean." He said. Freddie chuckled. Ash raised an eyebrow and walked over to him. The two were about the same height so Ash could look him in the eye. "What's so funny?"

Freddie stepped back. "You didn't even pat us down. How can you say we are clean? The knife on my hip alone says we are very definitely not clean."

It was Ash's turn to laugh. "That isn't what I was looking for. Your weapons are of no use here." Freddie looked puzzled. Chris laughed now and slapped Freddie on the back. "Now do you believe me?"

PENANCE

Freddie looked at Chris skeptically, "No."

Reese stepped from the shadows. "Hello Chris." Freddie's brow furrowed. "Where do I know you from?"

Chris stepped in between Reese and Freddie. "From the Top Spot. The day Denny died." Chris turned to face his friend. "She killed him." Freddie's face darkened and he moved towards Reese.

She smiled slowly at him and took a quick breath. Freddie stopped in his tracks and his hands flew to his throat.

"Reese please! Denny was one of our best friends. You have to understand. Don't hurt him." Chris pleaded. Reese flicked her eyes to him. "You brought him into this. AGAIN!" she seethed. "His damage is on your head." She took another small breath in, and Freddie dropped to his knees, gasping.

Chris grabbed Reese by the arm, and she flung him back against the door. He slumped to the floor. "OW!" he grumbled. He got up and leaned back against the door.

"Killing him would teach you a lesson Chris. Maybe then you would listen to instructions." Reese seethed through clenched teeth. She was no longer amused.

Freddie raised his hands. "Now, now, let's just talk about this. I'm really not interested in dying today." In the distraction of Chris, Reese had let Freddie go. She turned her gaze back to him and he felt a quickening in his chest.

"Speak." She said.

"Look, Chris can be…an ass. Yeah, he doesn't generally listen, and he usually thinks he is the smartest guy in the room." Ash snickered at that. Freddie looked at him and

229

then back at Reese. "But his heart is always in the right place. Usually. If he brought me, he did it for a reason. He's a fighter, but I have always watched his back. Every fight Chris has ever been in, I have been there to back him up, and usually get him out of it alive." He backed away from the group and towards Chris who was still catching his breath. "Maybe he feels I can be of help?"

"He's the toughest guy I know." Chris rasped from his spot against the door. "If there is anything that I have learned in the short time I spent with you and Marlon is that I need some kind of backup."

Reese's lips formed a thin line and she turned on her heel and headed for the kitchen. Freddie shot Chris a quizzical look. "Tea. If I am right, she is making tea."

"Tea?" Freddie asked.

Chris nodded. "Yeah, she does that when she is in a mood." Tiana shot Chris a look. "A mood?" she asked. "This is a bit more than a 'mood'."

"And we know that how lady?" snapped Chris. "We have barely made it through the door, and we have been sniffed, doused in water and tossed around."

Tiana snapped her mouth shut and spun around, stalking off to the kitchen. Cynthiana, who had been observing all of this from the archway to the living room, let out a laugh.

She walked over to Chris and Freddie and stuck out her hand. "I'm Cynthiana. That was my mom Tiana, and the blood hound is my twin brother Ash. Follow me."

She headed towards the kitchen with Chris and Freddie in tow.

Penance

"He's human! He can't be here!" Tiana said angrily. "One non-magical human is enough to protect. Two makes it complicated."

Reese stood at the counter. "He is not immune to me; I could just make him leave."

"I could compel him to forget." Offered Jayden. Reese looked at him with a raised eyebrow. "Right." He mumbled. "Never mind."

Freddie leaned against the wall closest to the door and remained quiet. Chris on the other hand didn't have that capability.

"What ever it is you need me to do, I need him to help me. If he goes I go." He tried to be the tough guy and Jordan laughed.

"Who is this guy?" he asked between laughs. "Does he have any idea what we are?"

Reese turned around with her cup of tea and smiled. "No." she looked at Chris and Freddie.

"He can stay. For now. I want to see how he reacts to what I am about to tell Chris. He has a certain...air about him. But he is no threat to us." She motioned Ash from his chair and nodded to Chris. "Have a seat."

Chris sat hesitantly. "What don't I know? You're a vampire, Marlon is your Renfield." He looked around the room. "Who...what are they?"

Reese pointed around the room. "Werewolf, Vampire, Witch and her magical children, who have the ability to manipulate nature and live a really, really, long time."

Chris stared at each one, mouth gaping. "This shit is

real? All the movies? Real?" Again, Reese's lips thinned into that line again. "Hollywood got a lot of things wrong."

"We are going up against a creature unlike anything you may have seen in a movie." Reese sat at the table across from Chris. "He has power you can't even fathom. He can do things you've never seen before; much like us. He got those powers from me. They all did."

Freddie pushed himself off the wall and leaned down onto the table. "What do you mean 'they all did'?" he asked quietly. Reese looked at him surprised. She had forgotten he was still there. Jordan got up from the table, freeing up a seat for Freddie. "What are you not telling us?" He sat in the chair, leaned back, and crossed his arms. Reese looked at him with amusement. He carried this air of toughness with him, a lack of fear, but she could feel, inside, he was cautious, nervous. He was good at keeping a poker face, his outside looked calm and disinterested.

The chair creaked as he shifted his 6'4 frame. He was a large man of solid muscle, and the poor wooden chair was objecting under the weight. "Who are 'they'?"

Reese waved her hand around the room. "They are."

Freddie nodded. "Okay. How did they get...whatever it is...from you?"

Reese gave a frustrated sigh. "I don't have time to explain the particulars, we need to get this plan into action."

"If you want Chris's help, then you will give us a bit more than what you have." Freddie said flatly. Reese's eyes flashed angrily. "Are you threatening me? Do you even know what I could do to you?"

Penance

Freddie sized her up. "I know you can steal my breath. I also know Chris seems to be immune to them. What you can *do* to me, is almost irrelevant because if you kill me, Chris will be no use to you. He will be to upset to focus. So, again, what is the full story?"

Tiana laid her hand on Reese's shoulder. "He's not wrong Reese. The length of time you have spent arguing with him, you could have told him the basics and we could be laying out the plan."

Reese yanked her shoulder away angrily. "Fine." She straightened and rose from the table. She leaned down until her face was level with Freddie's. "I'm going to say this once, so listen carefully." She straightened up. "This woman," she pointed to Tiana, "and these two men," she waved at Jayden and Jordan, "along with three others, felt it necessary to rip literal pieces from my body, eat them, and gain their powers. From there, they spawned 'children' if you will, and those children spawned children of their own and so on. Adrian, or Aaron as they know him, found a way to kill two of the originals, and absorb their powers. He was originally the Phoenix, Jayden made him vampire, and then he absorbed the power of Djinn and Shapeshifter. We are going to destroy Adrian. Now you are caught up." She walked to the window and stared out.

"Who is Marlon?" Freddie asked.

"Someone who means a great deal to Reese." Answered Tiana. "He has been with her for a very long time. He died and Adrian is holding his spirit hostage. We are going to get him back first."

Freddie pondered the information for a few moments while the rest of the room sat in silence.

"Marlon is dead?" Chris's voice broke the silence. Reese nodded slowly.

"His body is in the cellar. If we can get his spirit back, we can put it back into his body." Tiana explained.

"Um...ok then." Said Chris. He looked over at Freddie who shrugged. "So, what is the plan?"

Everyone except Reese and Freddie looked at Chris in surprise.

"I told you he rolled with it." Said Reese. She pointed to Freddie. "Any questions?" He shook his head. "Not yet." He answered.

Reese looked at Jordan. "You're up."

Jordan motioned for everyone to follow him to the living room. The whiteboard with the tree of The First Ones was still set up and Chris walked up to it curiously. Freddie, again, leaned against a wall behind everyone.

"What's this?" Chris asked.

Reese walked up beside him. "A family tree of sorts. My family tree."

Chris smiled at her, "Neat!" Freddie snickered from the back of the room causing Chris to shoot him a glare. He looked back at the chart. "So, all these people descended from you?"

Reese nodded. "Originally there were 6. Werewolf, Vampire, Djinn, Phoenix, Shapeshifter and Witch. Each had or created children of their own. Over the years, I was tracking down the descendants to get back to The First Ones, so I could destroy them and take back my power."

Chris looked around the room. "And now?"

Penance

Reese perched on the edge of the settee. "And now, all I want is to get Marlon back and destroy Adrian. After that, we shall see."

Everyone found a seat and Jordan moved the chart aside. He stood in front of the fireplace and looked around the room.

"Our first objective is the retrieval of Marlon's spirit. When Reese traced Adrian's energy back to him, she saw the box that he is keeping Marlon in. We need to grab the box and get it back here. Once we have that, we can put Marlon's spirit back into his body." The room was silent.

After a moment, Freddie spoke up. "Sounds easy enough. So, why haven't you done it."

Jordan glared at Freddie. "You're human, you, as far as I am concerned, shouldn't even be here."

Tiana got up and walked to Jordan, placing a hand on his arm. "Be nice." She admonished. She turned towards Freddie. "Adrian has sigils and wards painted all through the hotel. The minute a supernatural gets anywhere near the place, he will know."

"Ah, I see." Said Freddie. Chris knew that tone. He looked at Tiana. "What is the plan exactly?"

Tiana took a deep breath and before she could speak, Reese cut her off. "The plan is to get you, and now your friend, into the hotel, retrieve the box and get you back here. While you are inside, you will destroy some of the sigils so we can enter the hotel. After that, you are done. You will come back here."

Freddie nodded and walked over to the group. "Okay, but won't this Adrian notice that his little pictures, sigils? Is that what you called them? Won't he notice they have been tampered with?"

"Yes, definitely, but he won't be in the hotel so we are hoping you can get in and get out before he gets back." Tiana answered.

"Hoping?" Chris squeaked. "You are hoping we can get in and get out? What happens if we don't?

Freddie placed a hand on his friends shoulder. "I don't think you want to know buddy." His eyes locked with Reese. "I want a guarantee before we go in there."

"You aren't even supposed to be here! You have no right to demand things!" Jordan blustered. Reese raised her hand to silence any further tirade from him.

"You are not shocked by all that you have been told. Why is that?" she asked Freddie.

"You haven't met my wife. This is not the strangest thing I have heard." Freddie replied.

Reese smiled. "What do you ask of me?"

"If this all goes south, I want you to make sure our families are taken care of. Financially. Looking around this place, you can afford to make sure my wife wants for nothing if I don't make it home." Freddie spoke softly, his tone carried the seriousness of his words. "It's gonna be bad enough that I am going to have to listen to her 'I told you so' beyond the veil, I would at least like to make sure she does it comfortably. She may forgive me for following Chris then."

Reese nodded. "Done."

Freddie nodded back. "Now, how are the two of us

236

going to get into the hotel. I am assuming Adrian has money and it's not a cheap fleabag joint? We aren't going to just blend in with the regular clientele."

Jayden looked at the two, sizing them up. "We could change your clothes, a little hair mousse, and if you didn't actually speak…"

"Have you seen the tattoo's on Freddie?" Cynthiana asked. "He would have to wear long sleeves to hide them, and that would stick out like a sore thumb. What about repair men? Or janitorial?"

Reese shook her hand. "Adrian would have them all vetted, and bespelled. If there is one thing he is, it is paranoid, and he has had eons to perfect his particular brand of paranoia. No, I think the best way is right through the front door. Money comes in all flavors; things have changed since I was last among the people. High class has a new definition. With the right clothes, an airtight cover story, and…." She sized up Freddie. "A motorcycle, I think we can pull it off as two tourists living their best lives."

Chris looked down at his rock band t-shirt and jeans. "What's wrong with my clothes?"

Ash burst out laughing. "Come out of the 80's man!" he got up and looked at Chris carefully. "You are going to need a hair cut first. No one has hair like that now. Not unless you are willing to put it up in a man bun?"

Chris glared up at Ash. "How short are we talking? It took me a long time to grow it this long."

Cynthiana grabbed Chris's hand and tugged him towards the kitchen. "Don't ask. Just trust me. I cut Ash's hair all the time."

"He has a buzz cut!" said Chris. "It isn't that hard!" Freddie could no longer contain his laughter as he watched his friend being dragged to the kitchen. The way Chris made it sound; it was like he was being dragged to his death. He turned back and looked at Reese thoughtfully.

"So, why did you let me stay?" he asked. He sat on the couch across from Reese and stretched out his legs.

She sat back and folded her hands in her lap. "You seem to have a connection with Chris. This is the second time he has defied me for you. I have learned in my long life that you need to pick your battles. Sending you home is not a battle worth having. It also adds to the illusion we are trying to create to get Chris into the hotel."

"Why is Chris so special? Couldn't you use any human to do your bidding? You have some strong power, why not, what's the word, bespell, someone and make them do it?"

Reese's face became thoughtful. "Chris seems to be immune to my powers of suggestion. Yes, I can steal the breath from him, no one seems immune to that, but he is immune to the manipulations of the mind. He just does what I ask, because I asked it, not because I made him. I have a theory, but I will need Jayden to help me test it."

"What your theory?" Freddie knew that Chris liked to portray that he was the smartest guy in the room, but in all reality, he was wrong more often than he was right. Freddie thought that would make a person more susceptible to mind manipulation, not immune.

"I believe that much like Marlon, nature creates balances. Marlon can not deny what I ask, but he retains his own free will. It's his body that obeys me, not his mind. I think Chris is the ultimate balance. While I can take life

Penance

from him, I cannot control him, physically or mentally."

"Can you take life from Marlon?" Freddie asked.

"Yes, but at great pain to myself. It weakens me greatly, and if I were to die, Marlon would cease to exist, making him my weakness instead of my strength. Nature creates people like Chris, to counteract creatures like me. Although I have yet to encounter anyone else like me."

"Makes sense. Do you think this plan is gonna work?" Freddie asked.

Reese gave a heavy sigh. "You know what they say about best laid plans."

Freddie grimaced. "Great. It is not boding well for the humans."

Chapter Twenty-Four

The silly games we play

THE GROUP SPENT the weekend finalizing the plans to get the guys into the hotel. Freddie spent most of that time talking Chris out of punching Ash. They had cut his long curly hair to just above his ears. It was still shaggy and curly, but now in a more refined grown up manner. He no longer resembled some aging rocker. Ash borrowed his friends Harley, and Tiana and Cynthiana had gone shopping with Jordan. Not for his fashion sense, but to get him out of the house and away from Chris and Freddie. He seemed to have a distinct dislike for them, and no one could figure out why.

Reese spent a lot of time sitting in the back courtyard. She would listen to the bustle in the house, the faint murmur of tourists wandering the Quarter. They had put a deterrent spell around the house, so people tended to stay away from it. Reese didn't want any innocent people getting hurt. When she had asked Tiana to put it in place, Tiana had questioned her about Chris and Freddie. Reese laughed a little and told Tiana that they were far from innocent and could hold their own if need be. She also reminded Tiana that they had chosen to be there.

Reese closed her eyes and breathed in the life around her. She could feel the electricity and it always made her feel alive. They had still not been able to determine what she was, but in moments like this, she felt very, very human. Soft fluttering against her cheek caused her to open her eyes quickly. A butterfly fluttered around her face. She swatted at it, but it dodged her hand each time. Reese sat very still and metaphysically examined the energy around the butterfly. It didn't feel like Adrian's, so she relaxed just a little. It felt full of life, so full it almost vibrated. She reached up her hand, gently this time, and the butterfly landed on her index finger. A jolt of electricity and power went through her body, and she gasped.

"You are not alone."

The words whispered on the breeze that had stirred up in the courtyard. Reese scanned the area for any sign. "Who are you?" she whispered.

"One who has searched for you, but been with you, since you first began." The voice replied.

"Where are you?" Reese asked.

"I am everywhere, and nowhere." The voice replied.

Frustration began to filter through Reese. "Stop

speaking in riddles. You have come to me before, always with the same words. Yet you never reveal yourself. I grow tired of these games."

The butterfly danced around on Reese's finger and a small trickle of blood appeared. Reese could feel the breath being slowly drawn from her and her skin began to wither.

"Do not push me." The voice, now thundering, echoed through the courtyard. "I made you, and I can unmake you."

Reese took deep gasping breaths and within seconds things were as they had been before. The butterfly now lay dead in the palm of her hand. She placed her other hand over it and closed her eyes. She was sad that something so beautiful, so fragile, had fallen victim to not only her anger, but the anger of the one who had used it as a messenger. She placed her hands in her lap, the butterfly still between them.

Tiana came out into the courtyard. "What was that? Reese are you alright? Was it Adrian?" she rushed to Reese's side.

"No, it wa…." Reese stopped speaking mid word. She could feel a fluttering against her palm. She opened her hands, and the once dead butterfly was again vibrating with life.

"OH!" she exclaimed as it flew off. She looked at Tiana, shocked. "It was dead not a moment ago! What did you do?"

"I didn't do anything. I came to check on you." Tiana replied. Reese looked down at her hands. "Then how?" she asked looking up at Tiana.

Tiana sat in the other chair at the table. "When we first started watching you, life flowed around you. Everywhere you went, beauty grew. Plants flourished; things lived. Even when it was impossible, you could touch something, and it would be healed. After that night, death followed you. I thought it was because I had taken that part of you. That it was woven into the magic."

She took Reese's hands in hers and turned them over and back, examining them. She saw the small pinprick on the tip of Reese's finger. "What is this from?" she asked.

"The butterfly. It bit me." Said Reese.

"Butterflies don't have teeth." Said Tiana softly.

Reese stood up angrily. "We don't need another damn mystery to solve! We have enough on our plate with Adrian, now we have some mystical being that can make a butterfly bite?"

Tiana tried to calm her friend. "Have you seen this thing before?" she asked.

"I've heard it before, but this is the first time it has manifested."

Tiana thought about that for a minute. "It didn't really manifest, it took an already existing creature and made it bite you, it basically just gave it a mouth. So, if up to this point, all you have had is an auditory manifestation, I think we have a bit of time before we have to worry about it for real."

Reese took a deep breath. "I hope so, I can't handle anything else right now."

PENANCE

Tiana put an arm around Reese and walked her to the kitchen door. "Dinner is ready. Let's go eat and have one night of fun before battle. Shall we?"

Reese hugged her friend around the waist. The two entered the kitchen to a good natured argument between Ash and Chris over music. Cynthiana was at the stove stirring the big pot of gumbo that Tiana had made, and Freddie was putting a salad together. An unlit cigarette dangled from his lips.

Tiana snatched it from his mouth and tossed it in the trash. "That is a filthy habit, and I won't have it in my house."

"Hey!" Freddie said. "I was going outside to smoke it!" Tiana waved her hand over Freddie's face and mumbled a few words.

"There, now you don't have too. Addiction, cured." She huffed as she pulled a bottle from the wine fridge. She then grabbed a bottle of red from the rack above it and set both on the table, along with some beer steins. Jayden looked at them with distaste. "Such an unrefined palette is that of a beer drinker." He murmured.

Chris had stopped arguing with Ash and was filling one of the steins. "Not everyone enjoys that snooty tootie wine you drink. I think it tastes like old socks."

Jayden walked over to Chris. "Remember, wine is not my first choice, but I will not sully my taste buds with something called Old Milwaukie." Chris stared at Jayden blankly. "What would be your first choice?" he asked.

Freddie came over and took one of the steins from the table and handed it to Chris. He took the full one and put himself between the two. He then turned and looked at Chris.

"Blood dude. His first choice would be blood. He's a vampire remember? How is it that you are the chosen one to balance out Reese and yet, you can be so dense sometimes?" Chris scowled at Freddie and poured another beer. "Shut up." He mumbled.

Jordan clapped his hands together to get everyone's attention. "Let's eat! I'm starving!" The group all sat at the table and bowls of gumbo were passed around. Thick warm bread was pulled from the oven and placed on the table with freshly churned butter. Wine, beer, and conversation flowed around the table easily. Very quickly this group had become friends, for the most part. Jordan still didn't like Chris and Freddie, and Jayden didn't express emotion. In a very short time people understood why Freddie was there. Chris, although immune to any kind of magical influence, was not the brightest and his mouth had a way of getting him into trouble. It had been decided that when they checked in at the hotel, Freddie would do the talking. He had a golden tongue and could talk his way out of just about anything.

The meal began to wind down and Cynthiana got up to clear the table. Jayden got up with her to help. Freddie nudged Chris. "Go help them." He whispered. Chris opened his mouth to object but caught the look in Freddie's eyes.

Freddie got up and moved down the table to sit by Reese and Jayden. They were discussing the plans for the morning and stopped talking when Freddie joined them.

"Don't stop on my account. It's my life on the line

tomorrow." He said.

Jayden sat back in his chair and looked passed Freddie. "You are a means to an end. Nothing more. We are discussing the real work."

Reese let a little of her energy out at Jayden. He gasped in pain as a wound opened on the back of his hand. No blood ran as he had not fed yet, but it caused him pain. His eyes shot to Reese.

"That *means to an end* is going to get Marlon back. That is more important to me than anything. Do not forget why you are here. Do not forget that it is I who allows you to live." Reese released a bit more energy and Freddie backed away from Jayden just a bit. More wounds appeared on his hands and his face.

"I can destroy you with a thought. I can destroy all of you." Reese stood and stormed from the room.

Freddie looked at Jayden. "You might want to curb that disdain. You are the reason this mess even exists. You all are. Your greed and obsession broke what I can only imagine was a beautiful creature. You created what she is. Just as she created all of you. Push her and I see her taking you out without a thought." He got up and followed the direction Reese had gone. He found her standing at the fireplace. Her body was tense, and he knew she was trying to calm herself.

"Reese?" he said quietly.

"What?" she replied through gritted teeth.

"Don't you think you are overreacting just a bit?" he asked. She spun around, her eyes wild. She went to speak but stopped. Freddie watched as she examined what she was feeling and her reactions.

"You are right. Something *is* wrong. This level of emotion isn't me. Certainly not over a misuse of words. I know Jayden is analytical and emotionless. To him, this would just be a means to an end. He understands the importance to me, and he is afraid of Adrian, but beyond saving his own hide, he has no further investment in this fight."

She sat on the edge of the couch. "There is no way for Adrian to get in or out of this house. He can't send one of his slaves to do anything either."

Freddie stood by the fireplace now, a thoughtful look on his face. "So, other than Chris and I arriving, what has changed? Anything out of the ordinary happen?"

Reese quickly looked down at her finger. The tiny red spot almost mocked her. "A butterfly bit me." She said flatly.

Freddie opened his mouth to speak, and Reese stopped him. "Yes, I am aware, they can't bite. Something, or someone sent it here, but it didn't feel like Adrian's energy. It was new, yet familiar, if that makes sense."

Freddie laughed. "Lady, none of this makes sense. Until this morning, I didn't know any of this existed except in Chris's mind."

Reese laughed as well. "Fair point." She got up and called Tiana into the room. "Sweep me." She said as she stood in front of Tiana with her arms stretched out at her sides like she was being frisked by a cop.

Tiana ran her hands up and down Reese just above her body. "There is something new. It's not Adrian's. It's not any of us. But it has a connection to you. Which doesn't make sense. If it is connected to you, it should be connected to us." Tiana furrowed her brow. "Let me just push a little fur...." Within seconds, Tiana was on her butt on the floor. "Why did you do that?" she asked, her voice laced with shock.

Reese looked at her stunned. "I didn't."

Freddie observed the scene. "It reminded me of the built in security systems that we had at...at...well where I hung with my friends. You get to close; you get a zap, and it discourages any more curiosity."

Reese helped Tiana up. "Did it feel like a 'zap'?" she asked. Tiana thought about it. "No, not really, more like a push. But not a harmful one, just a forceful one. Maybe Freddie is right, you seem to now have a built in security alarm."

Reese smiled. "That is the first useful thing to come out of all this!" she exclaimed. Cynthiana and Ash came out of the kitchen. Ash was yawning. "We are gonna head out Ma." He said. The twins kissed their mother on the cheeks, and both headed out back to the RV. Tiana clapped her hands together, suddenly all business. "Let's go Freddie. I have you and Chris set up in Ash's old room. It's not much but it is a bed and a beautiful view of Royal Street."

Freddie followed Tiana into the kitchen to retrieve Chris.

Reese sat back down on the sofa and stared at the fireplace. It was too hot for the humans to have a fire, but she didn't experience temperature the same way. Hot or cold, she could feel it, but it didn't alter her reaction to it. The human experience, no matter how well she could portray it to the outside, was one that was still hard to understand. She waved her hand and the hearth blazed to life.

"Little warm for the humans, don't you think?" remarked Jordan from the doorway. "Little warm for me, for that matter." Jayden walked passed him and sat on the sofa across from Reese. "It's just perfect for me." He mocked.

Jordan stayed at the doorway and looked at Reese. "You ready for tomorrow?" he asked. She gave a heavy sigh and looked down at her hands. Marlon said that her eyes always gave away a lie, so she chose not to look at them.

"Yes. It should be easy enough. We get Chris and Freddie to check in, the more money they flash, the higher they are placed in the hotel and the higher they are, the closer to Adrian's quarters. Once inside, we can use the laptops and cell phones to communicate."

Jayden squinted his eyes at Reese. "You neglected to mention Adrian. How are we going to get him out of the suite so that Chris can retrieve the box?"

Reese looked up at Jayden and he could see the pain in her eyes. "I will take care of that." She said. "The less you all know, the better chance we have of this plan working. Chris knows the bare minimum because he can't be influenced. Freddie knows even less."

Jayden nodded, stood up and left the room. "I don't trust those two." Said his twin Jordan, from the door.

Reese gave him a look. "You don't have too. I do." Jordan opened his mouth to speak again, but, seeing the determined look on Reese's face, decided against it. He turned and joined his brother.

PENANCE

Reese sat alone staring at the fire. This plan had to work. They had to get Marlon back. If they didn't, than there was no point in moving forward. She knew how she would do it, should the plan fail. She would not let Adrian destroy her. She had a spot picked out, the tomb waiting. If they could not retrieve Marlon's soul, she would go back into seclusion. Alone.

"You are not alone."

She heard that voice again and got to her feet angrily. "Well if I'm not alone, then stop playing these stupid games." She barked angrily.

"You are not ready."

Reese let out an exasperated huff and stormed off to bed. Tomorrow was going to be a hard day; she needed some kind of rest.

"Leave a message then and get back to me when you think I am ready. I don't have time for your games."

Chapter Twenty-five

Call my bluff

THE SUN BEGAN to lighten the sky as Reese stood at the kitchen counter looking out onto the courtyard. The house was starting to stir. She flipped the switch on the coffee maker, shuddered just a little, and laid out the bagels, croissants, and beignets she had picked up earlier. She knew Tiana would give her hell about going out without protection, but she was hoping all would be forgiven once they tasted New Orleans best.

Tiana was the first through the door. She spied the breakfast fare laid out and turned to berate Reese. Then her head swung back to the table.

"Café du Monde?" she asked. Reese nodded and smiled. Tiana scooped one up and bit into it. Her moans of ecstasy echoed throughout the kitchen. Ash and Cynthiana came in the back door with their hands over their ears.

"MA!" exclaimed Ash. "There are just some sounds a son doesn't need to hear!" Cynthiana spied the bagels and snatched one up, giving it a good smell. "Ohhhhhh." She moaned.

Ash stuck his fingers farther into his ears and glared at both his mother and his sister. "You guys are killing me!" Reese walked over and shoved a cup of coffee in his hand. "This will make you feel better. Ground fresh this morning, same place they made the beignets."

Ash took a sniff and his eyes rolled back in his head. Cynthiana saw him and immediately blurted out. "Don't you start!"

Jayden and Jordan were the next to join them. Jayden went straight for the coffee and Jordan the fridge.

"Man can not live on carbs alone." He said as he pulled bacon and sausage from the meat drawer. Soon the kitchen was full of chatter and the smells of breakfast. Reese stood leaning against the counter and just watched her motley little family interact. They had become family, even against her better judgment. Jayden came and stood beside her sipping his coffee.

"They look like children on Christmas morning." He remarked. Reese giggled. "What does that make us? Mom and Dad?" she joked.

Freddie and Chris wandered in finally and took a seat with the group at the table. Jayden poured them each a cup of coffee and sat it in front of them, then grabbed his cup and sat down at the table.

PENANCE

Chris stared at him. "You drink coffee too? Do you eat food? Can you go outside in the sunlight? What about garlic and crosses?"

Reese came and joined the group. "I told you; Hollywood got a lot of things wrong."

Jayden smiled. "I enjoy coffee, and yes, I enjoy food, just as Reese does. I do not need it to survive, but I do enjoy the taste."

Chris looked at Freddie, shaking his head. "After this, we need to sit down and rethink all our horror movies." Freddie took a long swig of his coffee and looked at Chris, expressionless. "Nope. Somethings are better left alone."

Everyone ate breakfast and chatted. To an outsider it looked like a nice friendly meal. To those at the table, the tension was palatable.

Tiana stood up, picking up her plate. "We have stalled this long enough."

Chris and Freddie stood up as well. "I guess we better get a move on." He moved towards the front door where their suitcases waited. Cynthiana had exchanged the duffel bags the boys had brought for expensive suitcases. Appearances needed to be accurate. Ash handed them both an Amex Black Card. Those credit cards were reserved for the most prestigious and were given out by invite only. "These will draw attention, which is what we want."

Cynthiana spun Freddie around and checked his appearance. Then she spun Chris and let out an exasperated sigh. With a quick yank she pulled the price tag from the back of the jeans he was wearing. She pushed the two out the door towards the Harley Davidsons that waited for them at the curb.

Freddie let out a low whistle. "The wife would never let me ride one of these babies." They strapped their luggage to the back of each bike and climbed on. Both started up their respective rides and both giggled like schoolboys.

Reese came forward and put stood between the two. "Once you are in the room, text us. From that point, we will switch to the computer and correspond by email only. Jordan will send you step by step directions into Adrian's inner sanctum."

The two nodded and sped off. The plan was in action. No turning back now. A small knot formed in the pit of Reese's stomach. This had to work.

Once the two men were gone, the rest went to work. Tiana set all the protection spells in place and Cynthiana set up the disillusionment spells. It was now Reese's turn. She walked into the living room where she was alone and thumbed through her contacts until she found the number she was looking for. She pushed call and held it to her ear.

"Ma cher. This *is* a surprise." Adrian's voice drawled down the phone line. Reese's stomach clenched. He chuckled. " I felt that."

"Hello Adrian." Reese said. "I would like to meet you for coffee. We have some things we need to discuss." She opened herself up just a little bit more. She let him feel hunger and fear. Two of his biggest turn-ons.

Caution laced his next words. "I am wary of you. You were not so congenial the last time we spoke. As much as I would enjoy seeing you in the flesh, the desire to protect mine comes first."

PENANCE

"I understand that." Reese replied. "I too am wary. How about we call a truce? So that we may speak."

She could feel Adrian considering it. If there was one thing she knew about Adrian, was that she was his biggest weakness.

"Very well. Somewhere public. Of my choosing." He said. A small smile played across Reese's lips. "Very well." She agreed.

"Café du Monde." He said. Her heart gave a little skip of joy. She knew he would chose that restaurant. Adrian was a creature of habit. He had been frequenting that establishment since it opened in 1862. He had a table reserved in a far back corner where he could observe the tourists, enjoy the fresh air, and protect himself. He had bespelled the owners to ensure that it was always available. It was his comfort zone. The finished up the conversation, set the time and Reese hung up.

"You gonna tell Mom?" Cynthiana asked from the door.

"Tell me what?" Tiana asked as she entered the room with her laptop.

"I am meeting Adrian for coffee." Reese said.

Tiana stood still, blinking at Reese. She then sat down on the couch, opened her laptop, and hit the keys; a bit more vigorously than she needed too. Her displeasure was more than clear judging by the aggressiveness of how Tiana was hitting the spacebar.

Jordan walked into the room, and immediately his attention was drawn to Tiana. He looked around the room with a raised eyebrow. Cynthiana pointed at Reese.

"I am meeting Adrian for coffee." She repeated.

Jordan's lips formed an 'O', and he sat on the couch. Tiana snapped the laptop shut and sat it aside.

"When were you going to tell me?" she asked Reese angrily.

"I just did." Reese said.

Tiana jumped up in frustration. "I meant before the actual event! How are we supposed to prepare for this? How are we supposed to protect you?"

Reese walked over to Tiana, took her by the hand and sat down. "If I told you, you would have tried to talk me out of it. This whole plan is contingent on Adrian being out of the hotel. I am a sure bet. He can't resist trying to get me back, to dominate me."

"She is right." Said Jayden. "I do not like it either, it is not safe, but I don't think a fire in one of this other properties would have worked as quickly or as effectively as using Reese as the bait."

Tiana pulled her hands free, sat back and crossed her arms. "I still don't like it."

"You don't have to like it. Just know that I am not unprotected. Why do you think I went out this morning? To that particular Café? Adrian is predictable and paranoid. I knew he would choose that as neutral ground. Both on the fact that he feels comfortable there and the fact that to him he will still feel as if he has the upper hand. He has had the Fernandez family bespelled since they took over the Café. What he didn't anticipate was that today, the day I chose for the rescue, is the day of a big family event. Only the hired staff will be there. They are under my control. I have also placed sigils of protection around the outside, under tables and around his table. Sigils that are hidden, just as you have shown me."

Reese looked at her watch. "I must go."

She stood and looked at the last three of the team. "Rescue Marlon. That is the mission. The only mission. Stick to the plan, no matter what happens. Also, know that I am always in complete control of myself. No matter what. If innocent death occurs, I will pay my penance later."

Reese got into the Uber that was waiting outside. Five minutes later she arrived. She could feel Adrian long before she could see him. Sitting smugly at his table. She allowed herself to admire him as he sat, legs casually crossed, observing the crowd from behind his Ray-Ban's.

He looked up in surprise as she approached the table. "You come protected ma cher."

"Yes, did you think I would not?" Reese asked matter of factly.

"No, I supposed not. That is why I chose this place." He waved his hand absently. "Sit. Coffee?"

"Have they added tea to the menu yet?" she asked. Adrian laughed. "No."

"Café au lait then." She said disappointedly.

Reese felt her phone vibrate in her pants pocket and knew that the boys were in the hotel.

"We need to discuss Marlon." Reese said.

"What is there to discuss?" Adrian asked. "I have him, you want him back, I am not returning him."

"He is of no use to you without a form." Reese reasoned. 'Give me his spirit and I will leave New Orleans. You can return to ruling your city and I will return to my life elsewhere."

Adrian laughed. He removed his sunglasses and sat them on the table. Reese felt her phone buzz in her pants pocket again. The boys were on the move. The waitress brought their beverages and a plate of beignets.

"Let us enjoy one of the best parts of this city and discuss nicer things. War should never be discussed over a shared meal." Adrian took a sip of his coffee and sighed.

"This is not a meal Adrian. This is what people do to discuss awkward situations, make plans, resolve differences. If there is one thing I have learned about this era, is that 'going for coffee' is a euphemism for dealing with ones problems." Reese took a dainty bite of the beignet and Adrian laughed. He leaned over and gently wiped powered sugar from her nose and chin. "You can not eat those like a lady, have you forgotten everything?"

Reese smiled. When Adrian was in good spirits he could be quite charming. They drank their coffee and chatted about nothing in particular.

"Adrian." Reese said.

"No Reese. I will not give you Marlon's spirit. I rather like how he makes my Soulbox glow. Unlike any human soul. You may ask for anything else, but not that." Adrian's phone rang, startling Reese.

"Speak." Adrian said. Reese pretended to be watching the crowd, but she kept a close eye on him. Within seconds, his countenance changed. His face darkened and the air around him crackled with power. He stood abruptly, shoving his phone in his pocket.

PENANCE

"You lied to me Reese. You lured me here, while you sent in humans, humans, to do your dirty work. I expected more from you. Much more than a common thief." Adrian snapped his fingers and Reese stood. Try as she might she had no control over her body.

"Yes, I knew about your sigils. Do you think me stupid?" Adrian marched the two of them out of the Café. He put Reese into the backseat of his waiting limo and walked around the car and got into the other side.

"How?" she asked.

He laughed at her. "I own the building. I own the block. I own the whole damn city!" he bellowed.

"You only needed to bespelled the owners, why own the building?" Reese asked.

"Why not? It's prime real estate. Also, keeping it in the Fernandez name, I can use it as a place to hide money."

The car sped toward the hotel, and to the unsuspecting Freddie and Chris. Reese kept trying to move her arms, she tried desperately to connect mentally with Tiana, but all to no avail.

They pulled up in front of the hotel and Adrian dragged her in the back to the private elevator. Within minutes the doors whooshed open, and they stepped out into the dim coolness of Adrian's suites. He motioned towards the large couch and Reese immediately sat. From her angle she could see down the darkened hallway. Two figures moved along in the shadows. She knew they were Chris and Freddie. She tried to send them some kind of signal, but she still couldn't move. Her arms lay useless at her sides.

"Concentrate." She heard a voice in her head. "I am."

261

She snapped back. "No, you are focusing on to much. Bring your focus smaller. Your pinkie finger."

Reese lowered her eyes until she could see just the tips of her fingers. She stared at her pinkie finger and willed it to move. The voice in her head chuckled. "That isn't how you do it."

"You're not helping!" Reese growled at the voice in her head. Adrian walked into the room and looked at her sitting on the couch.

"You look quite lovely sitting there so quiet." He smirked. He strolled to the bar and poured himself a brandy. Reese glanced quickly back down the hall and saw Freddie and Chris had retreated back into the bedroom. She pulled her energy into herself and pushed it into a very small ball. Adrian sat in the wing backed chair across from her.

"Cat got your tongue ma cher?" he laughed at his own joke. He looked down the hall and then back at her, all mirth gone from his face. "I am aware they are skulking in my boudoir. That elevator is the only way out. They are not going anywhere, and you do know how I love to toy with my food."

Anger flared in Reese, anger and protection towards Chris and Freddie. She had put them in danger. Her love for Marlon had caused her to be weak. Her own selfishness had put two humans in the path of a psycho. She needed to find a way to break Adrian's hold and help them.

"You *are* power." The voice said.

Adrian looked around the room. "Who was that?" he asked. Reese was just as surprised as he was that he had heard it. She decided to use it.

"You said I came protected." She said calmly. She focused on that ball again and this time she felt her pinkie jump just a bit.

"Keep focusing." The voice said. This time Adrian jumped from his chair. "Who is there?" he yelled. He paced the room looking for the source of the voice.

"Push Reese." The voice said.

Adrian stormed out of the room in search of the voice. Reese gave her energy one final push and the bond broke. She could move. She jumped to her feet and ran down the hall to the bedroom.

"Chris?" she whispered.

The closet door slid quietly open, and Chris popped his head out. Reese motioned for them to follow her. She hit the panel on the wall above the bedside table. If Adrian was anything he was predictable. The panel popped out and she hit the button to open the secret door. The wall opened and a bathroom and playroom lit up.

"In here." She motioned. Freddie looked around as they entered. Reese raised an eyebrow at him.

"Weapons. I'm looking for weapons." He said.

Chapter Twenty-six

All is not well that ends well

CHRIS AND FREDDIE armed themselves with things they found in Adrian's playroom. Reese sent her energy out, not only searching for Adrian, but also the voice. Adrian was still stomping around the apartment looking for the source of that voice. Reese knew they couldn't make a run for the elevator; Adrian was too close. She knew that Chris and Freddie didn't stand a chance against him either, but she did. Now that she knew what his level of power was at, she had gleaned that much when he bound her. He could mimic the power that he absorbed, but he couldn't sustain it and it didn't become part of his original power. The only extra boost he had was that of vampire, which was limited. Both of which he had received from her. However twisted

Adrian had made those powers, they were still a part of her, and she believed she still had some control over them.

"I'm sorry we got caught." Chris whispered.

Reese looked over at him and gave a small smile. "It's not your fault. I was cocky and should never have put you two in danger. You are human, not like us."

Freddie gave a snort. "No one is like Chris." Chris shot him a glare. "We aren't completely helpless. We have run with some pretty tough guys." He whined, just a little.

"It wasn't a complete loss." Freddie said. He pulled the small wooden box from his knapsack. The top glowed a soft blue. Reese gasped. It was Adrian's Soulbox. It was Marlon.

Freddie tossed it to Reese. The minute she caught it a jolt of power went through her.

"Use that power." The voice said.

"What the fuck?" exclaimed Chris.

"I will not." Replied Reese. "It is Marlon. I will not take from him."

"You are not taking, you are sharing." Said the voice.

Before Reese could reply, the hidden door slid open. Adrian stood in the doorway, illuminated by the light from the room behind him. His face was in shadow but the energy that rolled off him in waves almost took Reese's breath away. He was not amused. Play time for Adrian was over.

"Come out, come out, little mouse." He used the pet name he had given her a century ago. "Let us play with the meal you sent to me." He flipped a switch and the room lit up. She rose from her spot and walked towards him. She had a plan, a desperate one, but one she hoped would buy them sometime.

"No Adrian." She said calmly. "We don't need them. We have a whole city to feed on. Let them go. They are nothing. A mistake I made."

She placed a hand on his chest and let her energy surround him. His gaze was locked with hers and she slowly led him into the center of the room, Freddie knew the move. She was clearing the door for them. He motioned to Chris and the two inched slowly towards the door.

"We could rule, just like you want." Reese purred. Adrian's hand came up to caress Reese's cheek. His fingers brushed along her jawline and tangled in her hair. He yanked her head back and forced her down to her knees.

"Oh, ma cher, we will rule. You will be mine, but do not for one moment think that I will fall for your charms again. You will obey me. I am the power now. I am the ruler; you are merely entertainment. You can not bespell me." He flung her across the room, and she crashed into the glass wall. It shattered sending shards of mirrored glass everywhere. He turned and snapped his fingers. Chris soon joined her on the floor. Bleeding. Freddie after that.

"If we are going to play ma cher, then it is going to be in the playroom. That is what it is for. I do not want blood all over my suites." Adrian was rolling up the sleeves of his linen shirt. He grabbed a cat of nine tails from the wall to the right of him and began whipping it skillfully.

"This particular piece I had custom made. So many whips either tear the skin, or merely mark the flesh. You must use force to slice it clean. I had little blades added to the leather to split the skin and not waste your energy." He aimed for Chris and Reese threw herself along the floor to cover him. Her shirt tore open and her back had red lines streaked down it. Within seconds they began to bleed.

"You protect this human." Adrian commented. "Interesting." He walked over to Freddie and pulled him up from the floor. "What about this one?" He drew a line with his nail along Freddie's jaw. Blood followed his finger.

"Stop." Reese stood. She flicked her finger and Freddie was across the room in the hallway. "I told you; they will go free."

Adrian lashed out at her with the whip. Her shirt opened in the front and long gashes appeared on her abdomen. She staggered a bit but struck back. She reached forward and pulled her hand back, taking Adrian's throat with it. The flesh flapped wetly as he desperately tried to hold it together. His mouth gaped trying to take in air. She could feel him drawing his energy to repair the damage. She walked towards him slashing her hands left to right. Wounds opened along his chest, down his arms. His once white pants were now blood red.

He dropped to his knees. Hands still at his throat. He fell and let his head fall forward. Freddie had slipped in and picked Chris up from the floor and moved them both out into the hallway. Freddie's heart almost stopped when the elevator doors opened. Jayden, Jordan, Tiana, and the twins emerged. As soon as Freddie saw them, his adrenaline gave out. Help had arrived.

"Red room, down the hall. Reese has him on his knees, but I wouldn't trust him." Freddie said.

Before anyone could move, a scream shattered the air. It was Reese. It was the sound of excruciating pain. It was the scream of terror.

Jayden, Ash, and Jordan ran down the hall. Tiana saw to Chris's wounds and Cynthiana set out to break the sigils that were binding their magic.

Jayden stepped into the room and immediately put his hand out to stop Jordan and Ash. Reese lay atop a marble altar, she was naked. Her arms and legs were strapped down. Adrian was wearing his cloak from so long ago. Reese was writhing and screaming in fear and pain, her eyes darting around the room wildly.

"He kept it." Jordan said in shock. Jayden nodded. "Yes." His voice was laced with disgust. The very same altar they had used, the very same cloak, so many moons ago, sat in the middle of Adrian's playroom, with Reese once again strapped to it.

Adrian walked around the altar, trailing a long obsidian blade up and down her skin. "I took power from the others, when I took their lives, but it never lasts." He stopped at her head and forced her to look up at him. "Now, I will do what I should have done the first time. I will take all of you, every piece of you, into me. I will be so much more than you ever were."

Ash tried to push into the room, but Jordan stopped him. The noise drew Adrian attention.

"Ah mes amis!" he said. "Come! Come!" he motioned them into the room. The three entered, cautiously and stood against the wall.

"Aaron you can not withstand the full ingestion. You know this." Said Jayden matter of fact. "That is why we split it as we did. No one person could sustain such power."

Adrian smiled. "I have not heard that name spoken in that voice, in a long time." He slid the blade down Reese's shoulder and nicked her forearm. "One last taste?" he offered.

The room smelled of blood, but the smell of Reese's almost broke Jayden's control. He shut his senses off and walked around the room. "I will not. We made a vow that night. One I still hold too."

Adrian laughed. "You always were a stickler for rules."

"You cannot take in all her power Adrian. You will not be able to contain it." Jayden tried to reason with him again.

Again, Adrian laughed. "Once, yes, that was true. But that was when I was a mere human. Now, I am so much more. As phoenix, no, I would not have withstood it either, as my body remained human, but with the ability to regenerate after death. But you my friend, you made me something other than human. You made me immortal."

Jayden looked sharply at Adrian. "You sought me out. Our meeting was not chance." He said flatly.

"No, it was not." Replied Adrian. "I kept track of everyone. I was not destined to be what I was given. I was destined for more and you robbed me of that. I was given the worst of the powers. That was not what we had agreed too. Now, I will remedy that mistake."

He cut a piece of flesh from Reese's breast. As he brought it to his lips, Jordan, in full wolf form, hit him full on. He had Adrian by the throat before they hit the floor.

Jayden also flew across the room to aid his brother. Ash set to work on the leather straps that held Reese down.

A yelp was ripped from Jordan as Adrian pushed him

off and sprung to his feet.

"You will pay for that dog." He hissed.

Jordan growled and moved slowly around him. Jayden pulled at Adrian, and he slid along the tile floor towards him.

"I am your Master Adrian. I have dominion over you." He roared. He raised Adrian off the floor and flung him into the wall.

Ash had freed Reese and was about to scoop her up when the others joined them.

"We have broken all his sigils. We can bind Adrian to this place and go." Cynthiana rushed toward Ash and Reese. Jordan had changed back into human form and he and Jayden walked towards the door.

"Do it." Said Jayden.

Tiana stopped them as they turned to leave. "The mission. We must get the box."

"I got it. I gave it to Reese." Said Freddie from down the hall. He was holding up a very weak but very much alive Chris.

Tiana looked around the room. "We need to find her clothes." She cast a wary eye at the still prone Adrian. He had not moved since Jayden and thrown him.

The group spread out gathering the knapsacks and Reese's clothing.

"I have it!" said Chris. He held the box up, waving it. A look of shock spread across his face, and he looked down.

Adrian's hand burst through his chest, holding Chris's heart. He pulled back and Chris dropped to the floor, eyes staring blankly. Jayden, faster than the eye could see, caught the box before it hit the floor and returned to the door with the others. Freddie lunged forward. "NO!" he yelled as he watched his best friend fall. Ash and Jordan held him back.

Adrian took a large bite out of the heart. Blood ran down his chin and dripped onto the floor. He tossed the rest of the heart aside and approached the altar. Reese still lay atop it. He ran his hand down her face, leaving a trail of blood. He brushed her lips with his fingers and her tongue flicked out.

"Ah, there she is." He said. Reese opened her eyes, but Adrian had bound her again. Not with the straps but with his magic. Blood always made his borrowed powers stronger. No one at the door moved. Some out of fear, some out of curiosity, some because they just didn't know what to do.

Adrian retrieved the blade from the floor, donned his robe once again, and began the ritual. Jayden rushed into he room closely followed by Ash and Jordan. Freddie was in too much shock to be of any help. Cynthiana and Tiana had begun the binding and gently pushed Freddie down the hall towards the elevator.

"I can't leave without Chris." He said. He tried to go back down the hall, but Cynthiana held him back. "He is gone. I am so sorry Freddie." She said softly.

"Then how do we kill Adrian." He said emotionless.

Tiana hugged him. "We let Ash, Jayden and Jordan handle it and hope that Reese is still in there somewhere."

PENANCE

Within seconds they could feel the crackle of power. The three ran back down the hall to the room. Adrian was circling the altar, Jayden, and Jordan on the other side circling. Ash lay motionless and bleeding on the floor. Cynthiana ran to him and began a healing spell.

"This will happen. You can not stop me." Adrian bellowed. "I will not allow it." Replied Jayden. Jordan lunged across the altar and Reese's body and tried to tackle Adrian again. This time Adrian was ready and struck back. The sound of bones breaking echoed through the room and Jordan landed on the floor behind Adrian.

Jayden's eyes blazed and his steely control broke. He flew at Adrian and the two met mid-air. Adrian was again prepared and as soon as he made contact with Jayden he broke his neck. It wouldn't kill him, but it would incapacitate him long enough to complete the ritual. He drew is power into him and plunged the blade into Reese's chest.

Tiana screamed from the doorway. Ash held her back. He knew there was nothing more they could do. Adrian held all the power now. The best they could hope for was to escape. Adrian circled the altar, watching Reese and the blade.

After a few moments the blade began to glow. The obsidian seemed to take on an inner light and the blackness took on a luminescent quality. Adrian stepped back, grinning. He could feel the power building. His power. He would claim it.

Cynthiana had roused Ash and they had moved towards the door. Adrian kept circling the altar. When he had reached the far side, Cynthiana ran to Jordan. Adrian had

273

broken his back and it would take all she had to knit the bones back together, but she had to try.

Adrian looked over at Cynthiana. "Let the dog die." He sneered. "You will all be dead when this is over anyway."

"Reese." The voice that Adrian heard earlier floated through the room. "Move."

Reese sat up. Adrian spun around, looking all around him. "Who are you?" he demanded.

"I am her. She is me. We are one and we are many." The voice replied. The air crackled with electricity. The air snapped and the glow from the blade became brighter. Reese pulled it from her chest and light shot from the wound. She threw her head back and screamed. The walls shook, the floor rumbled. Everyone in the room put their hands over their ears. It was a deafening sounds.

Adrian raised his hands towards her, pushing his power at her. "You will not take this from me!" he screamed. His power forced her back onto the slab, the blade falling from her hand. The voice again spoke. "Remember. You are power. You are life. You are unending." The light streaming from her wound surrounded her. Slowly her body began to rise from the altar, as it had once before. Adrian froze. He could feel the change in the energy.

Her screams echoed through the room once again. This time it was one of primal instinct, of the earth and the wind, the air and of fire. It was power. Slowly she came back to rest on the altar and sat up. She swung her legs over the side and slid down onto the floor. Her hips swayed slightly as she walked towards Adrian. The glow was almost blinding as it filled the room, emanating from her. Adrian tried to turn away but found that he could not move. She smiled at him. Her eyes glowed and the air around her moved like a brisk wind.

When she spoke, it sounded like there was more than once voice coming from her. "You are a fool. You cannot take from me what I do not give you. Not anymore." She ran her hand up his chest and stopped where his heart was. She dug her fingers in just enough to draw blood.

"I do not have the power to kill you and have you stay dead. Not yet. But I will. You will never best me Adrian. I made you, and I will unmake you."

She snapped her fingers, and a small flame sprang to life at the tips. Adrian's eyes grew in fear. He knew he wouldn't stay dead, he would regenerate, he always did, being vampire made it harder to kill him, but fire, fire was the one thing that both phoenix and vampire could not fight. Reese trailed her hand along his shirt, little flames caught on the cotton and began to burn. Adrian tried to scream, but Reese had not only taken his ability to move, she had taken his voice. All he could do was stand there as he burned. Once his body was fully engulfed, she stepped back. His was a supernatural flame so there was no risk of damage to the room around him.

He would be nothing but ash in moments and the room would remain untouched. She turned to the group and the minute she locked eyes with Tiana she collapsed. Tiana and Cynthiana rushed to her side and dragged her from the room. Tiana wrapped her in a bath sheet they had pulled from the bathroom and Ash scooped her up in his arms. Freddie and Jordan and picked up Chris.

Reese looked at Freddie. "I am sorry." She said.

Freddie nodded. "Let's just get out of here before that

ash is walking and talking again."

"This was not how this was supposed to go."

"No," Tiana said, "All is not well that ends well."

Chapter Twenty-Seven

Do not go gentle

RAIN DANCED IN puddles and dripped off the tips of the umbrella's. It was perfect weather for a funeral. Freddie wanted Chris buried. He needed that closure. Jayden didn't understand that sentiment, but when he was reminded that he almost had to face that with the loss of his brother, he grasped the concept a bit more. He had memories of being human, but the actual sentiments had faded. Tiana purchased a crypt for her family when she had first settled in New Orleans.

Since they had an unusually long life, it had sat empty. Until today. Today they would lay Chris to rest inside. She had even arranged a Second Line to accompany them from the funeral to the cemetery. Complete with horse drawn hearse. Freddie had remained stoic as they walked the streets of New Orleans following behind his friend. Reese had walked beside him, but neither had spoken a word.

They stood outside the crypt after the crowd had died down. There was nothing more popular than a good second line and Tiana had gotten the best. Freddie stood staring at the crypt as it was closed up.

"He would have loved this shit." He said. Reese looked up at him. "Are you sure he wouldn't have objected about the music?" she asked. Freddie cracked a bit of a smile. "Yeah, he would have."

Jayden came and stood with them. "May I say something before we go?" Freddie nodded.

Jayden looked at the crypt. "I did not know you well, but you were braver than any human I have ever met. From what Reese said, you lived life with innocence, arrogance and an acceptance for strangeness that was rare."

He laid his hand on the wrought iron fence that surrounded the crypt.

["Wild men who caught and sang the sun in flight,

And learn, too late, they grieved it on its way,

Do not go gentle into that good night."]

"That was beautiful." Tiana said. She had joined them during Jayden's little speech and hadn't wanted to interrupt.

"It is Dylan Thomas." He replied.

Reese smiled. "He wrote about fighting death, living your life to the fullest. Very appropriate." Freddie nodded. "Chris would have hated it because he didn't understand it." Everyone laughed. "Ash has brough the car around. When your ready." Tiana said.

Freddie turned from the crypt. "Let's go."

The group walked back to the car and rode back to Tiana's house in silence. Each deep in their own thoughts. When they arrived back, Cynthiana had laid out a small lunch, but no one was really hungry. They all sat around the kitchen table quietly, making pleasantries. Finally, Freddie sighed.

"Enough of this. He's gone. He isn't coming back. Bawling in my beer isn't going to help. What is our next move? Adrian is still out there; we have a glowing blue box on the mantle in the living room and a corpse in the cellar that isn't rotting but isn't getting any fresher."

"Tiana and Cynthiana need to put Marlon's spirit back into Marlon's body." Reese said. Tiana stood and put the kettle on. She stood very quietly at the counter.

"Tiana." Reese said. "What's wrong? You can do it right? You said as long as his vessel stayed in good shape you could put him back."

"I did say that." Tiana replied. "But he has been in 'good shape' far longer than any normal dead body. There is something keeping his from rotting. I don't know what that is."

Reese jumped up from the table. She grabbed Tiana's arm and spun her around. "Well find out!" she barked. "Chris died. For Marlon's soul. We have to put him back or that death was for nothing." She stormed from the room.

"Mama, what is really going on?" asked Ash. He knew his mother better than anyone, much to Cynthiana's chagrin. He knew she wasn't telling the whole story.

"There is a magic, an energy, around Marlon's body. Every time I try and do anything to it, I find myself elsewhere. This morning I tried to get a grasp on the energy and found myself three blocks over! In my pajamas and slippers!"

"Why didn't you say that?" Reese asked from the door. Tiana looked at her surprised. "I didn't want to upset you any more than you already were." Reese turned on her heel and headed down to Marlon's body.

He lay, just as he had from day one, looking very much like he was sleeping. She touched his face and it felt warm. She picked up his hand and it didn't feel wooden and cold like it should.

It felt like it had life in it. Which she knew was impossible. She had seen him die; she had been the one to kill him. She knew the box upstairs held his soul.

"Why does it feel like you're still here?" she whispered.

"You know why."

She hadn't heard the voice since the night with Adrian, even though she had called for it many times.

"Enough of these games! I need to know who you are. I need to know why Marlon does not decay and why Tiana can not get her magic close to him." She paced the room, sending her energy out, looking for the source of the voice.

"You." It said.

Reese found a small flicker and pulled at it. A glow began in the back of the room, she pulled harder, and a shape started to take form. Within minutes a man stood before her. Hair the same color as hers, Features similar.

She immediately took a defensive stance around Marlon. "Who are you?"

Tiana and Cynthiana came running from upstairs. They had felt the shift in power as well. The boys were not too far behind.

"I am your brother. Your twin to be exact." He said.

"My what?" Reese asked.

"Your twin. Dark to your light, male to your female, death to your life."

"I don't remember you."

"No, I became part of you the night of the ritual. Your light turned to dark, which is what I am, so your power absorbed me into you." He explained.

"Why are you here now?" she asked.

"Because your light is returning. You have once again learned to love, to have empathy and protect others. That is what you were created for. To love, to bring life, to shine. But they destroyed that light. This man, here, brought it back. He was created to ignite that flame in you again." He walked towards her. "There is no room for complete darkness within you anymore, there hasn't been for centuries. But you denied that part of you. It wasn't until you lost this man that I was able to pull myself from you. You heard me the night they took from you, that was when you drew me into you.

"You heard me again on the cliff because you had given up your self-punishment. Your penance. Today, you grieved for someone you cared for. That was the final push I needed."

Reese waved her hand. "This is all well and good, but it still does not explain why Tiana can not put Marlon's spirit back into his body."

The man laughed. "But it does." He walked over to Marlon and Jordan let out a low growl. "It is fine Wolf. I will not harm him. Not unless it is willed." He touched Marlon's chest.

"Touch him." He said to Reese. She laid her hand on his chest opposite the man's. She could feel something moving just under the surface. Her eyes flew to the man's. "That is your magic. You are keeping him whole; you are keeping him protected. Which is why your witch can not touch him. You will not allow it."

"How?" Reese asked. The man shrugged. "I do not know. It just is. How is the hummingbird able to fly like a flurry but cannot walk? Why is each snowflake different? It just is."

Reese placed her other hand on Marlon's chest. The stirring she had felt earlier got stronger. "I can bring him back with my will alone?" she asked.

"Yes." The man said.

Reese push her energy at the man, and he fell back. "Now I know you lie. I have willed him alive since the day he died."

Jayden and Jordan took up position between Reese, Marlon, and the man. "Speak now." She said.

The man got up off the floor, dusted himself off and glared at Reese. "I do not lie. We are not capable of it. You may have willed him alive, but it was a human willing, a weak willing, one trapped by the laws of what you believe to be nature. Look beyond what you think you know."

Reese laid her hands back on Marlon. Again, she felt that strange stirring. This time she reached out to it, felt it with her hands. It held heat, energy, it held life. "Go get the Soulbox." She said quietly to Tiana. She didn't trust this stranger, but she had never felt anything like this before. Everything he had said had rung true to her ears. Somewhere inside her she knew he was not lying. She also knew they were connected somehow.

Tiana returned with the box, and she brought it to Reese. Reese instructed her to place it on Marlon's chest. The minute Tiana placed it on Marlon, the glow intensified. The stirring that Reese had felt, became more of a wave.

A pulse that she could push through his body. She closed her eyes and remembered what his chest had felt like when his heart had beat. The thump, the rise and fall with each breath.

"OH!" Cynthiana exclaimed. Reese opened her eyes and looked down at Marlon. His chest was rising and falling. The glow from the box was now outside the box. She pushed it off his chest and the glow remained, hovering over him.

"Push it back into him." The man said. "You were created to give life. Give it to him."

Reese reached out her hand and touched the glowing orb. It felt like pure love. It felt like Marlon. She gently pushed downwards until her hand was flat on his chest. The room was silent, and everyone waited. Reese stepped back and looked at Tiana. "It didn't work." She said. Tiana's eyes welled up and she opened her arms. Reese fell into them. "I really thought it would work."

"It did."

Reese spun around and stared. Marlon was sitting up looking at her. "Come here." He said. His voice was hoarse from misuse. She flew into his arms. "Don't you ever leave me again." She said. Marlon chuckled. "Don't kill me again."

Marlon looked around the room. His eyes settled on the man. "I know everyone else here, you, are new." His grip tightened a bit more around Reese.

"I am her brother." The man said.

"Your name?" Marlon asked.

"I do not have one." He answered. "When we were created there was no need for a name. Humans give labels to things to identify them. We are beyond that."

Marlon looked over at Tiana. "This guy for real?" Tiana nodded. "'Fraid so. He showed up just before you did."

Reese pulled back. "Lets get you upstairs, cleaned up and filled in. Hungry?" she asked.

Marlon jumped down from the table and followed Reese to the stairs. "What about naked boy over there?" he asked.

Reese turned and walked back to the man. "You say that it was my power that brought you into this world."

The man nodded. "Then it is my power that can send you back." Reese pulled up all the power she had and pushed it at the man. He laughed. "I am a part of you, and you me. I came from you, you can not [push] me back."

Reese listened to him and realized that he was speaking literally. She took a breath, and the man began to shimmer.

PENANCE

She took a bigger breath, and he began to look like a mirage. She took a huge breath and within seconds the man was gone.

"You know I am still here right?" he said, this time in her head. She sighed heavily. "Yes, but you are somewhere I don't have to worry about right now."

The group headed upstairs. "Brother eh?" Marlon asked. "What else did I miss?"

"Lots." Ash replied.

Reese put up her hand. "That can all wait. Let's go and get some food, Marlon needs a change of clothes, and I need something stronger than tea."

"We still have to discuss what we are going to do about Adrian." Tiana said.

"We do, but not today." Reese gave Tiana look that told her the discussion was over.

Marlon got cleaned up, and they all sat around the kitchen laughing and just being happy to be alive. Freddie stood up and took Tiana's hand. "Thank you for all you did for Chris today. I appreciate it. I know we came here as strangers, but I feel like I am leaving as a friend."

Tiana stood and hugged him. "You are and you are always welcome here." Everyone got up and said their goodbye's to Freddie. Even though he was a great help, they wanted him as far away from Adrian and any upcoming danger, as possible.

That and his wife had been calling, wanting him home. He still hadn't told her that Chris was dead. That was a conversation he needed to have in person.

Reese had decided to let Freddie keep the motorcycle so once he had his things strapped to the back, he hopped on and set off down the street.

Marlon pulled Reese close and kissed the top of her head. "I do believe there are some things you aren't telling me." He said.

She looked up at him and smiled. "There are. Adrian is still alive. I apparently have a brother, and a power I didn't know I had. We need to find a way to kill Adrian and deal with my new familial situation." She hugged him close. "But that can all wait until tomorrow."

"I know one thing that can't." Marlon said. "There was something that I wanted to hear, from your lips, in person. Not in spirit and not in a puppet."

Reese smiled. "Oh? I don't remember."

He picked her up and carried her into the house. She giggled and squealed as he carried her, fireman style, up the stairs. He flipped her unceremoniously onto the bed. He fell down beside her. Rolling onto his side he took her chin in his hand. "I love you Reese. I always have."

She looked into his eyes. The ones she had longed to see open and sparkling again. "I love you Marlon. Always."

Across the city, Adrian sat in the dark staring out the window at the glittering lights. He had felt when Marlon had returned to life. He seethed in the dark, rage fueling him. He would have his revenge. He would have her power.

The End

About the Author

Stephanie J. Bardy is an accomplished author, poet and editor. She is Editor in Chief at *The World of Myth Magazine* and has held an editing position with them for over 5 years. She is also Editor in Chief for *Dark Myth Publications* and holds a position on the Board of Directors for *The JayZoMon Dark Myth Company, LLC.*

Her published works include *Eternally Bound, Eternally Bound PCE Exclusive Edition, The Chosen, Musings From Me, The World of Myth Anthology Volume 3* and *Volume 4,* all under *Dark Myth Publications.* She also appears in *Full Moon & Howlin: A Werewolf Anthology, Monsterthology 2, Natural*

Instincts Tales of Witches and Warlocks and *Unwelcomed Stories of Hauntings and Possessions* published by *Zombie Works*.

She has several short stories to her credit on *The World of Myth Magazine,* and several works of poetry.